COMING UP ACES

The Hounds of Zeus MC
Book 9

By Faith Gibson

Copyright © 2025 by Faith Gibson
Published by: Bramblerose Press LLC
Editor: Candice Royer
Proofreader: Kerstin Meier
First edition: February, 2025
Cover design: Jay Aheer, Simply Defined Art
Cover photography: Golden Czermak, FuriousFotog©
ISBN: 979-8991426121

DEDICATION

For you, the reader. Thank you for sticking with
me.

Be on thy guard against the Gryphons,
the keen-mouthed unbarking hounds of Zeus,
and the one-eyed Arimaspian host,
who dwell around the stream flowing-with-gold,
the ferry of Plouton.

— Aeschylos

Author's Foreword

Coming Up Aces takes place immediately following *The Ripley Effect* and during *Sultan's Pride*. I didn't intend to write it that way, but sometimes (okay, all of the time) the characters dictate how and when their stories take place. If you've read Sultan's book, you know a bunch of Gryphons are involved, which means Ace needs help elsewhere. I won't spoil the why, but that help comes from some of the Stone Society Gargoyles. With Lucy back in the mix, that means her Gargoyle mate, Tamian, is along for the ride, and with him, some familiar faces. If you haven't read the Stone Society series, I've tried to give a teeny bit of back-story so you aren't completely lost. I won't give too much away in case you decide to go back and read those books too.

I'm only listing the main players in this book so you aren't looking for characters who are off on a different adventure. I won't say this is the last Hounds of Zeus MC book, but I have written it so that the main story arc is complete. I have also included an epilogue looking a few years forward, which I haven't done with the other Hounds books. So, sit back, grab a drink, and enjoy.

PROLOGUE

RAYNA KEPT HER eyes peeled for wildlife as she drove the back way toward New Troy. Headlights shined behind her, and when they brightened, Rayna slowed down. Big mistake. The car sped up, moving into the oncoming lane, then rammed into her rear quarter panel. Rayna was a skilled driver, but the car fishtailed a few times before the other vehicle rammed into hers again. The force of the impact had her rear tires sliding toward the shoulder. The other car continued pushing until Rayna was in the weeds, then wedged against a tree. By the time she regained her bearings, her door was flung open, and a strong hand grabbed her left wrist. The seatbelt held her in place as she struggled against her attacker.

"Let go of me!" Her claws popped out on her right hand, and she raked her sharp nails across the attached arm.

"You fucking bitch!" a familiar voice shouted, his grip faltering.

Rayna disengaged the seatbelt, but as soon as she was free, the man struck again with his

1

uninjured hand, punching her in the temple. Fuck. Her head throbbed, and her vision dimmed. The man once again pulled her left arm, and Rayna grabbed for purchase, missing the steering wheel, and her claws dug along the door's interior. The male's grip was strong. Since she didn't want her shoulder to be dislocated, Rayna allowed herself to be dragged from the car.

Drawing on her beast's abilities, Rayna twisted, landing on her feet. The man had a gun trained on her, but she was fast enough to claw him a second time on the wounded arm holding his pistol. He screamed, releasing both her wrist and his weapon. Rayna didn't give him time to retaliate. She popped a front kick into his stomach, sending him flying. She retracted her claws, picked up his gun, and moved toward him, but another voice stopped her in her tracks.

"Stop right there, Agent Bellamy."

Rayna raised both hands in the air, finger on the trigger guard, and turned. The second man stood on the far side of his vehicle, shielded. His pistol was aimed at her chest.

"What's going on?" Rayna allowed her voice to tremble.

"What the fuck are you?" he asked.

"Shoot her!" her attacker yelled. "Look at what she did to me!" Rayna didn't have to look to know his arm was torn apart, dripping blood.

2

When the man raised his gun, Rayna screamed, "No!"

Chapter One

Rayna

BOOM!

The unmistakable sound of a rifle blasted from somewhere on the compound, followed by glass shattering. Rayna jumped out of the chair where she was knitting. Tossing the yarn aside, she rushed out of the cabin she shared with a woman named Lisa Ann.

"Melinda!" her cabinmate called after her, using the alias Rayna had given when coming to Haven. Rayna didn't stop. She ran barefoot down the dirt road toward the other end of the compound where the sound had come from. Haven, one of The Ministry's locations, was heavily guarded, and Rayna's skin crawled at not having her FBI issued weapon. Being undercover sucked ass, especially in a cult where Rayna had to pretend to be a subservient female. *Fuck that noise.*

Speaking of noise, her King Cheetah rumbled in her chest.

Down, girl.

A few more shots were fired in quick succession, and Rayna dove to the ground on instinct, covering her head with her arms. After a few seconds with no further shots, she looked around, using her cat's superior vision. When she didn't see a shooter, she climbed to her feet and took off behind the cabins so she could run without being seen. When she got to the area where the barns were, Rayna skirted behind the closest building. She edged her way to the corner and sneaked a peek. What she witnessed didn't make sense. Haven's guards were on their knees with their hands clasped behind their heads, and holding them at gunpoint was a group of men in jeans and T-shirts. She recognized some of the men as members of the Hounds of Zeus MC. Had the bikers killed some of the guards?

GIA agent David Spencer had a shit-ton of information on the club, and he readily turned it over after he was taken into custody for kidnapping his adult daughter, Rhiannon, who the members of Haven called Anna. David claimed the bikers were mercenaries instead of the do-gooders they were purported to be. He also had a shit-ton of information on Haven and Josiah Talbert. David alleged he had been undercover at Haven, but Rayna found that hard to believe. Ten years on a UC operation wasn't the norm. At least it wasn't in the

FBI. Still, Spencer claimed he was innocent of any wrongdoing, vowing he took his daughter to keep her safe. However, when Special Agent Seth McCauley arrived at the scene, Rhiannon gave a different account. The FBI had received evidence against David Spencer, albeit anonymously, and were holding the man until they could figure out the truth.

Voices in the loft of the barn caught Rayna's attention. She glanced up at the shattered window.

"*Glory! Oh, Sunshine,*" a male rasped. Glory? What was she doing back at Haven? According to Sandra, Glory had run away from the market a couple of weeks ago when she'd gone with others to help sell items they made to earn money.

"*I'm okay,*" Glory assured the male. "*I'm fine, Rip. Look at me. I knew you'd come for me.*" After a few seconds, she added, "*And thank you for saving me.*"

"*I'm sorry you had to see that, Sunshine,*" Rip said.

"*I'm not. Thomas was going to kill me.*"

"*But you threw up.*"

"*Not from that. My stomach is wonky. I also threw up on Josiah's face.*" Josiah was back? The leader hadn't been seen around Haven lately. If he had returned, Rayna needed to get eyes on the man.

"*Glory, who saved you from Josiah?*"

"*I saved myself.*"

"*You killed him?*" Rip asked, his voice awe-filled. Wait. Glory killed Josiah? Oh, shit.

6

"If he's dead, then yes. He was going to force Rhi back here, and I couldn't let that happen. What's going on outside?"

"We voiced the guards and took their weapons. I'm so sorry we missed that one." Voiced them? What did that mean? And who else was up there? Rayna needed to get inside to see for herself.

"I'm just glad he couldn't aim," Glory muttered. "Can we get out of here? I want to check on my mother. She agreed to come with us if you managed to rescue me."

"Anything you want."

Rayna eased her way around the building, intending to enter from the front. She needed to get inside, but there was someone standing guard. He turned when Glory and Rip exited the building. Rip and the man had to be brothers. Rip led Glory over to the other one, who grabbed Glory and wrapped her up tight. While he was hugging her, he asked, "Where's my mate?"

"In the loft waiting on you to bring her clothes. She was something fierce," Glory told him.

Mate? And why was she waiting on clothes? What the hell was going on? Rayna sniffed the air, and there was something different about them. Then why wasn't her Cheetah on edge?

"Glory?" Marjorie, Glory's mother, called out to her. Marjorie, like most women at Haven, was meek. Even though her husband had disappeared, she was a good little sheep, behaving the way

7

Josiah, then Thomas, instructed.

The older man kept his arm around Glory when her mom approached. Glory jutted out her chin. "I told you Ripley would come for me."

Marjorie eyed the man. "Thank you for taking care of my girl."

"Oh, no. I'm her father-in-law." He gestured toward Rip. "This is her husband, my son, Ripley."

Marjorie did a double take. Rayna didn't blame her. The man didn't look much older than his son. If the female upstairs was his mate, she could be a shifter. They all could be, and that would explain why father and son appeared close in age. In the cheetah world, they stopped aging in their forties. Were these creatures also cats? Rayna's grandmother had said those of their species were rare, but wouldn't it be wonderful to find more of her kind?

"Oh, uh, well, thank you. Glory told me you and your wife bought her a piano. That's very nice of you."

"It was nothing. Glory deserves everything this world has to offer, and we were more than happy to provide for her. Now, if you'll excuse me." The man took off toward the barn with a bag in his hand. Rayna listened in on Glory's conversation with her mother as she waited for Ripley's father to come back outside. When he did, he was holding hands with a pretty blonde who also appeared too young

8

to be Ripley's parent.

Rayna went back around the building to observe the men holding the guards at bay. They weren't speaking, and the guards weren't moving. A man Rayna recognized, Sutton Lazlo, father to five of the Hounds of Zeus, approached from the woods and gestured to one of the kneeling Haven guards.

"You will gather everyone to the church, then you will return to this spot, and you won't move." The air shifted with his command. The guard rose and went to do as he was told without question. Rayna darted between the buildings, then made her way back to her cabin for her shoes.

Lisa Ann was waiting in the open doorway. "What's going on? Who were the guards shooting at?"

"I'm not sure, but it appears there's been a takeover. We're supposed to meet in the chapel." She found the simple shoes they were provided and slipped them on. The meeting bell rang, and when she and Lisa Ann stepped outside, other doors were already opened with people looking out.

"Meeting in the chapel. Now." The guard stood in the middle of the road until every cabin was empty. Rayna kept an eye on the guard, and when he got to the chapel, instead of entering, he walked toward the barn. She and Lisa Ann followed other Haven members into the large building where the

9

elders had their version of church. Rayna spotted Glory and Ripley against the back wall, so she veered off, putting on her game face, and rushed to the younger woman.

"Glory! Oh, my god. What are you doing here? Sandra said you ran off from the market." Rayna sniffed the air, but doing so didn't give her a hint as to what Ripley was. Her Cat purred.

Yum. He smells delicious. Like our mate.

Who? Ripley?

No, the other one.

Rayna turned to face the male standing on the other side of Glory. Hooded eyes met hers as she took in his spiked hair and stacked body covered in ink. Yum indeed.

"I did run off, and now I have a new family. This is Ripley." Glory patted her man's stomach. "And this is his best friend, Ace." Glory thumbed Yummy's direction.

Rayna stepped toward Ace, and his scent washed over her. It was all she could do not to throw herself at him. She maintained control and extended a hand. "Melinda. It's a pleasure."

It would be a pleasure to get him naked.

Melinda ignored her Cheetah as Ace gripped her hand between both of his. "The pleasure's mine."

"If I could have your attention, please," Sutton called out when he climbed onto the stage. Rayna

10

didn't want to move from Ace's proximity. She wanted to bask in his arousing scent, but she had a part to play, so she excused herself even though she wanted to remain at Ace's side. When she found her seat next to Lisa Ann, she turned and looked at Ace over her shoulder. She couldn't help but smile at the man. Instead of returning her smile, he inclined his head, then focused his gaze on the man at the podium.

Sutton placed his hands on the lectern, looking around the congregation. "I'm here tonight because your former leader, Josiah Talbert, kidnapped Glory Yearwood, and brought her back to Haven where he intended to trade her for a woman you know as Anna Spencer." Some of the congregation murmured, and Rayna expected Nadine to stand and defend her husband. She didn't. Nadine wasn't sitting with the married women. Instead, she was with the unwed females. That would be strange if the leaders didn't discard their wives for younger ones.

Sutton commanded the crowd to get quiet, and they did. "Josiah had Glory call her boyfriend and demand the exchange, and when she made the call, Glory alerted us to where she was being held. While we were on our way, a guard confronted Josiah, and the two got into an argument where the guard stabbed Josiah." *Okay, so that's how they're playing it to protect Glory.* "Thomas, who was in on the kidnapping, took off through the woods. You are now without a leader, and your guards have been relieved of their weapons. My family and I welcome anyone who wants to leave Haven to come with us. We are not here to take over, only to help those who were held against their will, like Anna, or those who wish to have a different kind of life, like Glory. We have a safe place for you to stay while you get back on your feet. Clothes, food, and shelter will be provided. Life skills will be taught for those who need them, all at no cost to you. For those of you who want to leave, meet us outside after gathering anything you wish to take. If you're staying, remain seated until I dismiss you."

Rayna looked around, unable to believe the men who served under Josiah weren't moving. Weren't complaining. They sat like zombies. A handful of single women rose from their seats and headed to the door. This was her chance to leave. Now that Talbert was dead, there was no need to stick around, no matter what her assignment had been. Besides, there was something off about the whole situation, and she couldn't figure out what that was if she remained. Rayna turned to Lisa Ann. "Come with me."

"What? I can't, Melinda. This is my home. I thought it was yours too."

"I came here hoping to find something, but it didn't happen. It's been great having you for a cabinmate, but this is what's best for me."

Lisa Ann nodded, her eyes misty. "I understand." Rayna hugged the older woman, then slid out of the row and made her way to the door. She glanced over at Ace, but he was talking to Ripley. Sutton's next words caught Rayna's attention before she exited the building. She stopped at the door to listen.

"For those remaining, you will not remember we were here. What you will remember is the police came and took Thomas away, and when they left, they offered for those who wanted to leave to do so. While you are waiting for Abraham to find a new leader, all of you men will be respectful of the women. You will not engage with them if they do not wish you to. If one of the elders holds bible study, you will read from the New Testament, telling of Jesus's love, not God's damnation. Bible study will not be required of anyone who doesn't wish to participate. The children will spend time daily with their parents, and they will not have to memorize scripture as part of their lessons."

What the hell? Rayna looked over the congregation. Everyone sat stone still. No one contradicted the man. If Abraham did show up, it wouldn't be to the same Haven he'd tasked Josiah and Thomas with leading. She had no idea how Sutton was mesmerizing the crowd, but he was doing something to them. Rayna was torn between going back to stand by Ace and leaving. If her Cheetah was right, Ace was their mate. Still, she needed to get while the getting was good, so she exited the building and joined the others who were leaving. She could find Ace once she was free.

It didn't surprise her that the women leaving were all younger, and she couldn't blame them for wanting to get away from the cult. In the few months she'd been inside Haven, Rayna had witnessed how they were treated as nothing more than hired help, only they didn't get a wage. Not only that, but they were chosen as wives for the older, single men, whether they wanted the male or not. None had gone back to their cabins to retrieve items they wanted to take with them. They weren't allowed to have anything of value. Rayna had been permitted to keep her purse, but her fake ID had been confiscated upon arrival. She didn't bother retrieving it.

Glory and Ripley exited the church and met up with her mom and sisters as well as her sister Hope's husband. They piled into a waiting van, while Rayna and the single females were escorted into another. She didn't see Ace, but she couldn't worry about the hot male. Rayna had a job to do.

A pretty redhead named Kerrigan drove the van. She reiterated what Sutton said about Providence House, the place she was taking the women to stay until they were ready to get back out

14

into the world. Rayna wondered where they got the money to fund such a place. Kerrigan also explained how she'd been taken to Sanctuary, The Ministry compound run by Josiah's brother Gideon, then rescued by Warryck Lazlo. David Spencer was adamant the Hounds weren't good people, but hearing how the Lazlos banded together to rescue a woman they'd never met put a check in the positive column.

Most of the women were silent, so Rayna chatted with Kerrigan who talked about helping others who'd been taken against their will. By the time they arrived, Rayna felt as though she'd made a new friend. The two vans pulled into the driveway at the same time, and they all piled out. Rayna was curious about the place but not enough to hang around all night. She was ready to go home, soak in her tub, drink a beer, and eat copious amounts of junk food even though it was late.

The couple who ran Providence House, Lynette and Branson Miller, met them outside. Before greeting everyone, the couple rushed to Glory and hugged her. Only after being assured she was okay did they welcome the others and usher them inside. They were introduced to a young woman named Julia who was also a resident. Lynnette gave them a quick tour since it was late before showing them to the rooms where they would live for as long as they wanted to. Rayna followed along, taking note of the conditions. The house was spotless, and each room was well-appointed with its own en suite. No one would have to share. Lynette explained that each woman's suite was their sanctuary, and no one was allowed inside without permission. Rayna was impressed.

As the others were choosing their bedrooms, Rayna made her way downstairs. She spotted Branson in the kitchen and strode his way.

"Excuse me, Branson. Do you have a phone I can borrow?" He set down the mug he was holding and retrieved a cell from his back pocket, handing it over. "Thanks. Providence is great, but I have a place to stay with a friend."

"That's wonderful. If it doesn't work out, you're welcome to come back."

Rayna smiled. How could she not? He and his wife were amazing. Spotting the back door, Rayna exited the house. Her Cat wanted to shift and run through the woods. Having spent months at Haven, she'd not been able to let her animal free, and it was itching to do so. It also wanted her to find Ace.

Soon, she promised. Rayna knew better than to bypass her boss. Assistant Director Frederick Hanson was a hardass, but after the way he dismissed her from interrogating David Spencer, well, he could go fuck himself. Instead, she called her partner, Seth McCauley. When he didn't answer, she left a message. "It's Rayna. Please call me back on this number." She ended the call and waited. It took less than a minute for him to call back.

"Rayna, are you okay?"

"Yes. I'm no longer at Haven, and I need a ride. I'll explain later."

Seth hesitated. "Did you call Hanson?"

"No. I'm not sure I trust him."

Seth sighed. "Okay. Send a pin of your location, and I'll be there as soon as I can."

"Yes, Sir," Rayna quipped. Seth was her partner, not her boss, but she still respected the hell out of him. Rayna opened the map app, dropped a pin, and sent it via text message. She then cleared the text as well as the call from the device. Sure, that would look suspicious, but if asked, she would say she was protecting her friend. Rayna needed time to get her story straight. It wasn't that she didn't trust Seth. She did, but outing the Hounds if they were shifters wasn't something she could trust anyone with. She returned inside and handed the phone to Branson who was leaning against the kitchen counter once again sipping from his mug.

"Thanks. My friend will be here in about forty-five minutes," she said, estimating the drive time.

"Would you like some coffee while you wait?" he offered after subtly sniffing the air.

Shit. He was a shifter too. She hadn't sensed that about Lynette, but she was more focused on leaving

17

than those around her. Rayna was slipping. It was probably from spending too much time at Haven and not using her skills as an agent. Time to get her head back in the game.

"Thank you for the offer, but I'd like to wait outside and get some fresh air." Rayna calmly walked out the back door, but her nerves were frayed. She prayed Seth hurried the hell up.

Chapter Two

Ace

ACE FOLLOWED RIPPER and Glory outside after the meeting. He searched for the female who had his Gryphon agitated. No, not agitated – intrigued. Melinda stood with the other females who were leaving Haven. Ace hadn't missed how she sniffed the air. He had also inhaled, only more discreetly. When their skin touched as they shook hands, his Gryphon perked up, recognizing another predator as well as someone it wanted to get to know. She didn't smell like a Gryphon, so what was she? And why would a shifter be at Haven? There was only one way to find out.

Rip touched his shoulder, getting his attention. "We're going to ride to Providence with Glory's family. Can you bring the Camaro to us?"

"What about your bike?"

"I'll come back for it later. It should be safe for now at the campground."

"Okay. I'll meet you at Providence as soon as I

can."

"Thanks, Brother."

They clasped hands, then Ace walked behind the barn where he wouldn't be seen and entered the woods, locating his carry pouch. After removing his clothes and storing them in his bag, Ace took to his Eagle and flew to where he'd parked his bike. He searched the area to make sure he was alone, then shifted and got dressed.

As he rode back to New Troy, Ace couldn't stop thinking about Melinda. The brunette was girl-next-door pretty. The way she moved gracefully reminded him of the female Gryphons when they were in their Lion form. He intended to find out more about the woman when he got to Providence. Granted, he needed to give her time to get settled, but he would speak to Lynette and Branson and have them keep an eye on her.

By the time Ace pulled up at Providence after trading his bike for Rip's vehicle, the vans were gone. He parked the Camaro and angled out of the car. Since he was without wheels, he ordered a ride. Rip and Glory had both been through hell, and he wouldn't keep them from getting back to the hotel any later by having to drop him at home. Instead of disturbing them, Ace texted Branson to meet him outside.

The Hound came out the front door a few minutes later, and Ace tossed him the keys. "Give those to Ripper, please."

"Will do. You need a ride home?"

"Nah. I've called for one." He hesitated before asking, "Uh, did Melinda get settled?"

"She's not staying. She asked to borrow my phone to call a friend to come get her."

Ace looked around, hoping to catch a glimpse of the female. "Isn't that unusual?"

Branson turned his back on the house. "Yeah, it is. What's more unusual is the person she phoned? She called him Sir. She also deleted the call and text. I wouldn't say that's unusual, but it did make me wonder what she's hiding. She's still waiting on whoever it is to pick her up." Brick hesitated, then asked, "Ace, did you notice anything different about Melinda?"

"Like?"

"Like she doesn't smell human."

Ace twisted his neck, popping the tendons. "I did, which is all the more reason to keep an eye on her. Can I borrow your truck?"

Branson narrowed his eyes. "What are you going to do?"

Ace rubbed the back of his neck. "Something about this feels off. I want to follow her."

"The man could be her father, or—"

"Someone higher up the chain. I don't like this, Brick." Ace had always trusted his instincts, and they were screaming at him that he needed to keep an eye on the female.

"Neither do I. Let me grab my keys. Meet me at the side of the garage." Branson went to retrieve his key fob, and Ace walked around the house to where the detached garage was located. Branson met him a few minutes later, handing it over. "She said it would take about forty-five minutes for her ride to get here, and that was thirty minutes ago. I'll call you when they arrive."

Ace clapped the male on the shoulder, then entered the garage through a side door. He got into Branson's truck and canceled his rideshare. While he waited for Branson to send the alert, Ace leaned his head back and pondered the female. His Gryphon took notice when he and Melinda shook hands, and that never happened.

Ace didn't feel romantic stirrings until he'd formed a solid relationship with whomever he was dating, male or female. By the time that happened, his partners had written him off. Ripley was the only one who knew that about Ace. Not because the other Hounds were homophobic, but because Ace didn't want the others looking at him with pity when each relationship crashed and burned. And they always did. Not that he was looking for something with Melinda even if she had his beast taking notice. There was something going on with the female, and Ace planned to figure out what.

It was half an hour later than expected when his

phone pinged with a text from Branson. Ace started the truck, pushed the button to open the garage, and when the door was fully raised, he pulled out with the headlights off, then closed the door behind him. He eased his way around the house, catching sight of Melinda's ride. The vehicle was a black SUV with tinted windows. Two factions drove such vehicles – the government and the mafia. Okay, maybe he was stereotyping, but Ace had a bad feeling about whoever was driving. Ace didn't move until the SUV was almost out of sight. Keeping the headlights off, he followed from a distance. He kept them off until they were in traffic. The vehicle merged onto the onramp for the highway, and Ace kept several car lengths between them. They traveled west until they came upon the exit for New Latham. Ace was familiar with the town since that's where Spyder's mate, Charlie, lived and worked when the two first met. Ace and Rip had guarded The Blooming Boutique, or BB's, as Charlie called her shop, when someone from The Ministry had targeted Charlie's cousin.

Ace had to back off, as traffic was non-existent in the early morning. Speaking of BB's, Ace pulled into the lot where he parked and got out. Knowing someone at Zander "Zero" Andino's security company was monitoring the cameras, he waved, then skirted around the building and stripped. Calling forth his Eagle, Ace took to the sky and flew hard in the direction Melinda's ride had gone. It took a bit of backtracking, but he spotted the SUV backing out of the driveway of a nice two-story house. Ace circled above the home. There was a kid's play fort in the backyard, which was fenced in. There were tall trees and flowering bushes. Potted plants lined the covered patio. If this was her home, did she have kids? Why had she gone to Haven, and who had taken care of the plants while she was away?

There was only one light on in the house, and it was in a top-story room where the blinds were closed. Ace settled in one of the trees at the back of the yard and waited. Ten minutes later, the light went out, and the home was bathed in darkness. His beast urged him to remain in the tree until she rose later that morning, but he had no good reason to do so other than his gut told him something was off about the female. Instead, Ace flew to the front yard, took note of the address, then made his way back to the truck. After getting dressed, he climbed into the cab and sent off a text to Bishop, hoping he didn't wake the Hound.

As he returned to New Troy, Ace turned the radio on and did his best to focus on something other than the woman. It didn't work. Too many things didn't make sense, and they all tumbled around his brain. Once he arrived home, Ace strode to his den, opened the French doors, then snagged a half-full bottle of tequila. He didn't bother with a glass, instead opting to drink from the bottle. As a shifter, the clear liquor wouldn't get him drunk, but the burn soothed his mood. Ace leaned against the doorframe and gazed at the crescent moon. It was something he did often; staring at the sky, wishing on stars, wondering why he wasn't like others. He'd long ago given up on expecting an answer to that last one. His phone pinged with an incoming text. He should have known Bishop would research the house as soon as he got the inquiry.

Bishop: *The house is owned by Joseph and Delia Edwards. Two kids, ages six and nine.*

Me: *Can you check if either have a sister named Melinda?*

Bishop: *Hang on a second.* Ace tipped the bottle back and took a generous swig. *Neither has sisters, only brothers.*

Me: *Okay, thanks for checking.*

Bishop: *Anytime.*

Okay, so maybe they were friends of Melinda's as she had told Branson. Or she could have gone into a different house. Either way, Ace needed to put the female out of his mind. She was safely away from Haven, and that was all that mattered. At that conclusion, Ace shoved the cork back in the bottle and set it on the bar before heading to his bedroom. He didn't bother calling Branson since there was nothing to report.

The next morning, Ace drove by Providence to pick up Branson. They were helping Ripley at the house he and Glory were moving into. When he pulled down the driveway, Branson met him outside and dropped a toolbox into the bed. Ace opened the door to move to the passenger seat, but Branson waved him off.

"You don't want to drive?"

"Nah. I like having a chauffeur," Branson joked.

As they traveled across town, Ace relayed everything that happened after he left the night before.

Branson scrubbed his chin, looking out the windshield. "Maybe we have this wrong, and she was looking for something at Haven. When she didn't find it, she opted to leave."

"True, but why would a shifter go to Haven?"

"Why would anyone go there?" Ace tapped the steering wheel with his thumbs. When he glanced at Branson, the male was studying him. "What?"

"Did you feel a connection to Melinda? Is this why you're so intrigued with the female?"

Ace squeezed the leather, then relaxed his hands. "No. I..." Ace cleared his throat. Branson was a good male. A good friend. "I don't feel connections the way most others do. I have to get to know someone before I—"

"Oh, you're demi, like our son, Brooks. Nothing wrong with that."

"Except by the time I get to the romantic feelings, the other person has moved on."

"Yeah, Brooks had that problem too. Always felt like there was something wrong with him. Luckily, Daniel, his partner, was willing to wait. Patient as a saint, that one." Branson clapped Ace on the shoulder. "I hope you don't feel the way Brooks did. Some of us are just wired differently, but that doesn't make it wrong. When it's right for you, he or she will be patient."

Ace cleared his throat and blinked back the wetness forming in his eyes. "Thanks, Brick. I, uh, haven't told anyone other than Ripper, and now you." Ace gave the Hound a weak smile. "I'm glad I did."

"I'm honored you shared that part of yourself with me."

Branson had promised breakfast for those helping with the furniture, so they stopped and picked up the order he had called in at a local bakery. When they arrived at Rip's, Ace pulled down the long driveway that cut through trees on both sides. The house was situated on seven acres with two of those being cleared for the house and yards. Ace couldn't be happier for his best friend. Ripley, Conrad, and Sutton were waiting on them. After devouring breakfast, Rip gave Ace and Branson a tour of the house while they waited on the furniture to arrive. When it did, Ace helped assemble the king-sized bed going in the master suite, and Branson installed the washer and dryer. They had most everything in place by the time Glory and Ripley's mom, Regina, arrived.

Ace found the two females in the kitchen. Glory was unloading the dishwasher, and Regina was folding dish towels. "What do you know about Melinda?" he asked Glory.

Glory pulled out the plates, stacking them in a cabinet. "Not much. She was only at Haven a few months, and she didn't really talk about herself." Glory closed the cabinet door. "What's wrong, Asher? Why are you asking about her?"

"Who's Melinda," Regina asked.

"She was one of my cabinmates at Haven. I thought I saw her get in one of the vans last night, but when we got to Providence House, I didn't see her."

"That's because she borrowed Branson's phone and called for someone to come pick her up. She left while you were talking to your family."

"That's a good thing, right? It means she had someone she trusted to come get her."

Ace ran a hand over his spiked hair. "Maybe."

Regina stopped folding the towels and placed her hand on Ace's arm. "What's wrong, Son?" His heart warmed every time she and Conrad claimed him. His own parents had passed away many years ago, leaving Ace on his own.

"There's something off about the female. She addressed the man on the phone as Sir, which Branson and I found odd, so I followed her after she was picked up. Since it was late, I couldn't follow too closely, so I parked behind one of the mate's floral shop and shifted to my Eagle. I saw the vehicle backing out of a driveway. I had Bishop check ownership of the house, and it belongs to a married couple with two kids. Neither has a sister, so maybe it was friends of hers?"

Sutton called his name, so their conversation was cut short. He followed the older Hound out the back door. "What's up?"

"Since Viper is watching Abraham's compound, I'd like you to keep an eye on Haven. Now that Josiah and Thomas are dead, I want to know if Abraham shows up or sends someone else in to lead."

"I can do that. As soon as we're finished here, I'll head that way." It had been almost five months since they began patrolling Oasis, the compound Abraham Goodman oversaw. Neither he nor his wife, Rhiannon's grandmother, had been spotted, and that didn't bode well for the Hounds. According to Rhiannon, her grandmother was aware of Rhi's abilities to heal people with her energy. After her mom passed away, her father, David Spencer, had taken Rhi to Haven instead of Oasis. According to him, it was to protect Rhi, but

Josiah had used her for the cult's gain. He brought in new members who had health issues, promising to heal them if they lived at Haven and gave Josiah all their money. With Abraham knowing of her abilities, Rhiannon wouldn't be safe until the man was found and taken out. Ryot wasn't letting Rhi and their new baby girl out of his sight, sending other Hounds out on mercenary jobs. Ace didn't blame him.

"You don't have to go tonight, but I wouldn't wait too long."

"Will do, Boss."

Sutton clapped Ace on the shoulder before heading to his SUV.

Ace spent a few more hours at Ripley's, then when everyone left Ripley and Glory to enjoy their new home alone, Branson dropped Ace off at his house. Once inside, Ace called Spyder and asked if he could use BB's as a hiding spot and why. The Hound assured him Charlie wouldn't have a problem with it, but he promised to call her and fill her in. Ace hopped in his car and drove to the floral shop. He was cutting it close to getting there before closing time. As he drove, he also called Zander to tell him he'd be parking at BB's.

The bell jingled when he pushed open the door to the shop. Kristoff was behind the counter, and when he saw who it was, his face lit up. "My Ace of Hearts! I've missed you."

Ace grinned at the young man and sauntered up to the desk. "How are you, Kristoff?"

"Better now." He fanned his face and batted his lashes. The male was cheeky and cute, but he was too young for Ace.

"Kristoff, what have I told you about flirting?" Charlie asked as she came from the back room where she put together her floral arrangements. She rolled her eyes as she approached, holding out a set of keys. "Here you go."

Ignoring Kristoff who had his chin propped on his fist watching, Ace said, "Thanks. I shouldn't need it too long."

Charlie waved him off. "Use it as long as you want, and when you're finished, you should come by for dinner."

"I can do that." Ace wrapped his fingers around the keys. "I'll get out of your hair so you can close up."

"Come back soon!" Kristoff husked. Ace grinned at the cutie, shaking his head. As he left the shop, he thought about the young man. Kristoff was a force of nature who couldn't sing for shit. He was funny and talented in other ways, but Ace hadn't given into the flirtations while he and Rip were guarding BB's. It wasn't that Ace didn't find Kristoff attractive. He did, but he worried the man wanted that instant love, the kind he probably read about in romance novels where Ace would sweep him off his feet. Then again, maybe Ace wasn't being fair. Either way, he had someone else he needed to focus his attention on.

Not wanting Kristoff to know Ace was hanging around, Ace got in his car and drove across the street, parking at the end of a strip mall. When Charlie and her assistant left for the evening, Ace returned. He parked around back, then went inside to wait until dark since he didn't want to chance anyone seeing him shift into his Eagle. He sat in the breakroom until the other stores closed for the night, then locked up behind him. Once again, he stripped and shifted, heading to the house a few miles away.

CHAPTER THREE

Rayna

WHEN SETH FINALLY picked Rayna up from Providence, the first thing she did was ask about his wife and kids. Vanessa was Rayna's best friend and had been for years. Only after he assured her they were all good did Rayna tell him what she'd found at Haven. It wasn't anything they didn't already know. What she didn't tell him was that Talbert was dead.

"What took you so long?" Before Seth could answer, Rayna eyed the exit leading home, which he passed. "You missed my exit."

"I know. I'm taking you to Delia's."

"Delia's? Why?" Delia was Seth's sister. Rayna had hung out with the woman, her husband, Joseph, and their two kids several times over the years. Her house was a good thirty minutes away from Rayna's.

Seth let out a deep breath. "Because David Spencer was released after you went undercover.

According to Hanson, Deputy Director Grissom and someone at the GIA made a deal."

"What kind of deal? And released to whom?"

"That's above my paygrade, but I'm assuming he's in GIA custody."

"Then why are you taking me to Delia's?"

"After he sent you to Haven, Hanson stopped allowing anyone else into the interrogation room. When I tried to access the recordings, I was told they were locked down for security purposes."

"And you think what?"

"I think it's possible Hanson and Spencer are working together. Call it a gut feeling, but until I know for certain, I don't think you should come in. There was no good reason for you to go undercover, Ray. I think Hanson did it to get you out of the way."

"And what about you? Why aren't you hiding?"

"As far as the higher ups know, I'm being a good little sheep. Between cases, I've been trying to find out if the GIA really made a deal, or if Hanson let Spencer go free. So far, I've hit nothing but dead ends. I've also been watching the Hounds, and there's nothing about them that indicates they're bad people."

Rayna thought back to what she'd seen and overheard at Haven. She was still on the fence, but for now, she was giving them the benefit of the doubt.

"I told you that before I went to Haven."

Seth scrubbed a hand down his face. "I needed to see it for myself. You know how convincing Spencer was." He gestured toward the house. "Delia and Joseph took the kids on vacation to Disney and the beach, so you'll have the house to yourself for the next two weeks. I stopped by your place and packed a couple of bags so you'd at least have your own clothes and toiletries. That's why I was late. I also put a burner phone in your laptop bag along with some cash and one of my credit cards so you don't have to use yours. Until we know what's going on, I don't think you should use your phone or computer. Not yet anyway. If you need to go somewhere, take Delia's car. I need you safe, Ray."

"Yeah, well, I need you safe too."

"Hanson sent an inner office memo stating he would be out of town a few days, so at least I have a reprieve from him watching my every move."

"That's even more reason I should come back to the office. I can help you while he's gone."

"No," Seth barked. Rayna moved as far back as her seatbelt allowed, and he shook his head. "I'm sorry. Just do this for me. Stay at Delia's and keep your head down. I'll keep you posted if I find out anything."

"Fine."

When he pulled in the driveway, Seth didn't get

out. Rayna didn't blame him considering the late hour. Instead, he handed over the house keys and gave her the security code. Rayna thanked him as she grabbed her bags from the back seat. Seth waited until she was safely inside before backing out of the driveway.

Rayna reset the alarm, then dropped her laptop bag on the sofa. It was odd being in someone else's home, even if she had met them. She took her duffel and suit bag, searching the house for a spare bedroom, finding one upstairs. She hung the garment bag over the closet door and unzipped the duffel. Rayna removed the toiletries and went across the hall to wash her face and brush her teeth. When done, she changed out of the pajama-like clothes of Haven into a T-shirt. She climbed under the covers and wanted to cry. Damn, but she'd missed a regular mattress. If she never went undercover again, it would be too soon. Instead of falling asleep quickly, her mind spun with questions about David Spencer, the GIA, and her boss. Her dreams were filled with random images of Ace. Rayna's dreams were never cohesive, so that wasn't unusual.

Even though it was late when she went to bed, the next morning, Rayna was up before the sun, being used to starting early at Haven. She made a pot of coffee, then showered and dressed in cutoff shorts and a tee. It felt odd yet comforting to once again wear her normal clothes, even if they were a little tight from not working out over the last few months. She grabbed the burner phone and Seth's credit card, taking both to the kitchen. She poured a cup of coffee, then rummaged through Delia's kitchen for breakfast food. There wasn't a lot in the fridge, but that made sense, considering the family was out of town for two weeks. Rayna did find a box of cereal, so she opened the package and munched on the fruity gems while making a list of groceries she would need for the next few days, which consisted mainly of frozen meals since her skills in the kitchen were worse than lacking.

Rayna took the box of cereal and her coffee to the living room. She placed her mug on the end table, located the controller, and turned the TV on. She had missed having access to electronics. No phone, no scrolling the internet, no movies, no music. Since she wasn't going into the office, Rayna planned to take a full day to lounge in her shorts and binge some of the shows she'd missed while at Haven.

She wanted to boot up her laptop and do some snooping, but that would alert the higher ups that she was no longer where they thought she was. Her Cheetah was restless, but she couldn't let the animal out. She'd noticed more than one camera throughout the house, and she had no idea if Delia would check it while Rayna was there. She cursed her boss for not being able to go home. Her place was small, but it was her sanctuary.

After binging several hours of a program about firefighters, Rayna's stomach rumbled. First, she ordered a cheeseburger with all the fixings, French fries, and a strawberry shake from her favorite fast-food place. Then she found the local grocery store app and ordered the items on her list. The food arrived within half an hour, and she relished the meal, dunking her fries in the shake instead of ketchup. With a full belly, Rayna went back to the sofa and watched a couple more episodes. By then, the groceries were delivered.

Rayna put them away, but instead of going back to the sofa, she found a blanket and headed outside. There was plenty of daylight left, so she spread the blanket on the ground and lay down, letting the sun's rays warm her skin. She remained outside until it was dark, then she went inside and popped a frozen meal in the microwave. Once it was ready, she ate it on the sofa while watching more mindless television. All in all, it was a good day.

The next morning, Rayna took her coffee out to the covered patio. The backyard boasted tall trees, flowering plants, and the kids' play fort. Birds were singing, and several dogs barked somewhere in the distance. Rayna's Cheetah bristled, and she looked around. Using her Cat's superior eyesight, she studied her surroundings. The only thing out of the ordinary was a large eagle in the top of a neighbor's pine tree. It was stunning with its white wings. She'd never heard of such a creature. Could it be an albino? Was that even a thing? The bird didn't move. It stared at the ground below, most likely searching for its next meal. When her cup was empty, Rayna rose to go inside for a refill and breakfast. As she did, she took one more glance at the magnificent creature, but it was no longer there.

Rayna had purchased some breakfast scramble kits, so she opened one, cracked an egg in the bowl, stirred it around, then popped it in the microwave. It wasn't gourmet, but she still savored the food. It had been months since she'd eaten anything besides oatmeal and toast for breakfast. That in itself was reason enough to hate her boss. After downing her food, she poured another cup of coffee and took it to the sofa to binge another one of her shows.

Instead of focusing on the fantasy featuring a hot mage, Rayna's thoughts went back to the brooding biker with spiked hair and hooded green eyes. That led to thoughts of her last night at Haven and where Glory killed Talbert, and Sutton convinced the congregation of things happening differently than reality. What the hell was she going to tell Seth? She'd managed to avoid his question of how she'd gotten away, but she knew her friend. He wouldn't be satisfied with not knowing everything. Rayna wanted to help him find Spencer, but she couldn't do that hiding at Delia's. Rhiannon needed to know her father was possibly no longer in custody.

Before going undercover, Rayna spent hours studying the Hounds. She mainly focused on the Lazlos since Ryker, the oldest son, was Rhiannon's boyfriend as well as the President of the MC. Rhiannon had been several months pregnant, so by now, she would have given birth. Instead of calling and having Ryker ignore the unknown number, Rayna decided to visit their house and inform Rhiannon that her father was possibly loose. Rayna cleaned up her breakfast trash and washed her mug, then made her way to the guest room and changed into one of her pantsuits. Just because she was hiding from her boss didn't mean she wasn't still an agent. Hopefully, that fact would give her some leeway with the biker when she went to speak to his female.

Rayna checked her firearm before sliding it into the holster beneath her arm. She was putting on her coat when her Cat bristled. Rayna eased down the stairs, pulling her weapon as she went. She hit the bottom stair just as the doorbell rang. She padded on silent feet to the front door and looked out the long window beside it. "What the hell?" The male standing on the front porch was delectable in jeans that hugged his legs and a tight black tee that accentuated his build. It was his eyes, though, that

40

Rayna had dreamed about.

Rayna holstered the gun, punched in the alarm code, undid the locks, and opened the door. "Good morning, Ace."

"Hello, Melinda. May I come in?"

Her Cheetah purred, but Rayna ignored it. "May I ask how you found me?"

"I followed you when you left Providence. I wanted to come by and see how you are now that you're no longer at Haven."

Rayna glanced past his shoulder but didn't see a vehicle. Her skin prickled. "I appreciate your concern, but as you can see, I'm fine. Now if you'll excuse me..." Rayna pushed the door only to have it blocked by Ace's hand against it.

"You should let me in so we can talk about why you're dressed like an agent of some sort." The air shifted with Ace's voice. Was he trying that voodoo Sutton used? She didn't want him to know it didn't work on her, so she stepped back, holding the door for him. As he walked past her into the living room, her Cheetah purred again.

Mate.

Rayna closed the door and followed the male, ignoring her beast once again. If Ace was her mate, they would get there. Eventually. She gestured to the sofa. "Please, have a seat."

"Thank you." Ace lounged on the sofa, and Rayna stood far enough away so that she could get to her weapon if he turned out to be dangerous.

"I am curious about your attire. If you are some type of agent, that means you were possibly undercover at Haven. I think we could help one another by sharing information."

"What type of information would that be? The type that tells a government agent what really happened to Josiah Talbert? Are you willing to share the truth, Mister...?"

"Asher McMurray, and yes, I'll tell you the truth if you promise to do the same with me."

Asher. What a fabulous name.

Ignoring her Cat, Rayna asked, "So?"

"Why don't you go first?"

Rayna knew a diversion when she heard one, so she admitted, "I overheard Ripley and Glory talking in the loft after she killed Josiah."

"Fuck," he muttered as he scrubbed at his face. "Are you going to arrest Glory?"

"No." Rayna sat in one of the overstuffed chairs, crossed her legs, and propped her elbows on the chair arms. "Josiah Talbert was an evil man, and from where I'm sitting, the world is better off without him. But I am in a pickle, Asher. What Sutton told the congregation happened and reality are two different things, yet I can tell my boss neither. I also can't explain what Ripley's mother was doing in the loft as I didn't see her, but from what I overheard? It sounded as though she took

42

out Thomas. And then her mate had to take her clothes to her." Rayna arched a brow and waited to see if he would confirm her suspicions.

"What do you mean what Sutton told the congregation and reality are different?"

"Come on, Asher. You were there. Sutton told Haven that one of the guards killed Josiah and that Thomas ran away. We both know that's nowhere near the truth. I thought it odd how everyone went along with his words, then I realized he was voicing them."

His eyes narrowed. "Voicing?"

"Isn't that what the Hounds call it when they're manipulating others?"

Asher's eyebrows rose. "How do you know that?" His face was so expressive. Rayna usually enjoyed making those she interrogated uncomfortable, but she felt bad doing it to this male. Not that she was interrogating him per se.

"I wouldn't be a very good agent if I weren't aware of all the players and what they're capable of," she hedged.

"True, but I'm curious as to where you learned the term."

"Ripley used it when he and Glory were talking in the loft, and for the record, it doesn't work on me."

"Shit. I apologize for trying to do so earlier, but I didn't think you would let me in to speak with you

43

otherwise."

Rayna waved off his apology. "No harm done."

"I need you to keep that information to yourself." The air rippled again, and Rayna kept her face impassive, waiting. Asher thunked his head against the sofa and stared at the ceiling. When he returned his gaze to hers, he swallowed hard. "Melinda—"

"Rayna. My name is Rayna Bellamy."

"Oh, that's a beautiful name."

"Thank you. And don't worry. I won't spill the Hounds' secrets. Speaking of secrets, I'm assuming the Hounds, at least some of them, are *different* if they have mates, and before you deny it, I'll admit I'm also different."

Asher leaned forward, propping his forearms on his thighs. "That explains it."

"Explains what exactly?"

"Why you sniffed the air when Glory introduced you. It was subtle, but I noticed."

Rayna studied the male her Cat was so interested in. Since King Cheetahs were rare, it made sense they wouldn't have to find another of their kind to mate with. Rayna's grandfather had been a regular Cheetah, and her father was human. He and her mother never secured their bond. They met while Rayna's mother, Colette, was filming a movie in Italy. Colette was more interested in her career than having a mate or a child, so she never

44

informed the man he was going to be a father. She said it was because he was human and couldn't know the truth about them, but it still hurt Rayna's heart that she didn't know him. Hell, Rayna didn't even know his name. Colette left Rayna with her grandmother while she continued seeking fame as an actress.

"When you borrowed Branson's phone, he overheard you use the term Sir, and that sent up a red flag. Since you know the truth, you can understand why we wanted to find out who you were speaking with. Again, I'm curious as to why you were undercover at Haven."

So polite, and Rayna was enamored. She was more interested in what he was than discussing Haven. "Are you dodging the elephant, Asher? How about I go first? I'm a King Cheetah."

"Oh, wow. That's a new one."

"Are you some other type of cat?"

"Not exactly. I'm a Gryphon. Half eagle, half lion. If I choose to do so, I can shift into either animal separately. Zeus called his Gryphons *hounds*, thus the name of our MC."

"Zeus, huh? I was raised to worship a goddess. Does that bother you?"

"It doesn't. The wolves I know also worship the goddess, as does Rhiannon. I'm assuming you've heard of her since Sutton mentioned her during his speech?"

"Wolves…" Rayna bit her bottom lip. Gryphons and wolves and cheetahs. What other types of shifters were there? Getting back on task, she said, "Yes, I'm aware of who she is. Rhiannon is the reason I went undercover. When her father was taken into custody, David Spencer vowed his innocence. Said he took Rhiannon to keep her safe from the Hounds."

"Yeah, that's what he told her, but she didn't believe him. If he wanted to keep her safe, he would have never taken her to Haven where…" Ace snapped his mouth closed.

"I thought we agreed to share the truth?" Rayna urged.

"It's not that simple. Let's just say Rhi is special and leave it at that. What I can tell you is Spencer is a dangerous man, and with his stepfather being the leader of The Ministry, he—"

"His stepfather?" How had she not known that? Spencer left out that bit of information during their talks.

"Yes, Abraham Goodman married David's mother, Ruth. After Rhi's mother died, David took Rhi to Haven instead of Oasis to keep her away from them, but Josiah Talbert used Rhi for his own gain, and David did nothing to stop it. The man put tracking chips in his young daughter, for Zeus's sake."

"That's appalling." If the man could do that, he

could have lied about the Hounds being mercenaries. Rayna had to tread carefully.

"It is. It allowed James, one of the men from Haven, to track Rhi when she escaped. James was the man Josiah had promised Rhi to even though she didn't want to be his wife. Whatever else Spencer claimed, I can assure you the Hounds are honorable, Rayna. We were created to do good, and while there have been a few Gryphons who turned from our ways, the majority are decent, and we do what we can to make the world a better place."

Rayna slid her elbows back and tapped her fingers against the chair arm. Making the world a better place could include taking out the trash. There had been times Rayna wanted to put a bullet between someone's eyes when there wasn't enough evidence against them, or they walked on a technicality and went back to their heinous ways. Maybe being a mercenary wasn't such a bad thing.

Asher continued, "David Spencer provided crates of guns to Haven. He used his computer skills to invest their money while hiding their involvement with governments."

"How do you know that?"

Asher sat back and propped an ankle on the opposite knee. "When James found Rhi, we were able to subdue him. We questioned him about the tracker as well as David's position within Haven."

"And you're certain he was telling the truth?"

Asher rubbed the back of his neck. When she angled her head waiting, he dropped his hand. "Yes. We, uh…"

"You voiced him."

"We did," Asher admitted.

"I've sat in on the interviews with Spencer. He's very convincing."

Asher scowled. "Most sociopaths are."

"On that, we can agree. Why do you think Spencer is convinced Rhiannon isn't safe with the Hounds?"

Asher toyed with a loose thread on the cuff of his jeans. "Rhi lived at the cult for years, so she would know they aren't the God-fearing community they claim to be. She knew they raised the boys to be soldiers. On top of that, she has knowledge of who her father truly is, and if she shared that with the Hounds, we could expose him for the liar he is. It isn't that Rhi's not safe; it's David's fear of her talking." Asher narrowed his eyes. "I'm confused, though. Why were you sent undercover inside Haven? You said it was because of Rhi, but she hasn't been there for almost a year and neither has David."

Rayna didn't have a plausible answer. She'd wondered that herself when her boss insisted her time was better spent inside the compound gathering intel on David from the cult members and Talbert than looking into the Hounds.

"That's a good question, one I asked myself several times. My boss said he wanted intel on David from the members. What he didn't realize is that I wouldn't be allowed to talk to anyone who had that information."

"How is that possible? From what I understand, the FBI has been looking to take down The Ministry ever since they claimed responsibility for the apocalypse. Surely in the last thirty plus years, they have garnered knowledge of the inner workings of the cult. Rayna, are you sure you can trust your boss?"

CHAPTER FOUR

Ace

ACE HATED TO put doubt in Rayna's mind, but nothing about her going to Haven added up.

She spread her hands. "Can we ever really trust anyone?"

"Yes. I trust the Hounds with my life. I would apologize for asking about your boss, but it doesn't make sense. The FBI and the GIA have been after Haven as long as we have. Lucy St. Claire, nee Lazlo, worked for the GIA, and her job was to search for connections between The Ministry and governments. She wasn't the only analyst assigned to doing so. David Spencer was in the same department, so who better to know the inner workings of the cult?"

"Okay, playing devil's advocate here. Spencer knew all about The Ministry from a computer perspective, but infiltrating them from within would give him the evidence needed to put Talbert away."

"Then why didn't he do so early on? Why supply them with more weapons and boost their bank accounts for ten years? He wasn't doing that to protect Rhi. I think the man got a taste of power and wanted more. And if a GIA agent could be swayed, why couldn't someone from the FBI? You and I both know there are corrupt men and women in all factions of the government."

"Dammit," Rayna muttered and stood, pacing the living room. "I think you might be right. When Spencer was first brought in, I sat in on the interrogations. I questioned him extensively, blowing holes in his statements. More than once, he would look at my boss questioningly, like he was asking Fred to step in. I thought it was nothing more than he didn't appreciate a female bearing down on him. But now…"

"Now?"

Rayna stopped pacing and sighed. "Spencer was moved after I went to Haven. Where to, we don't know. That's why my partner brought me here instead of taking me home. My boss informed Seth that the GIA and Deputy Director Grissom arranged for Spencer to be turned over to the GIA. When Seth tried to access Spencer's files, they were locked down."

"Are you sure you can trust your partner?"

"Absolutely. Seth was the agent who arrested Spencer, but he's also one of my best friends."

Unexpected jealousy reared its head. Ace didn't do jealousy. He had no claim on Rayna. She pushed her jacket back to place her hands on her hips, exposing the weapon at her side. Fuck. Ace was glad she hadn't pulled the gun on him when he tried to voice her.

"If your partner has you hiding out here, were you planning on going to the office?" Ace gestured at the way she was dressed.

"No. I was on my way to see Rhiannon and let her know her father may be roaming free. I thought it best to dress professionally instead of showing up in shorts and a T-shirt."

"If Spencer is no longer in the FBI's custody, Rhi isn't safe, and I doubt you are either. The male has skills with a computer that are unbelievable. When Spencer was after Rhi and Ryker was taking her somewhere safe, Spencer remotely took over control of their vehicle's computer system. If he and your boss are working together, they might have someone inside Haven keeping tabs on you."

"I think I need to get out of here." Rayna's fear was tangible.

"Come home with me," Ace offered. When she opened her mouth to argue, he stood and held up his hands. "Just until you know who to trust. Rayna, I vow on all that's holy I will keep you safe. I have plenty of room at home, and no one will suspect you are staying with me in New Troy. Leave your phone here. I have a burner you can use to contact Seth if you need to get in touch with him."

Rayna bit her bottom lip, staring over Ace's shoulder. Sighing, she acquiesced. "Yeah, okay. Let me change clothes." Rayna removed her jacket as she strode out of the room. While he waited, Ace walked over to the mantel and surveyed the photos. Joseph and Delia Edwards were a handsome couple with two adorable kids. His heart kicked up a notch thinking about having his own children someday. He would rather have shifter kids so he didn't have to watch them grow old and die before him. Then again, a long life wasn't guaranteed for anyone.

When Rayna returned, she was wearing cutoff shorts, which accentuated her toned legs, and a faded band T-shirt with sneakers. Her long hair was no longer in a severe bun. Instead, it hung loose past her shoulders. She was carrying a duffel over her shoulder with a garment bag draped across her arm. "I hate leaving my laptop here, but it's also traceable."

"Is there any information on it you need? If so, we can take it by the security firm run by one of the Hounds, and they can clone your hard drive."

Rayna shook her head. "I'm afraid to turn it on. If it's powered up, someone at the office could be alerted, then they'll know I'm not at Haven. That, or they'll think someone else is tampering with it. Since I'm supposed to be undercover, it's best it remains off."

"Then bring it with you but don't turn it on." Rayna hesitated but eventually slid the case's strap over her shoulder. Ace reached out and took her bags from her and headed toward the back door. "I parked a few houses down, but it's best we don't go out the front, just in case."

"I wondered when I didn't see a bike in the driveway. Do you have an extra helmet?"

Ace waited on the patio while Rayna set the alarm, then pulled the door closed behind them. "I drove my car. It's less conspicuous."

Rayna muttered, "Some agents we are, not picking up on a tail."

Ace grinned. "Being a shifter means I can see well, so I was able to maintain a bit of distance."

They cut through several yards with Ace searching the area for anyone who shouldn't be there. When they got to his vehicle, Rayna whistled. "Damn, I think I'm in the wrong line of work."

"I don't splurge on much, but I did in this case." Ace was proud of his car. Where most of the other Hounds drove SUVs or trucks, he'd chosen the high-end sedan for comfort as well as style. He opened the passenger door for Rayna after clicking the locks. Once she was seated with her laptop bag at her feet, he tossed her duffel into the back seat, placed the garment bag carefully on top of it, then angled around to the driver's side. He started the motor and pointed to the large display screen. "Choose whatever you'd like to listen to."

"Even if it's today's pop music?"

Ace figured she was testing him considering the shirt she wore. "Sure. I'll listen to most anything except country, but if you like it, I can suffer through it long enough to get home."

Rayna chuckled and chose a hard rock channel. Ace kept his eyes peeled for anyone following. With her boss possibly lying about Spencer, Ace needed to call Bishop and have him investigate Fred. "What's your boss's full name?"

"Frederick Hanson, why?"

"I'm going to call Bishop, our computer expert, and have him dig into the man. See if he can find any dirt."

Rayna propped her elbow on the doorframe. "Goddess, I hate this."

"Maybe I'm wrong, and he's one of the good guys."

"Maybe," she mumbled.

Ace called Bishop and explained what he needed. Afterward, he and Rayna made small talk. The getting-to-know-you kind. Ace was amazed when Rayna said she only knew of three King Cheetahs – her, her mother, and grandmother. Others of their kind had either died off or traveled abroad. Her grandfather had been a standard cheetah shifter. "When I said my species is rare, I wasn't joking. I was raised by my grandmother since my mother wanted to focus on her career." It turned out that her mother, Colette, was known to the world as Francesca Ormond, a famous Hollywood actress. Rayna had only seen the female a handful of times since being left with her grandmother, Fern. "I have no idea who my father is. All my mother would say is he was a human she had a fling with while filming in Italy."

"And your grandmother doesn't know his identity?"

"Nope. Colette Bellamy is the most stubborn creature I've ever met. Every time she bothered to visit, I would ask. She said it didn't matter. That as a human, he couldn't be part of my life. I think it's one reason she stopped coming around."

"Well, that's bullshit. Most of the Hounds' mates are human."

"Do you have a mate?" The question was innocent, but Ace felt it to his soul.

"No. I keep hoping I'll find someone who's patient enough to deal with my issues." Did he trust the female with his secret? Not that she'd given any indication she found him attractive or felt a spark. Fuck it. "I'm demisexual. I've been in relationships in the past where I thought the person could be my mate, but by the time I got around to romantic feelings, they had grown tired of waiting."

"Oh, Asher. That's…" Rayna turned toward

him, as much as her seatbelt would allow. "Then they weren't the right one for you. I have no doubt you'll find your perfect someone."

Wanting to get the focus off him, he asked, "Where's your grandfather? I hope that's not a sensitive topic."

"It's not. He passed when my mother was young, so I never knew him. Gran keeps him alive with stories and photos, but it's hard to miss someone you never met."

"Both my parents are gone and have been for a while, and I never knew my grandparents."

Rayna squeezed his arm. "I'm sorry about your parents."

"Thank you. I miss them, but Ripley's parents sort of adopted me."

Rayna sighed, and Ace glanced over at her. "You should have seen the look on Glory's mother's face when Conrad said he was Glory's father-in-law, then pointed at Ripley, saying he was Glory's husband. Did they really get married?"

"No. Not yet anyway. But it's easier to say they're married than mated."

"Oh, that makes sense. I really like Glory, and I'm happy her life turned around. Her father is a piece of shit."

"Was. He's no longer of this earth." When Asher realized what he said, he whispered, "Fuck."

"Hey, right now, I am Rayna Bellamy, civilian.

57

Anything you tell me stays between us."

"Why is that? You took some type of oath, didn't you?"

"We promise to uphold the Constitution." Rayna reached over and squeezed Ace's arm. "I promise you can trust me, Asher."

You can.

Ace trusted his Gryphon, so he told her, "Amos Yearwood and William, the male Glory had been promised to, burned down Ripley's house trying to flush Glory out, not knowing if they were inside. Thank Zeus they weren't. The Hounds captured both men, and let's just say Ripley's mom was not happy with Amos for how he treated Glory. She was one angry momma Lion."

"Then he got what he deserved. Like I said, a piece of shit. There are more men at Haven that probably deserve the same fate. How exactly did Glory get away from the market?"

Ace chuckled, then told Rayna about Ripley's antics while Natalia snuck Glory out of the restroom. He then told her how Rhiannon escaped.

"Spencer gave my boss a ton of information on your MC. None of it's good."

"And I have no doubt it was all fabricated. After Ryker rescued Rhi from the dumpster, we found out a young man named Elijah was being held in solitary. He'd been at Sanctuary, Gideon Talbert's compound, along with Ryker's daughter,

McKenzie. That's another convoluted mess in itself, but long story short, Elijah and Mac fell in love, but Mac had been promised to one of Gideon's guards. The guard raped Mac, and when Elijah caused a scene, he was sent to Haven. During the time we were hiding Rhi, Josiah sent some of his men to look for her. Since Haven was heavily guarded, we couldn't chance storming the compound to find Elijah, so we convinced those men to bring not only Elijah but also a case of weapons and ammo. Ryker videotaped the men's 'confession' and sent it to the FBI along with where to find them. Spencer somehow recorded the Hounds walking into the warehouse. He also intercepted the video of the confession, so when your fellow agents arrived and found the Haven men dead, Spencer made it appear as though Hounds had killed them. Luckily, we have someone good with computers, and he was able to provide the original video and show the one Spencer handed over had been manipulated. The man can't be trusted."

"Goddess, that's awful. No wonder the Hounds want to take down The Ministry." Rayna took a deep breath. When she blew it out, she said, "Asher, Spencer claims the Hounds are mercenaries."

Ace flipped on the blinker to take the exit to New Troy. As he merged right, he contemplated trusting Rayna with the truth. While he did, she shocked him. "If you are... If you can look me in the eye and promise you only take out those who are evil, I'll drop the subject."

Ace rolled to a stop at the bottom of the ramp and turned to her. "I promise."

Rayna nodded as she admitted, "I've thought more than once about putting a bullet in someone who walked on a technicality. Those rapists and drug lords and pedophiles and human traffickers who find their way back onto the streets, continuing as though they're untouchable."

Ace relaxed at her admission. He pressed the accelerator and told her, "I can assure you those are the very ones the Hounds take out. They have a handler who vets every contract, and if it's someone wanting their wife killed for insurance money, those are passed over. I can't say someone less ethical doesn't take the hit, but the Hounds do not."

"You said *they*. Are you not a merc?"

"I'm not. I prefer to help Sutton where The Ministry is concerned. He's tasked me with patrolling Haven to see if Abraham shows up or sends in someone else to run the place."

"How will you do that without being seen?"

"In my Eagle. I will park well away from the compound, then fly in. But now that I'm protecting you, I'm going to ask him to have someone else patrol."

"Protecting me? You do realize I'm a trained agent, right?"

Ace turned down the street he lived on. "I do, but until we know whether your boss is helping Spencer, I'm not letting you out of my sight."

"Do you not think I'll be safe at your house? I don't want you to put your life on hold for me."

As he pulled in the driveway, Ace hit the button to open the garage door. "Yes, you'll be safe here as long as you don't contact anyone other than Seth. That is if you're one hundred percent sure you can trust him." Once in the garage, he closed the door behind them and turned off the motor.

"I trust him. His wife, Vanessa, and I are best friends, and I'm their kids' godmother. If he even thought of betraying me, she would string him up by his balls."

Ace chuckled. "Ouch. Let's get your things inside, and I'll show you around." He took her bags, but instead of following, Rayna walked over to inspect his Harley.

"So cool," she muttered, smoothing her hand over the leather seat.

"Have you ever ridden?"

Rayna shook her head. "No. I've never known anyone with a bike."

"Would you like to? I can get you a helmet. Just say the word."

"If you promise not to dump me off the back," she joked.

Ace rarely doubled anyone, but he would

Rayna. He would also purchase a backrest so she wasn't worried about falling off. "I promise."

He inclined his head to the door, and after taking one last look at the bike, she joined him. The door opened to a short hallway with the laundry room on one side and a pantry on the other. Past that was a modern kitchen Ace had spent a lot of money on. Living alone, he had learned to cook for himself many years ago, and other than the den, it was where he spent most of his time. "The fridge and pantry are well stocked, but you can let me know what you like to eat, and if I don't have it, I'll place a grocery order."

"I'm not picky, but if I never see oatmeal again, I'll be happy."

"Noted." Ace led her through the house, showing her each room until they arrived at the spare bedrooms. "There's one bedroom and a bonus room upstairs. My bedroom is down there." He pointed to the door at the end of the hall. "Both guest rooms down here are equally appointed, and the bathroom has plenty of linens."

"This one is fine." Rayna entered the room closest to the kitchen, so Ace followed and placed her bags on the queen-sized bed. "I appreciate this, Asher. While I'm here, I'll help out around the house to pay you back."

"That isn't necessary, but I do want you to make yourself at home. And if you want to cook, I won't say no."

Rayna scrunched her nose. "Yeah, you might feel differently after you taste my food. I can burn water."

Ace laughed, and she smiled. "Then we'll leave the kitchen duties to me. Why don't you unpack, and I'll go grab a burner phone for you?"

"Sounds good."

Ace left her to it and retraced his steps to the front of the house. While he waited on Rayna to unpack, Ace called Ryot. There was no need to barge in on the little family when a phone call would suffice. Ryot exploded, exactly as Ace expected. That was another reason Ace preferred to deliver the bad news over the phone. What he didn't share with his Pres was the fact that Rayna was staying with him. It wasn't that he didn't trust Ryot, but the fewer who knew of her whereabouts, the better.

His Lion wanted to come out and meet Rayna's Cheetah. There was no reason not to, so he agreed he would suggest it once she got settled. The sounds of Rayna moving around the guest room settled something inside Ace, and for the first time in forever, he was at peace. He didn't understand why, though. It wasn't like they were mates, so maybe it was just having someone else in his otherwise empty house. Whatever the reason, Ace was going to enjoy it while it lasted.

Chapter Five

Rayna

IF RAYNA WEREN'T both a shifter and a trained agent, she would never have agreed to stay at Asher's, even if her Cheetah thought they were mates, but what better way to judge his character than to live in the same house? So far, the male had been charming and kind. And honest. He apologized for trying to voice her, and she hadn't felt the odd sensation since she admitted the compulsion didn't work on her. Spencer hadn't been wrong about some of the MC being mercenaries, but if Asher had been truthful about the things David did to Rhiannon? Rayna would trust a merc any day over someone who put tracking chips in his child, then dragged her off to live in a cult.

She unzipped her duffel first. Removing her firearm, Rayna placed it on the nightstand, then put her casual clothes and underwear in the new-looking dresser. She hid the burner phone Seth gave her underneath her shirts. Until she knew without a doubt she could trust Asher, she wasn't going to tip her hand that she had another way to contact Seth. Her suits she hung in the closet. Then she took her toiletries across the hall to the bathroom. She was pleasantly surprised at how clean his place was. For a bachelor's home, it was charming, decorated in soft blues interspersed with beige and gray. Rayna had expected something different for a biker, which went to show you shouldn't judge a book by its cover, no matter how sexy said cover was.

Asher stating he was demisexual was an even bigger surprise. Not that he was demi but that he admitted it after such a short time. If her instincts weren't misleading her, Asher was decent and caring. Even before going through training, Rayna considered herself a good judge of character. If she had been wrong about her boss, was she also wrong about Asher? She didn't think so, and neither did her animal. Rayna's Cheetah certainly thought he was the shit, and she wanted to come out and play with Asher's Lion. It had been months since she'd been able to let her other half free, so now that she was unpacked, she planned to ask if he minded. She found him in the kitchen where a burner phone sat on the island.

"Here you are." Asher pushed the phone across the tiled counter, and Rayna closed the distance to take it. "Fresh out of the package," he added.

"Thanks." She set it down on the counter and twirled it. "Should we go see Rhiannon?"

"I've already called Ryker and warned him. And throwing this out there, I also told him about you. Since you planned on going to their house, I didn't think you'd mind."

"No. That's fine, as long as they know I'm on their side."

"I assured them you were."

Rayna picked the burner up, giving her hands something to hold onto. She was nervous, but with some prodding from her Cat, she asked, "Would you mind if I shifted? It's been months, and my Cheetah is itching to come out."

"I don't mind at all. As a matter of fact, my Lion wants to meet her, if that's okay?"

Rayna grinned. "That's perfect. I'll just go..." She thumbed over her shoulder toward the bedroom. She wasn't going to get naked in front of the male. She wasn't ashamed of her body, but she didn't want to seem too forward. Not after what he shared about his sexuality.

"Me too. It's unfair the dire wolves can shift with their clothes on."

"I've never heard of them."

"I hadn't either until one of the Hounds mated with one. They're bigger than regular wolf shifters. Anyway, I'll meet you in the living room? I need to close all the blinds before we shift."

Rayna agreed, then retreated to her room to undress. She had to leave the door cracked so she'd be able to get out, so she waited until Asher walked past to get to his bedroom. As soon as she was in her fur, her Cheetah purred. They padded down the hall to the living room and waited. When Asher's Lion prowled toward her, her Cheetah rolled onto her back like a hussy. Since it considered Asher her mate, it made sense her Cat would show her belly.

Asher's Lion chuffed and shook its large mane. He closed the distance and stretched out next to her. Both she and her Cat were smitten with the majestic animal. Rayna wondered what her mother would have done if she'd met another shifter instead of a human. Would she have mated the male? Or would she have tossed him aside the same way she did Rayna's father?

Rayna didn't date often. It had been over a year since she'd gone to dinner with someone, and there had been no spark, so she didn't accept the second invite. She saw no use in dating for dating's sake. Unlike her mother, Rayna wanted a mate. Someone to share her life with the way her grandparents had. As she spent the morning with Asher in their fur, she let her imagination run free. What if she weren't an agent who worked long hours? What if she and Asher hit it off and she moved into his house permanently? Rayna could be patient, becoming friends first, then lovers later. It had been years since she had sex with anyone, so waiting wasn't a problem. Rayna mentally rolled her eyes. Who was she kidding? The male was gorgeous, and she was nothing special. Just because he was nice and offered her a safe place to stay didn't mean he was interested in her. He had to get to know someone before becoming romantically involved, and Rayna had nothing to offer. She had no hobbies outside knitting and watching TV. She couldn't cook. Her looks were okay, and she was stubborn.

Her Cheetah rolled over and stood, then padded around the living room. It had been forever since she'd been able to let the animal outside to run. Maybe Asher knew of somewhere they could go to do so. Since they couldn't communicate in their fur, Rayna returned to the guest room, nudged the door closed, and shifted back. By the time she was dressed and walked down the hall, Asher was waiting for her in the kitchen where he was sipping a beer.

"Would you like something to drink? I have beer, soda, juice, and white wine. Oh, and all kinds of liquor in the den."

"Isn't it a little early for the hard stuff?" she joked.

"We're shifters. Unless your metabolism is different than mine…"

"I was just giving you a hard time. I'd love a beer."

Asher set his bottle down and retrieved one for her. After popping the top, he handed it over.

Rayna took a long pull, and after swallowing, let out an *ahh*. She'd missed drinking whatever she wanted. "Thanks, and thank you for letting me shift."

"No problem. Feel free to shift anytime you feel like it. It's easier for me since I can take to my Eagle and fly."

Something about that niggled at Rayna's mind. "Your Eagle wouldn't have white wings, would it?"

Asher rubbed the back of his neck, a sweet blush rising on his cheeks. "Uh, yes?"

Rayna grinned at him. "That was you in the tree watching me, wasn't it?"

"Sorry if that was creepy." He picked up his beer and took a swig.

"Not creepy. Beautiful. Do all Hounds have white wings?"

"No. We can call on one of the elements, and the wind is mine, thus the white in my feathers. Fire Gryphons have red wings, water Gryphons blue, and earth Gryphons have yellow or gold, depending on how old they are. We can also change the size of our bird to suit our needs."

"How big is your Gryphon?" Rayna couldn't wait to see the magical beast.

"Around eight feet. I should have shown you while we were both shifted. Next time I will, if you'd like to see him."

"Definitely. Now, don't you need to go check on Haven?" When Asher looked like he was going to protest, she raised her hand. "Asher, please. You're already going out of your way by letting me hide out here. I promise I'll be fine, hanging out, binge-watching television. I have several shows I need to catch up on." That would also allow her time to snoop.

Asher leaned his butt against the cabinet and crossed his arms over his chest. Rayna was drawn to the many tattoos on his arms, hands, and even his neck. Maybe one day, she would get to study the one on his chest hidden by his shirt. When he didn't say anything, she realized he was watching her checking him out. Instead of apologizing, she asked, "What do you say?" She arched a brow, waiting.

"I say you're stubborn. And I'll go, but not until tomorrow. Sutton already said to wait. That gives us time for you to tell me what you like to eat."

"You don't have to make anything special. I already said I'm not picky, and I meant it."

"I have to cook for myself, so it might as well be things you like. If you had to choose one food to eat the rest of your life, what would it be?"

"Cereal. The fruity kind, not the bran flakes with raisins. Blech." Rayna stuck her tongue out, and Asher chuckled.

"With or without milk?"

"Both. If I eat it for breakfast, with. If I have it as a snack, straight from the box. When I was a teenager, I'd grab a box of fruity loops and a two-liter grape soda, and that was my snack of choice while watching movies in my room. Drove my Gran crazy, but she kept the pantry stocked, indulging my addiction. Do you not have a guilty pleasure?"

Asher pushed off the cabinet and beckoned her to follow. When he opened the pantry door, he stepped back. Inside were all varieties of cheese snacks. "The fish are my favorite," he admitted. He then pointed to the top shelf where several boxes of fruity cereal were lined up.

"Yes!" Rayna pumped a fist. "We're going to get along just fine."

Ace frowned. "I'm still cooking for you."

"And I'll eat whatever you make." They returned to the island and picked up their beers. "At Haven, we didn't have meat often, but when we did, it was usually venison."

Asher retook his spot against the counter. "Yeah, Glory told us how she was the one who had to skin the deer once the hunters brought them in. What was your job at Haven?"

"Helping in the kitchen. Not cooking, mind you, but washing and cutting vegetables, then cleaning the dining room after everyone ate. At night, I knitted blankets to be sold at the market."

"Is that something you enjoy? Knitting?"

"It is. My grandmother taught me when I was young, and we would sit together and knit while watching TV."

"Do you still see her?"

Rayna downed the rest of her beer and looked around for the bin. "Do you recycle?"

"Yes. The bin is in the pantry next to the garbage can. You were too busy ogling the cereal to notice," Asher joked.

Rayna grinned at him. How could she not? She took her bottle to the pantry. When she returned, a fresh beer was on the island. "I don't see Gran as much as I would like since she lives in Arizona now, but I talk to her on the phone at least once a week. Or I did until I went undercover. I had to tell her about the assignment and how I wouldn't be able to call for a while."

"Too bad you can't do one of those DNA kits to find your father."

Rayna climbed on one of the stools and twirled the bottle between her hands. "I wouldn't even if it were possible. I don't want to disrupt his life, whatever that looks like. He's probably married with other kids."

"And you wouldn't want to meet your siblings?"

"I don't want to disrupt their lives either. It's not like I have free time on my hands to get to know them, if they'd even want that. Then there's the whole thing with my mother and who she is. Vanessa and Seth, and now you, are the only people aside from Gran and me who know that Colette Bellamy is Francesca Ormond. As far as the world knows, she's single with no children. She loves the limelight, but she's always managed to keep up that falsehood."

Asher tipped his head to the side, studying her. "Does it bother you that she doesn't claim you publicly?"

"It did when I was younger, but I'm used to it now. As far as I'm concerned, Fern Bellamy is my mother."

Asher's phone rang. He dug it out of his back pocket, studied the screen, then answered, "Go ahead, Bishop." Rayna used her shifter hearing to listen in.

"I've got an update on Fredrick Hanson. Up until four months ago, it appears the man was squeaky clean. Then a large sum of money was deposited into an offshore bank account in his name. Henry Palamo is the one who uncovered the money. I'm good, but Henry is better. Speaking of Rhi's father, Henry set up an algorithm to alert him if Spencer is seen on any CCTV cameras. So far, nothing."

"Can Henry link the money to Spencer?"

"Not yet, but he's working on it. I've already called Ryot. I'll keep you posted with anything else we uncover."

"Thanks, Brother." Asher disconnected and tossed the phone on the island.

"Who's Henry?" Rayna asked, not caring if he knew she had eavesdropped.

"He's a Gargoyle down in New Atlanta. Lucy, the female I mentioned who used to work for the GIA, is mated to Tamian St. Claire who is also a Gargoyle, tying the families together."

Rayna couldn't imagine what a Gargoyle would even look like. "How many types of shifters are there?"

"No clue, honestly. We know of four now that I've met you, but there could be any number."

Rayna tried to wrap her head around the fact that there were all types of creatures in the world interacting with humans daily. How many had she met and didn't realize it? "If Lucy's a Gryphon and her mate's a Gargoyle, what will their children be?"

Asher thought about it, and when he found the answer, he was grinning. "Total badasses."

Chapter Six

Ace

ACE DID HIS best to put on a happy face thinking of Lucy being pregnant, the same as he did when he was around the twins or Daisy and Patrick. He understood what females meant when they said their biological clock was ticking. He'd admitted as much to Ripley's mom, Regina, and she reminded him he could always foster kids or adopt. Ace had taken their talk to heart, and what no one knew, not even Regina or Ripley, was that Ace had begun looking into adoption. He had so much love to give, and while he'd prefer to have a biological child, he could adopt until that happened. If it happened. He'd all but given up on finding a mate.

"Are you okay?" Rayna asked, bringing him out of his thoughts.

"I am, but I'm also hungry. I skipped breakfast." Ace moved to the refrigerator to see what he could pull together quickly. "How do you feel about chicken gnocchi?"

75

"If you tell me you use sundried tomatoes, I'll be your best friend for life."

"Then consider me your BFF," Ace joked. As he gathered the ingredients, Rayna stood close and watched as he prepared their lunch.

Rayna sighed. "I need to tell Seth about Hanson. Since I'm hiding, he can be our eyes in the field."

"He needs to be careful. Men like that will do anything to protect themselves. Just look at how far Josiah was willing to go. He either had plastic surgery or found a talented artist to create some type of prosthetic." It reminded Ace of the masks the Gargoyles used.

"What do you mean?"

While Ace diced the chicken breasts, he explained, "Josiah changed his looks and called himself Jacob. After losing Rhi and David, Abraham was done with Josiah and told the guards to shoot him on sight. I'm not sure if Josiah thought getting Rhiannon back to Haven would return him to Abraham's good graces or if he was just a narcissist who felt he was above it all."

"What's so special about Rhiannon?"

Ace sauteed the diced onions in the oil from the tomatoes, then added the chicken and spices. He stirred as he considered telling Rayna the truth.

"Asher, you can trust me. Glory was willing to kill Josiah to keep him from getting his hands on Rhiannon. I've never met the female, but I do know she has a baby, so that alone is enough for me to want to protect her. Children are precious, and there's no way I could sit by while David or Abraham try to abduct her again."

Ace added the gnocchi and some chicken broth, stirring it all together. He covered the pot to let it simmer. His beast urged him to trust the female, so he admitted, "Rhi has a gift. I'm not sure exactly how it works, but she explains it as channeling energy into something or someone to heal them. Josiah found out about her gift and exploited it. Those trackers that David implanted were more than locaters. When they were activated, Rhi would become semi-conscious. Josiah recruited humans with life-threatening diseases, promising he could heal them in exchange for their money. He would activate the chip in Rhi, then have her use her gift to heal the person, only she didn't remember doing so. She would wake up having lost chunks of time. With David and Rhi gone, Josiah lost his income generators. He couldn't control David, but he thought he could control Rhi. Rhi's grandmother knows about her gift, therefore Abraham does as well."

"And David said he wanted to protect Rhi? Bullshit."

"Rhi's grandmother wasn't kind to her or her mother, saying since they were pagan, they were of the devil, but we both know how the men in The

Ministry feel about women having an opinion. Josiah, and now Abraham, didn't care where Rhi's gift came from, only how they can use it." Ace removed the lid, added the tomatoes, spinach, some heavy cream, and parmesan cheese. He stirred it all together, letting the sauce thicken. He opened one of the cabinets and removed two bowls. Rayna gathered forks, and when she opened the refrigerator, she asked if he wanted another beer. He did, so she grabbed him a bottle but chose a soda for herself. She took them to the island instead of to the table. Ace dished up the food and took the bowls to where she was sitting. He climbed on the stool next to hers and waited for her opinion.

Rayna blew across the food on her fork, and when she took the first bite, she moaned indecently. "So good," she mumbled around a mouthful. After swallowing, she asked, "How did you learn to cook like this?"

"My dad did most of the cooking at home since my mom was like you and could burn toast no matter what the setting was. He taught me when I lived at home, and after he passed, I watched online videos. I also made some adlib meals where I threw whatever in a pot to see if it worked."

"I would ask you to teach me, but my grandmother tried. For whatever reason, I just don't get it."

Ace stabbed a dumpling on his fork. "We all

have our strengths and weaknesses. You're smart, but that doesn't mean you're capable of everything. You're proficient with a gun, and I've never used one. You can knit, but I wouldn't have the patience to work on something long enough to make a blanket or sweater. I have no doubt there are plenty of things you're good at, so don't worry about your lack of skills in the kitchen."

"Why do you think I'm smart?" she asked, scooping up a bite of tomatoes, spinach, and chicken. He noticed she ate the gnocchi separately.

"I doubt the FBI recruits uneducated agents."

Rayna grinned. "I don't know. I've met some agents who don't seem to have their shit together."

Ace smiled back. They dug into their meal, eating in companionable silence. Rayna washed the pot after Ace put the leftovers in the fridge. It should have been awkward, having this stranger in his home, but it wasn't, and that scared Ace. It had been too long since he'd had someone else in his space. His last relationship, if he could call it that, had been several years ago. He had resigned himself to being single, thus the decision to start the adoption process on his own. Rayna mentioned children being precious, and he couldn't agree more. He'd bought his house with kids in mind. It had three bedrooms besides the master and a big, fenced-in backyard with shade trees. Granted, it didn't offer privacy for a shifter child, but he had enough money to buy some land the way Ripley had.

Instead of letting the melancholy take over, he plastered on a smile and asked Rayna if she wanted to watch TV.

"What did you have in mind?" she asked, drying her hands on a towel.

"You mentioned there were shows you wanted to binge. Any of those."

"Are you okay with hot firefighters?" she teased.

"Why wouldn't I be? Beauty is beauty, no matter the gender," he admitted. Rayna opened her mouth, then closed it. "You can ask. I won't be offended."

"It's none of my business, really." She grabbed her soda can and padded into the living room, taking one end of the sofa. Ace snagged another beer before joining her. He tossed her the remote, sat on the opposite end, and a few minutes later, a show about firefighters played. Ace mostly read or streamed movies, but he was quickly drawn into the drama while admiring both the male and female actors. Rayna explained the characters and the overarching plot since she had started with a mid-season episode. He wondered what she had considered asking, and he was sure it had to do with his sexuality. One of his earliest relationships ended when he admitted to being attracted to the person not the gender. The woman couldn't imagine being with a man who could have sex with another man. Ace didn't bother telling her he'd never had sex with anyone. No one alive knew that other than him.

After polishing off his beer, he set the bottle aside and raised the footrest. Ace linked his fingers on his stomach and closed his eyes. He'd spent the night before watching the house where Rayna was staying, plus his belly was full of gnocchi. He didn't plan on sleeping, but his body had other ideas.

Rayna

WHEN ASHER BEGAN snoring softly, Rayna eased off the sofa and padded down the hall to her bedroom. She opened the dresser and dug the burner from beneath her clothes, taking it into the bathroom and closing the door. Seth didn't answer, and she didn't want to leave a voice message in case someone intercepted his phone. A text came through almost immediately.

Seth: *Can you pick up the kids from practice? I have*

to work late.

Va.nessa: *Sure.*

Seth was smart to set her ID as his wife. So that he didn't confuse the two, he added the dot, but anyone who didn't know would hopefully overlook it. His message was a code they'd agreed when he dropped her off at Delia's. Since his kids didn't play sports, it meant he couldn't talk. She didn't dare send a different response. Instead, she replaced the phone in the drawer and returned to the living room. Asher was where she left him, so Rayna settled in for another episode. She was sure Asher wasn't into the show, but he didn't seem to mind her watching it.

Instead of the screen, she studied the male a few feet away. If he were different, she would have flirted with him just to see if he was interested. Earlier, she had almost asked if he was into both males and females, but it wasn't her business. And if he was? It didn't matter. Rayna knew a few humans who were bisexual, and although they were looked down upon by some, Rayna felt there was nothing wrong with being drawn to both sexes. In her opinion, it would be nice to have a bigger ocean to fish from. She could appreciate when another female was attractive, but they didn't interest her.

It mostly didn't matter because again, he was only being nice by offering her a place to hide. He didn't know he was her mate, and she wouldn't tell him. She slumped down on the sofa, leaning her head against the arm, and focused on the TV. Her mind drifted to her boss and Spencer. Rayna wanted to help find the former GIA agent. He needed to be stopped for good this time. She worried about Rhiannon, and even though she'd never met the female, Rayna felt sorry for the young woman. She couldn't imagine having a gift of healing, then being forced to use it without her knowledge. Rayna had no idea where to start. Where would an agent on the run go? For someone with his abilities, Spencer could be anywhere. He had over three months' head start on them.

"It's going to be okay," Asher murmured. Rayna glanced over at the Gryphon, but his eyes were still closed.

Rayna wanted to believe him. Since she couldn't focus on the program, Rayna turned the TV off, then stood and stretched. She headed to the back of the house and looked out the window. The backyard was spacious with a small shed in one corner where Rayna assumed the lawnmower was stored since it hadn't been in his garage. She spied lounge chairs on a covered patio, so she unlocked the door and stepped outside. Rayna dragged one of the chairs out into the sunshine and lay down. Her Cheetah begged to be let out so it could bask in the warmth, but that wasn't possible. It was one thing she missed about her grandmother's home where she was raised. The house had been secluded, and Rayna could shift whenever she felt like it. More than once, she asked Gran why the goddess had made them shifters who had to hide from humans. It wasn't fair to give them some wonderful abilities only to have to keep them tamped down. At least Asher could fly in his Eagle form. Wolves were common enough they could also shift without causing too much chaos. And Gargoyles? What did they even look like? She couldn't imagine it.

Rayna rolled her sleeves up to her shoulders to let her arms tan more evenly. She closed her eyes and attempted to let the heat ease her mind. She'd gone to Haven when the weather was just turning from cold to warmer, and she'd not been allowed to stay outside any length of time. Living in the confines of the compound had been some of the hardest days of her life. Rayna still didn't understand why any woman would want to live under such oppression. They had no freedoms. Even the married women were supposed to be obedient to their husband. There was no partnership. No equality. Very little love that she'd seen. Glory's sister and her husband were the one couple who had even smiled at one another. The older couples seemed miserable.

Asher had been correct that the FBI wanted to take down The Ministry and had ever since the cult brought the world to a halt almost forty years ago. They blamed it on Jonas Montague, the scientist who cloned the world's first baby, stating he was playing God, but the man didn't destroy cities. He didn't kill thousands of innocent people. He created life. Having lived among the cult members, Rayna couldn't find one good thing about them. They raised young boys to be soldiers. Not so they could defend their country but to defend the compound and anyone who opposed their backward lifestyle.

Then why was her boss working with Spencer? Maybe it had nothing to do with The Ministry. Spencer had proven he could amass fortunes using his computer. Was that it? Was Hanson so greedy he would allow David back into the world where he was a threat to his daughter? Money was often a great corrupter of morals. Maybe Hanson had no morals in the first place. Rayna hated that Seth worked so closely with the man. He had Vanessa and the kids to think about. Instead of hiding, maybe she should return to the office where she would have her partner's back.

No. Hanson had sent Rayna away for a reason. One she needed to figure out. But how was she supposed to do that from Asher's house? A shadow fell over Rayna. She opened her eyes to find the biker standing there with a phone in his hand. Damn, he moved silently.

"It was ringing. I thought it might be

important." When Rayna took it, she realized it wasn't the burner he'd given her but the one she'd hidden. He turned and walked back into the house on quiet feet. She sat up and unlocked the phone. There was one missed call notification and a text.

Seth: *Where are you? I stopped by to visit.*

Va.nessa: *Staying with a friend. With Spencer's whereabouts unknown, I didn't trust that he wouldn't track me down at Delia's. When exactly was he released?*

Rayna watched the dots bounce as Seth typed his response. The dots stopped, then started again.

Seth: *Two months, and what friend?*

Two months? What the actual fuck? Rayna's instincts were screaming at her that Seth was hiding something.

Va.nessa: *If Spencer's been gone for months, why didn't you pull me out of Haven?*

No dots appeared, so either Seth couldn't respond, or he was thinking of a plausible answer. Rayna slung her legs over the side of the chair and stood. She tapped the phone against her thigh as she walked toward the shade trees. She stopped at the far end of the yard, leaning against a tall aspen. While there had been trees at the compound, she'd not been able to enjoy them. Being a shifter, Rayna preferred the outdoors. Her Cat wanted to climb up the thick trunks and lounge on the branches while birds danced around her, toying with her Cheetah. It had been one of her favorite things to do as a teen.

She would never hurt another animal unless she was in danger, and small songbirds were a delight. The phone pinged, and she tapped the screen.

Seth: *Hanson thought you were safer there.*

Safer? From whom? Rayna's skin itched with unease. The only reason she'd been safe at Haven was because she was a shifter, but Seth didn't know that. She could have escaped if her life depended on it. She'd been lucky that she hadn't been paired up with one of the single men. When Rayna first arrived, she let Thomas know she was there for solitude, not to find a husband. Glory had befriended her and shared how she and her family came to be at Haven. Lisa Ann clutched her metaphorical pearls when Glory mentioned having sex as a teen, but then again, Lisa Ann was much older.

Seth: *At least tell me where you are.*

Rayna hesitated. This was Seth, so why was she hesitant to tell him the truth? Instead of typing a response, she padded across the yard and back into the house. Asher was standing in the kitchen, sipping a beer. He arched a brow, but she ignored him as she tore the phone apart. When she didn't find a tracker, she put it back together and powered the device down.

She blew out a breath and met Asher's eyes. "I need a favor."

CHAPTER SEVEN

Ace

WHEN ACE WOKE to a silent room, he worried Rayna had left, but his Gryphon informed him where she was. He scrubbed a hand down his face, then lowered the footrest. As he stood, a phone rang, but it was in the back of the house. He glanced outside to see Rayna resting on a lounge chair she'd pulled out into the yard so she was in the sun. She didn't move at the sound of the ringing, so he strode to the room where her things were. Was it an invasion of privacy to enter the room even though it was his? The device pinged, and Ace followed the sound, finding a burner tucked away under some of her clothes, only it wasn't the one he'd given her. Why didn't she admit she already had a phone when he offered her the new one earlier? Ace snatched it up and closed the drawer. He didn't try to open it to see who was contacting her. More than likely, it was her partner.

Ace retraced his steps and opened the back

door. Rayna didn't move. Either she was asleep or deep in thought. He stopped next to the lounge chair, and the female opened her eyes.

Holding it out to her, he said, "It was ringing. I thought it might be important." If she got pissed at him for going through her things, he'd ask forgiveness later. Ace returned inside, grabbed a beer, then leaned against the counter where he could see her. Rayna didn't return the call, but she did tap at the screen, sending a message. A few minutes later, she rose and walked to the back of the yard, leaning against a tree. Her body language was tense, and her pretty face was frowning. His beast wanted to soothe whatever was bothering her. That didn't bother Ace. In fact, he found it fascinating. What did bother him was her reluctance to trust him.

She trusted us to come here.

But not enough to tell me she already had a phone?

Maybe she thought it was a nice gesture and didn't want to hurt your feelings.

Rayna strode toward the house with purpose. Ace remained leaning against the counter as she entered the house. She pulled the cover off the phone and removed the battery, searching. She then put it back together but powered it down. When she spoke, she said, "I need a favor."

Ace inclined his head. "If it's within my power."

"Can you have Bishop run a discreet check on

Seth?" Rayna blew out a breath. "I have no reason not to trust my partner, but something isn't sitting right with me about this whole situation. I asked why he left me at Haven when Spencer had been released months ago, and he told me because I was safer there."

"Safer from whom?"

"That's what I asked. Myself, not him. I'm a trained agent, and my record is spotless. I've received several awards over the years. Not tooting my own horn; I'm just saying that I'm good at my job. If I was in danger from someone, why not just tell me who it is and what they want?"

"Have you considered Seth *is* protecting you?"

"Maybe, but my instincts are telling me something isn't right." Rayna paced the kitchen.

"Let me have Bishop run a search to put your mind at ease. Tell me about Seth. His family. What their day-to-days are like. What kind of house they live in, cars, etc. Better yet, let me get Bishop on the phone and you can give him the information. That way if he has questions, you can answer them."

"Yeah, okay. I hate this. I've never doubted him in all the years we've known each other."

Ace dialed Bishop. When he answered, Ace said, "Hey, Bishop. I need you to run another search. This one is on Rayna's partner, Seth McCauley. And I have her on speaker to answer any questions you might have."

Bishop cleared his throat. "Actually, I've already done that. Since Rhiannon's safety is threatened, I wanted to cover all our bases. I've also asked Zedra if she'll shadow the wife and kids."

Rayna leaned her arms on the bar and stared at a point over Ace's shoulder. "With this being the holiday weekend, Vanessa would have taken the kids to visit her parents over in Little Falls. They stay with their grandparents for the month of July. Vanessa should've been back in time to open her shop today."

"And Seth doesn't go with them?"

"If he's not on a case, but since he drove by Delia's and found me missing, he must be working on something."

"Thank you. That's helpful. As for Seth, I didn't find anything in his financials out of the ordinary. Rayna, can you tell me about Vanessa's life? I know she owns her salon, but what about after she leaves for the night? And with the kids staying with her parents, what does she do on weekends? Do they go to church? Does Seth normally go into the office on the weekends?"

Rayna gave Bishop all the information he requested plus some he didn't. It was clear Rayna was close with the McCauleys and knew details about their lives including the name of the older woman who watched the kids while Vanessa and Seth worked. "They don't go to church except at

91

Christmas when Seth's parents come visit. As for the office, he works all hours if he's on a case. I didn't ask him about his current one when he picked me up, though. His text said that Hanson is going to be out of town for the next week."

"Does Hanson use a company jet, or does he fly commercial?"

"A company craft. If it's for personal use, he's supposed to reimburse the cost."

"I was afraid of that, but it's helpful. Anything else you can think of that'll dictate whether anything is out of the ordinary?"

"Only if Vanessa didn't show up for work today."

"Thank you, Rayna. I can't imagine this is easy for you."

"It's not. Like I told Asher, I've never had reason to doubt Seth. If he is involved in any way, it's under duress."

"I'll keep you posted if I find anything suspicious or otherwise."

"Thanks, Brother."

Rayna propped her head against her hand. "This sucks. I'm not used to sitting on the sidelines."

"How long were you supposed to stay at Haven?"

"Two months. At least that's what I agreed to. When I was still there longer? I became both nervous and pissed off."

"I've heard about being in the cult from those who were there against their will. What was it like for you?"

"It was a culture shock of epic proportions. I had read case studies on The Ministry, so I had some suspicions of what it would be like, but living it... It was intense and hard for me to keep my head down and mouth shut. Women expected to heel, to be silent, to marry a man they have no interest in is ludicrous. It's like living in the Stone Age. If they were a loving group, only wanting to live off the land in a peaceful environment, it would be easier to assimilate to not having creature comforts like electronics. Being self-sufficient isn't wrong. When it's for less than peaceful purposes where the men rule with an iron hand, that I can't wrap my head around. The hardest part was interacting with Glory every day and not being able to help her. She has one of the brightest souls I've ever encountered. The night before the Hounds rescued her from the market, she came into our cabin with a mark on her face where Amos struck her. It was all I could do to sit there and not go claw his eyes out."

"Glory's safe now. She and Ripley moved into their new house yesterday, and Rip's parents are relocating from Florida to be closer. Conrad and Regina will more than make up for all the hurt Glory's parents caused."

"That's wonderful. I can't wait to see her

outside of Haven. I feel like we could be good friends."

"I'm sure she'd like that as well." Ace would too. If Rayna and Glory became close, it would give him the opportunity to spend time with his own best friend without feeling like a third wheel. He would love nothing more than to have Rayna on the back of his bike. For that to happen... "I need to run some errands. Will you be okay alone for a couple of hours?"

"I'll be fine. I'm going to go back outside and resume my nap in the sun."

"Help yourself to anything to eat or drink. I want you to feel at home here."

"I appreciate that." Rayna climbed down from the stool and walked outside. Once she was lying on the lounge chair, Ace headed to her room and opened the closet. He picked up a shoe to see what size she wore. Back in the kitchen, he grabbed his keys, then headed to town. His first stop was the bike shop where he purchased a backrest and a few helmets since he wasn't sure of Rayna's size. He also bought her some riding boots and a few T-shirts. He was going overboard for someone he'd just met, but it felt right. Still, he wasn't going to let himself get carried away thinking of a future with the female. That way lay madness, but a male could dream. With his purchases stored in the trunk, Ace turned the car to the grocery store where he filled a cart. If he bought more fruity cereal and several packs of grape soda, that was his business.

He returned home in just under two hours, and Rayna was where he'd left her, only now, she was on her stomach. Ace put the groceries away, then went to the garage to install the backrest on his Harley. It wasn't as cushy as some, but it would allow her to feel more secure.

"Asher?" Rayna called out.

"In the garage." He stood when she appeared in the door. "Come see." Ace gestured to the bike as Rayna closed the distance.

"Is that for me?" She ran her hand over the leather.

"It is. I also got you some riding boots and a helmet. Well, a few helmets since I didn't know your size. I'll return the ones that don't fit."

Before he knew what was happening, Ace had his arms filled with a happy female. "Thank you. It's been a long time since anyone did something this nice for me." Rayna hugged him tightly, her body fitting perfectly against his. Ace returned the embrace, setting his cheek against her hair. His Gryphon rumbled, and Rayna pulled back to look at him.

"Was that your animal?"

Ace ran his finger down her cheek that had an indention from the cushion she'd been lying on. "Yep. He likes hugs."

Rayna smiled as she leaned back in. "I do too. Anytime he wants one, all you have to do is ask." They remained in each other's arms for several minutes just being, and it was the most peaceful Ace had felt in years. "Can we go for a ride soon?" Rayna asked against his neck.

He pulled away, keeping his hands on her arms. "Sure can. Let's see which helmet fits." He walked around to the trunk where he'd left them. After finding one that worked, he handed her the other bags. "Here are your boots and some shirts. You'll want to wear jeans if you have them."

"I do. Let me get changed. I'll be right back." Rayna smacked a kiss against his cheek before rushing inside. Ace placed his fingers where her lips had been like a lovestruck fool. He didn't understand what was happening, and he would not allow himself to get his hopes up. Too many times he'd been optimistic and had his heart broken.

She's different.

You can't know that.

I can. Her Cheetah likes me.

Ace chuckled. Leave it to his Gryphon to puff up like a peacock.

We'll see.

While waiting on Rayna to change, Ace closed the trunk lid, then opened the garage door. He backed his bike out and turned it around.

Rayna jogged out of the house and held her

arms out. "Tada," she sang. "The boots fit perfectly. How'd you manage that?"

Ace admitted, "I snuck a peek at your shoes before I left. You look great." She'd braided her long hair and changed into one of her new T-shirts and a pair of jeans.

"Thank you. Not only for the compliment but also for the new duds. I love the shirts, and the boots are comfortable while being badass."

Ace couldn't help but smile at her. "You're most welcome. Let me lock up the house, then we'll hit the road." When he finished inside, Ace handed Rayna her helmet and helped with the chin strap. "I'll get on first, then you climb on behind me. The trick to riding with someone is to sit still. Don't try to lean with the bike."

"Don't lean. Got it."

Ace slung a leg over the bike and stood it up. Rayna placed her hand on his shoulder, her foot on the peg, and slid on behind him. He didn't have to tell her to wrap her arms around him. Leaning her chest against his back, she said, "I'm so excited."

"Then hang on." Ace cranked the motor, dropped the gear shifter into first, and eased off the clutch. There were no obstructions at the road like trees or hedges, so he pulled out when he saw no oncoming traffic. He kept to the backroads and took a route that was long and winding. Rayna sat perfectly still except for her hands that dug into his stomach when he took a sharp turn. It had been too long since he had someone to ride with. Only one of his previous partners was interested, but it didn't last long. Ace shook off the memory and focused on the present.

They'd been riding a couple of hours when Ace asked, "Are you hungry?"

"I could eat."

"The next town has a few restaurants, and there's also a state park that offers a buffet." Ace held his breath. The last female he'd been interested in had laughed at Ace for even mentioning a buffet, but the Hounds often stopped at state parks during their group rides since there was something for everyone.

"Oh, the state park please. I love buffets. I know some people frown on them, but I like being able to eat a little of everything. And they offer so many good desserts too."

Ace smiled to himself. How could he not? "Buffet it is." When they arrived, he pulled into a spot and placed his feet flat on the ground, turning the bike off. Rayna gave his stomach a squeeze before climbing off. Ace flipped the kickstand down, then dismounted. Rayna's smile was bright as he helped remove her helmet.

"Man, that was exhilarating. If I knew how to ride, I'd never drive a car."

Ace placed their helmets on the handlebars and

smoothed out his hair. Rayna didn't have to worry about "helmet hair" since hers was braided. "I can teach you."

Rayna clasped her hands together. "Really? Isn't your bike too big for me?"

"Nope. Several of our females ride their own bikes, and some aren't as tall as you. Plus, you have your shifter strength to keep it upright. We can start you off on something smaller, though. I'll give Havyck a call and have him on the lookout for a starter bike."

Rayna wound her arm through his as they headed to the door. "Let me know how much it is, and I'll transfer the money from my savings account."

Ace didn't argue, but he also wouldn't take her money. She would find he was a generous… friend. That's all they were at that point, but a male could dream.

CHAPTER EIGHT

Rayna

RAYNA HAD NEVER felt so alive. Riding behind Asher with the wind in her face had been amazing, and she couldn't wait to do it again. Yes, she wanted to learn to ride her own bike, just in case —

Nope.

What?

Don't even go there. Just be patient, and we'll get what we want.

Rayna trusted her Cheetah, and she could be patient with Asher. But that didn't mean he would want her romantically if she did give him time to get to know her.

His Gryphon wants us.

Hmm. That was intriguing, how the beast and the human weren't on the same page. Asher was proving to be generous, and they'd only known each other less than forty-eight hours. Not that she needed him to buy her things, but the gesture was appreciated. Rayna's mother had sent money to help Gran raise Rayna, and her grandmother invested every penny. While Rayna would have preferred to have Colette's love instead, she wasn't going to turn down the money. Growing up, she'd been content to garden in the summer and knit with Gran in the winter. Rayna loved being outdoors, running through the woods, climbing trees, and chasing smaller animals. Playing with them had been fun. Fern had given her all the love she needed while teaching her life skills (except cooking) and letting her be a kid.

Unlike others she went to school with, Rayna hadn't found her calling. She was content having fun and spending time with her grandmother, learning whatever Gran taught her. Being an agent hadn't been her dream. It was Vanessa who convinced her to change her major in college when Rayna couldn't decide on a career. Seth was already an agent by that time, and he talked at length about his job and what the requirements were. It sounded exciting, so she agreed. Her original plan had been to work until she was forty and then retire to find something else to fill her time.

Her job had been fulfilling up to the point she went undercover at Haven. Now, though, Rayna was considering retiring sooner. She didn't need the income. She also didn't need the headache that her boss continued to give her. If things with Asher worked out, Rayna would love to work with him and the Hounds in taking down The Ministry.

After they ate their fill at the buffet, Asher had taken the long way home. They settled on the sofa together and watched a movie before saying goodnight. The next morning, Asher left after breakfast to go spy on Haven. Rayna wished she could have gone with him. Instead, she was alone in his house with nothing to do. He'd left one of his credit cards and told her to order some knitting supplies or anything else she wanted since using her own card could lead her boss to where she was hiding. She asked if she could contact Glory, but she and Ripley were dealing with Glory's family. Feeling a bit sluggish, Rayna went through a circuit of push-ups and sit-ups. She jumped an imaginary rope. She did burpees. Then she did it all again ten times. After that, she showered. Then she found herself going over every inch of Asher's home. She wanted to learn more about the male.

There was next to nothing to tell her about his past. He had a couple of photos of him and who she assumed were his parents. There were a few with the other Hounds, including one of Asher and two of the cutest little boys Rayna had ever seen. She knew them to be Maveryck's twin sons from her time researching the club. Maveryck's girlfriend, Natalia Jones, had been a conundrum. When Rayna researched the female, she found little on the lavender-haired woman. Rayna concluded she was

Maveryck's mate since he was a Gryphon. Knowing the Lazlos were shifters put them in a new light. Ripley rescuing Glory added to the goodness. So did Sutton's voicing the members of Haven to behave better toward one another. Rayna couldn't wait to hear how the men were acting now that Sutton had convinced them to go against what they'd been taught by Josiah.

But she would have to wait, and that didn't sit well with Rayna. She didn't want to knit. She'd had her fill of that at the compound. She couldn't cook, so preparing a meal for Asher's return was out. What she wanted to do was help find Hanson, but being stuck inside without a computer made that impossible. Besides, she wasn't a hacker. She would have to wait on Bishop to find her boss. She could call Vanessa, but that would give Seth access to her. Instead, she retrieved the burner Asher had given her and dialed the one person she could trust.

Gran didn't answer, and Rayna didn't expect her to since the number was unknown, so she left a message and waited. It didn't take long for the phone to ring.

"Hello, Gran."

"Rayna! Oh, my goddess, child. How are you?"

"I'm… Well, I'm no longer undercover, but things are a little chaotic."

"Tell me everything." Gran's sweet voice washed over Rayna.

Rayna stepped outside, reclined on the lounge chair in the sun, and told Gran everything, including her feelings about Asher.

"A Gryphon? How exciting. I always wondered what other types of shifters were out there, and you've caught the eye of one. I'm so happy for you. But why do you sound sad?"

"I'm not sad, Gran. Just agitated. You know I don't like sitting around, and until my boss is found, that's exactly what I must do."

"Bah. Turn in your notice and find something you love."

Rayna flipped over to her stomach, placing the phone on the cushion while propping her head on her hand. "I don't know what that is. I didn't when I was younger, and it's why I let Vanessa and Seth convince me to become an agent."

"You have all the time in the world to figure it out. Or not. There's no rule that says you have to work. You don't need the money. Maybe instead of focusing on a career, you should give all your attention to Asher."

"I still need something to fill my time. He's only been gone a few hours, and I'm already going stir crazy. You know I don't do well sitting still. It about killed me at Haven."

Gran laughed. "We both know cooking is out."

"Thank the goddess Asher has that covered. And I knitted enough blankets these last four months that I don't want to look at yarn for a while."

"Does he have a garden or flowerbeds? You're good with making things grow."

"He has trees and shrubs and natural wildflowers. Maybe I'll ask if I can do a small vegetable garden in the backyard. There's plenty of room."

"He told you to do what you wanted, right? Why not surprise him? If he's handy in the kitchen, he'll appreciate having fresh vegetables. It's too late in the season to plant some things, but there are plenty that do well in the fall. And digging in the dirt, turning the soil, will expend some energy, which you obviously need to do. Heck, mow the lawn or trim the bushes. Those are things you used to enjoy. Share in the chores. Anything that will take something off his plate. If you truly believe he's your mate, show him you care by doing small things."

"Thanks, Gran. You always know what to say."

"You don't have to thank me, child. And my knowledge comes from living with your grandfather for over two centuries. I hated dusting, so he did that. I didn't mind laundry, but I would let it pile up after it came out of the dryer, so he put it away for me. He enjoyed mowing, but when it came to pulling weeds, he refused, so I took on that task. It's give and take. That's what makes a good

105

relationship. That and a lot of patience."

"You've given me plenty to think about. And as soon as this mess with my boss is over, I'm coming to visit. It's been too long."

"It has. Maybe you can bring your mate. I'll need to give my approval, you know."

Rayna could hear the smirk over the line. "Of course. I love you, Gran."

"Love you too, Rayna. We'll talk again soon."

Rayna looked around. The yard didn't need mowing, so she considered putting in a small garden and decided it would be something she enjoyed while gifting Asher with vegetables he could use in their meals. She studied where the sun shone and chose the best spot in her mind. Next, she rose from the chair and strode to the shed to see what tools, if any, Asher had. The inside of the small building was as neat as the house. There was a push mower, a weed eater, and hedge clippers. Asher had an axe, a hatchet, and both a leaf rake and garden rake. What he didn't have was a hoe, pick axe, or shovel. There were shelves which held boxes, but Rayna didn't rummage through them. She closed the door and returned to the house where she found a notepad and pencil in one of the kitchen drawers, then made a list of items she would need. She used the phone to search the internet for the nearest garden supply store. It was a short drive away, but Rayna needed things like compost that she wouldn't dream of putting in the trunk of Asher's sedan. There were smaller items she could get while she planned her little crop. With an idea in place, she changed out of her lounging clothes into something appropriate, then grabbed the keys and headed out.

Ace

WHEN ACE PARKED at the campground, he was surprised to find Ripley's bike wasn't there. He texted his best friend to make sure he had picked it up and it hadn't been stolen. Rip messaged back that his parents had retrieved the Harley. It felt odd for Rip to rely on someone else, but Ace wouldn't begrudge him his parents' help. Besides, Ace had Rayna to focus on. The whole ride toward Haven, Ace could think of nothing other than the female at his home, especially with his Gryphon singing her praises. It was odd yet welcomed.

Bishop called earlier stating he didn't have any updates, but Ace couldn't complain. He didn't have the knowhow to search for Rayna's boss or David Spencer. During breakfast, Rayna's restlessness had been palpable. She asked if she could visit Glory, but Ripley had texted the night before while Ace and Rayna watched a movie, updating him on Glory's family. Marjorie was being a pain in the ass – Ripley's words – and he was ready to throttle the woman. Glory was spending time with her sisters, and they wanted to go live with their grandmother. Marjorie was considering going back to Haven in case her husband showed up. Since the man was dead, she was in for a surprise if she did go back to the compound.

When Ace asked what hobbies Rayna had other than knitting, she claimed she had none, assuring him she was boring, but Ace didn't believe her. He found the female to be funny and energetic. Before he got on his bike, Ace gave Rayna a credit card and told her to purchase whatever she wanted. He would hate to be holed up in a strange place with nothing to do other than watch TV. He hoped she took him at his word and found something to fill her time.

Ace stripped, then stowed his clothes in the saddle bag. He shifted into his Eagle and took flight. He had no idea what to expect, but what he found when he circled above the compound was kids running around, men and women interacting, and guards strolling along the perimeter with no weapons. He spotted a good perch and settled in. By the conversations, Sutton's plan to cause peaceful chaos had worked so far.

A group of young men were huddled together, discussing the Bible and what they should teach at the next chapel service.

"I was raised on Jesus's love, not the fire and brimstone of the Old Testament. If He is the way to our salvation, shouldn't we teach the same messages He did?" the oldest-looking said.

"I agree. Kindness and tolerance." This male was younger, probably late twenties.

"And we should encourage the boys to treat our women with respect. Listen to what they have to say." This young man didn't appear much older than the boys he spoke of.

Ace found it interesting it was the younger men having that conversation. He searched the area for the older males. When he didn't find any, he left the safety of the trees and did another pass over the compound. Loud voices came from the house Josiah had claimed while he was their leader.

"I don't give a damn that Josiah's dead. Where the hell is Thomas? Why are the kids running around and not learning their verses? Why are the men and women talking freely amongst themselves? This is not how we run Haven! And where are the guns? Why are the guards strolling along like they don't have a fucking care in the world?" When no one spoke up, the angry man yelled, *"Someone fucking answer me!"*

"I'm sorry, Sir, but this is how things are. I don't

understand."

"What do you not understand? This is not *how things are."*

The front door opened, and Abraham stormed out. He strode to where the kids were. "Get back to your classrooms now!" The kids stopped playing and looked at one another. "Go, now." The kids scrambled to do as he said. Abraham then confronted those adults who were talking to one another. "Why are you not in chapel? Get to your cabins and wait there until I release you. And no talking amongst yourselves." The adults did as he commanded. Abraham watched them go, grabbing his hair and pulling. "What the fuck is going on?" he whispered.

When he noticed the group of young men huddled together, he stalked to where they were. "You. Why are you not in chapel?"

"We were just discussing what message to deliver today," the youngest one admitted.

Abraham frowned. "It's the same sermon we preach every day. There's nothing to discuss."

The older one nodded but disagreed. "Sure, there is. We were told to teach about Jesus and his love. That's what the Bible says we should do."

Abraham fumed, his face turning red. "Who told you that?"

The men stared at each other, not able to come up with an answer. Sutton had made sure of that.

Abraham fisted his hands. Ace expected him to hit the younger man. "Do you know who I am?" he asked through gritted teeth.

The third man shook his head. "Well, no, but it seems you could do with some of Jesus's love. You sure are angry."

If Ace had been in his skin, he would have laughed. Since he wasn't, he flew back to his bike and shifted. Pulling out his phone, he dialed Sutton.

"Ace? How's it going, Son?"

Ace couldn't help but chuckle. "Abraham is at Haven and losing his mind. It's glorious."

"Well, that was the plan. Can— Hang on a second. Dammit. We have a situation with Sultan and his mate. Go back to Haven and voice Abraham. I'm not sure how long this will take, so have him stay there, and once I'm finished here, I'll meet you at the compound."

"Since when does Sultan have a mate?"

"It's new, and it's also trouble involving the mafia or some shit. I need to go."

"Do what you need to do there. I'll be fine handling Abraham." The line disconnected, but it didn't bother Ace. If the mafia was involved with Sultan and his mate, Ace couldn't imagine the trouble they were in. He removed his clothes from the saddle bag and put them in his carry pouch along with his phone. After shifting back to his Eagle, he clutched the bag in his talons and took

111

flight. Ace landed in the woods behind the barns and took to his skin, dressing quickly. He shoved his phone in one back pocket, then folded the pouch and put it in the other. When he got to the spot he'd last seen Abraham, he wasn't there, and neither were the young men. Ace strolled through the compound, which was now void of people walking around. When he reached the main house, he tried the knob, finding it unlocked. Inside were several older men, sitting at the kitchen table drinking coffee. They didn't rise when he approached, but they did look wary.

"Where's Abraham?"

"He left earlier," one answered.

"Left the house or Haven?"

"The house. Are you our new leader?"

He added power to his voice when he responded, "Yes. Get up and go find Abraham. Have him meet me here if you find him before I do."

All four males rose, abandoning their coffee, and filed out the front door. Ace took a moment to look around the house. From what Glory and Rayna said, the cabins where most of the residents lived were sparse with nothing but single beds and chairs to sit on. There was also a small bathroom with a tiny shower stall. This house, though, had all the amenities one would need to be comfortable, including a sofa and armchairs in the living room. The master bedroom was appointed with a king-sized bed, while the smaller rooms held full beds. All had thick mattresses instead of the thin ones in the cabins. Another room's door was locked, but it was nothing for Ace to use his shifter strength to bust into what was an office.

He walked over to the desk where a laptop's screen was dark. Ace moved the mouse, and the screen came to life. Sitting down, he began scrolling through the various tabs, one of which was a porn site. He closed out of it, then clicked on the file icon. Ace didn't have the time nor inclination to go through them all, so he called Bishop who walked him through how to zip them and email them over.

The front door opened, and Ace rose to go see who it was. One of the men he'd sent to find Abraham stood in the living room. "Abraham left the premises."

"Shit." Ace brushed by the male, and when he hit the ground, he took off running across the compound. He stripped as soon as he was hidden, then took to the sky.

CHAPTER NINE

Ace

IT WAS WELL past suppertime when Ace pulled into his driveway. He sent Rayna a text earlier on the burner phone apologizing for being gone all day. When she didn't immediately reply, he almost called one of the Hounds to go check on her, but she finally responded, saying she was fine, making him curious as to how she spent her day. After parking his bike in the garage, Ace entered the house to find Rayna sitting at the island, her hair wet, as she ate takeout.

She wiped her mouth with a napkin. "How was your day?" she asked with a smile. He had never had that – coming home to someone asking about his day.

"Long." Ace sniffed the air. "Is that Korean?"

"Good nose. I ordered plenty, and it should still be warm enough." Rayna slid off her stool and got another plate, bringing it to the counter for Ace. "Chopsticks or fork?"

"Fork, please. I'm too tired to work at keeping rice on chopsticks." Ace plugged his phone into the charger, then washed his hands before plating some beef bulgogi and kimchi fried rice. Rayna grabbed him a beer out of the fridge, then retook her seat, expertly scooping rice with her chopsticks. He'd never really gotten the hang of using them. He dug into his meal, eating half before coming up for air.

"I take it you didn't stop long enough to eat lunch?" Rayna asked.

"No." Ace took a long pull off his beer. "Abraham showed up at Haven. It was rather comical. He didn't know what to do with a compound filled with happy people mingling. I left to call Sutton, and by the time I returned, Abraham was gone. I was able to spot him driving away, so I followed him to Oasis. Viper is there, so he's going to keep an eye on him. I had to fly back to my bike, and that took all day."

"I'd love to have seen that. Now what happens?"

Ace picked up his fork and scooped up some rice. "I'll have to ask Sutton, but I suppose we'll go in and voice Oasis like we did Haven. The main goal is to ensure Rhi is safe from Abraham and Ruth, then find out if they confided in anyone else about her abilities. With David out there somewhere, we need to eliminate all possible threats as quickly as possible." Ace took a bite. As he chewed, he studied

Rayna. She was calm, and if he wasn't mistaken, content. "How was your day? Did you find something to do so you weren't bored?"

"I, uh…" She took a drink of water, then cleared her throat. "I may have started a garden in your backyard. Just a small one," she assured him like he would mind her digging in his yard.

"Really? That's amazing. What did you plant?"

"Nothing, yet. I wanted to ask what you'd like. I did get the ground ready, though."

"I don't know anything about what to plant when, so I'll leave that up to you. Thanks for getting it started."

Rayna relaxed. "You're welcome. I enjoy getting my hands in the dirt. Gran and I used to have a big garden every year, and I've missed it. There's nothing like eating something you grew yourself. And I'll pay you back for all the supplies I bought."

Ace waved his fork. "I'm not worried about the money. Besides, I plan to take advantage of the vegetables, so I should probably pay you for your time."

Grinning, Rayna shook her head. "How about we call it even? Your land for my time?"

"Sounds good." Ace pointed to the containers. "You want some more?"

"I'm full. It's all yours."

As Ace dished out another helping, Rayna placed her chopsticks on the side of her plate and leaned back. "I called Gran earlier, and we had a good chat. After I told her what was going on, she encouraged me to retire and find something different to do, but I have no idea what that would look like. I don't need money, but I'm not good with sitting around. She said for now to do something productive, and that led to making a garden. So, I made a list of things I needed, and I went to the garden center, but on my way back, I had a feeling I needed to talk to Seth. I drove over to Harristown before I called him. If someone can trace the burner, they won't find me here," she assured Ace.

"He said Deputy Director Grissom showed up at the office looking for Hanson, and things went downhill from there. He also asked if I was still undercover, and Seth told him I was. If things are as chaotic at Haven as you said, no one will be aware I left other than Seth and the women who also left. I couldn't tell you a single one of their names, so I doubt they know mine either. Well, my alias. I didn't tell him I'm considering retiring, but I did ask how Vanessa and the kids are. He said they're good, but I wanted to hear her voice, so I called her. She was at her shop, so we could only talk a few minutes."

"Does she know you were undercover?"

Rayna took a sip of water. "Yes. We talk at least once a week, and we get together often, so if I went radio silent, she would have worried. I told her that

117

I'm undercover, and if anyone asked, she hadn't heard from me."

"Did she ask where you are?"

"No. Being married to Seth, she knows not to ask questions."

"I'm glad you have someone like Vanessa in your life. Ripley is that for me. He and—" Ace's phone rang. "Excuse me." He lowered himself off the stool and walked over to the counter to where his phone was charging. "Hey, Sutton."

"What a fucking day." Sutton explained what was happening with Sultan and the mob. No wonder he was stressed. "Please tell me you have good news."

"I think it is. I followed Abraham to Oasis. He was pissed about how things were being handled at Haven and insisted one of the men go there to take over. Not that it'll do any good."

"No, it won't. I'll call Viper and have him voice Abraham before he has a chance to go into hiding again. I'd appreciate it if you would head that way in the morning in case he needs backup."

"It'd be my pleasure. Once that's done, we'll only have Spencer to worry about."

"I spoke with Ryot earlier. We have several Hounds guarding him and his family. I've also called Lucy and told her we need her on this. Henry and Bishop are helping Sultan, so their focus is going to be there. Jonas Montague can follow up on any further trials with the serum." Ace was one of the few Hounds outside the Lazlos who knew what Lucy was doing in New Atlanta. Her adopted father left behind a journal that worked with shifter DNA to prolong human life. Lucy and Jonas had tweaked the formula and were successful. It was in the testing phase. Ace had no idea where they found test subjects, but it would be a life changer for the human mates of the Hounds.

"Lucy needs to be careful. She's good, but we both know she isn't on Spencer's level."

Sutton heaved a sigh. "I know, but this shit with the mafia is a definite, where Spencer is an unknown. Lucy will be home tomorrow or Wednesday at the latest."

"I'll reach out to her, and I'll call you when Abraham's taken care of."

"Thanks, Ace. I'm going to snuggle my mate. I will talk to you later." Sutton disconnected, and Ace felt a pang of jealousy. He wanted someone to snuggle with. He glanced at Rayna who was studying him. "What?"

"I wish I could go with you to Oasis." When he opened his mouth to argue, she raised a hand. "I know I can't, but I'd like to have your back." Rayna slipped off her stool and took her plate to the dishwasher.

"I appreciate that," he said earnestly. Ace's heart warmed at the sentiment, and he wished it as well. But there was no way...Actually, there was a way, but he didn't know whether he could make it happen. He tapped out a text to Lucy. She responded almost instantly.

Lucy: *I'm on it.*

Ace wondered what it would be like to have someone like Rayna for a mate. She was a warrior and a shifter who could hold her own. Would she be fierce and protective, the way Natalia was with Mayhem? Ace had no doubt, especially since his Gryphon had been chatting in his head all day, encouraging Ace to give her a chance. It wasn't that he didn't want to. He wanted it more than anything, having felt the spark when they first shook hands, which had never happened. Her being in his home was different. Maybe that's where he screwed up before. With her in his space, spending more time together than he had with previous prospects, he would get to know her quicker. He already liked coming home and finding her smiling at him. The fact that she had started a garden for him was a plus. Sure, it was to give her something to do, but she could have found a hobby that didn't benefit Ace.

"What types of vegetables can you plant late in the season?" he asked.

Rayna returned to the island with a notepad in hand. She pushed it over to him, and Ace was impressed with all the notes and diagrams. Rayna had put a lot of thought into the garden, including where to place it in the yard for maximum sun.

"This is a list of veggies, but I didn't know what you actually use in cooking."

"Everything but kale." Ace shuddered. "I know it has health benefits, but I find it's too bitter."

"Perfect. I won't be able to grow everything in the small area, but—"

"We can make it larger if you'd like. I'm happy to do the digging or whatever you need."

Rayna beamed. "I'd love for this to be a joint project, but I don't want you to neglect your duties to the Hounds. I honestly enjoy digging. What I do need is to either rent a truck or have the compost delivered. There was no way I was putting it in your trunk."

"We can borrow Brick's truck."

"Brick?"

"Sorry, Branson. Brick is his biker name."

"He and Lynette seem like nice people. I didn't sense that she's a shifter."

"Lynette is human, and they are one of the best couples I know, and I know many. As for the garden," Ace tapped the diagram. "Could we make it wider to include more rows?"

"Absolutely." Rayna picked up the pencil and sketched how it would look. "I didn't want to dig up half your backyard without asking."

"It's not like I use the space for anything. The

more garden, the less mowing I'll have to do."

"I love to mow. Honestly, I love anything to do with the outdoors. It stems from my childhood. I couldn't help Gran cook since I sucked at it, so while she was in the kitchen, I took care of the yardwork."

"Who does that for her now?"

"She does. Gran might be close to three hundred, but she's active and able to do anything she pleases."

"That's wonderful. Say, what time does the garden center close?"

Rayna glanced over at the stove. "In about an hour."

"Let's place an order for everything you need, and I'll ask Branson to pick it up in the morning and deliver it to you while I'm at Oasis. I shouldn't be gone all day, and when I get home, I'll help."

"He won't have a problem with me being here?"

"Not after I explain who you really are and why you're staying with me."

"If you're sure. I don't want to cause trouble."

"Branson and Lynette take in those who need a place to hide out, so he'll understand."

Ace led Rayna to his office and booted up his laptop. He had her place the order with the garden center while he called to ask Branson if he minded picking up their order after he explained who Rayna really was. Branson had questions, and Ace answered them all honestly. Once he was satisfied they could trust the agent, Branson said he was glad to do it.

With that taken care of, Rayna asked, "What do you normally do at night? Do you read or watch TV?"

"I drink and look at the stars. It's not very exciting, but..." Ace shrugged. He wasn't an exciting male.

"I could use a drink." Rayna winked at him, and something fluttered in his gut. Plenty of people flirted with him. Hell, Kristoff had, but never had Ace felt a stirring from a wink.

"Then follow me." Ace led her to his den where he told her to pick her poison.

She opted for tequila and asked, "Do you have limes in the fridge?"

"I do. Warryck Lazlo's mate taught me how to make delicious margaritas, so I try to keep the ingredients on hand for when I'm not drinking straight from the bottle."

"Do that often, do you?" Rayna didn't sound judgmental, just inquisitive.

"More than I should," Ace admitted. "But with my shifter metabolism, I never get sloshed."

"I'd love for you to teach me the recipe. I do love a good margarita."

"No time like the present." Ace grabbed the Casamigos Blanco, and they retreated to the kitchen.

"You're talking about Kerrigan, right?" Rayna asked as she settled next to Ace to watch.

"Yeah. How did you know?"

"She drove the van from Haven to Providence House, and we chatted on the drive. Her story was unbelievable. I already knew she was Warryck's wife from when I investigated the Lazlos, but to hear how he saved her? Remarkable."

Ace stopped mixing. "You investigated their family?"

Rayna placed her hand on Ace's forearm. "It was my job, Asher. I already told you Spencer made some wild accusations, and before I was sent undercover, I was tasked with looking into their family. Nothing I found was incriminating. On the contrary. Hell, even Seth said the same thing. He also looked into the Hounds after I went to Haven." It took Ace a second to focus on her words instead of her touch because his dick twitched at the contact. That never happened before. Ever.

When she pulled her hand away, Ace wanted it back. "No, I get it. A GIA agent is supposed to be respectable. But if he and your boss are working together, it would make sense that Hanson had you both researching the Hounds, if for no other reason than to take your focus off Spencer." Knowing how much Rayna loved fruity cereal, he didn't hesitate to substitute the orange liqueur for the raspberry flavored one. When the pitcher was full, he sliced a

124

lime, then grabbed two large margarita glasses from one of the cabinets.

"Salt or sugar rim?" he offered.

"Ooh, I've never tried it with sugar."

Ace retrieved the plain rimming sugar from the pantry, forgoing the flavored type since he'd already used raspberry liqueur. Rayna leaned her elbows on the counter, watching as he ran a lime slice around the glass before twisting the rim into the sugar crystals. He poured her margarita and handed it over while he prepared his own glass.

"Holy shit, that's good. Beats anything I've ever ordered. What did you do different?"

Ace grinned without looking at her and rattled off the recipe. "Kerrigan was a bartender before she was kidnapped. She has all sorts of tips for taking regular drinks and making them into something different."

Ace poured his drink and held out his glass. "Here's to new friendships."

Rayna tapped his glass with hers, her eyes twinkling as she took a sip. "Can we go outside and look at the stars?"

"Lead the way." Ace grabbed the pitcher, and Rayna opened the back door for him. He set the pitcher on the short, round table between two lounge chairs. Neither one spoke for a while as they sipped their drinks and gazed at the sky.

When Ace refilled her glass, Rayna muttered, "I

could get used to this."
Ace could too.

Chapter Ten

Rayna

RAYNA'S BEAST WAS purring, and she knew Ace could hear it. If she wasn't so content, she might be embarrassed. The margaritas were delicious, and the company was even better. Sitting under the stars in companionable silence wasn't something she ever thought she would enjoy. Rayna was a talker. She liked conversations. That was how you got to know someone. She thought she'd screwed up earlier mentioning how she had researched the Lazlos, but when she touched Asher's arm, she hadn't missed the way he tensed and not in a bad way. Maybe her Cheetah was right; Asher was warming up to her.

He emptied the pitcher, divvying up the liquid between their glasses. "Want me to make more?"

"If you don't mind. I'm not ready for bed."

Asher rose, squeezed her shoulder, then took the empty container into the house. Rayna basked in the effects of his touch. Her Cat rumbled. *Quiet.*

We don't want to scare him. It huffed, and she could imagine it licking a paw haughtily. Rayna chuckled as she sipped the fruity concoction. She'd never had a raspberry margarita, but it was now her favorite. She loved the tartness.

As she gazed overhead, a shooting star flashed through the sky, and Rayna made a wish. It was similar to the ones she'd made as a young girl, only this time, she had a face to go with the mate she longed for. Gran's love for her own mate never waned even years after he passed away. That was the type of love Rayna wanted for herself. The kind where souls were entwined for eternity. A true partnership with give and take from both parties.

Asher returned on silent feet, the ice in the glass pitcher the only sound in the otherwise silence. He had also brought fresh glasses with sugar rims. He poured her glass before filling his own. He placed the pitcher between them and took his seat. Rayna emptied her glass before taking the new one.

"I'm going to leave early to go to Oasis so I can get back and help with the garden, if that's okay."

Rayna turned her head in his direction. "Depending on what time Branson gets here, I might have the dirt prepared. I didn't put any plants or seeds on the list. I would like to choose those myself. If I get finished before you get back, I'm sure I'll be hungry," she hinted with a grin.

"Oh, I see how it is. You just want me for my

cooking skills." Asher's eyes were sparkling.

"You caught on to my evil plot." Rayna kept her eyes on him as she took a sip. Asher looked away, but he was smiling. "You mentioned that Ripley is your best friend. You were going to say something earlier before Sutton called. Will you tell me about Glory's life since she escaped Haven?"

Rayna was happy for her former cabinmate, but after hearing how Ripley and his parents had shown her such unconditional love and support? She was giddy for the young woman. "I can't wait to hear her play. I often sang for her at night when she had a hard time going to sleep," Rayna admitted.

"Maybe you, Glory, and Rhiannon could start a trio," Asher said.

"Rhiannon sings too?"

"Like an angel."

"I'm glad you told me. I can carry a tune, but I'm nowhere near good enough to sing with someone like her."

Asher reached over and squeezed Rayna's arm. "I bet you are."

Rayna's Cat rumbled in her chest at the praise. After yawning, she downed the last of her margarita. "I'm going to turn in. Maybe we can do this again tomorrow night? I really enjoyed it."

Asher rose and stood inches away. "Anytime you want. I enjoyed it too."

Rayna went to grab the empty pitcher, but Asher stopped her. "I'll take care of that when I lock up."

"If you insist." Rayna pressed a hand to Asher's cheek, and he turned his head, kissing her palm. Rayna swallowed a gasp.

"Good night." Asher grabbed the pitcher and retreated into the house without looking back. Rayna stood there, momentarily stunned. Her Cheetah itched to be released, and that was the impetus to get her moving. Rayna waited until she was behind the closed door of her bedroom before she did a little shimmy, biting the inside of her cheek to keep from squealing aloud. It wasn't a kiss on the lips, but it was affection.

Since she showered after working outside, Rayna brushed her teeth, changed into her pajamas, then slid under the covers. She pressed the same palm Asher kissed to her lips before turning onto her side and closing her eyes. She thanked her goddess for bringing Asher into her life and prayed he felt the same connection she did.

Ace

ACE WASHED THE pitcher and dried it, then returned it to the cabinet. His heart hadn't stopped racing since he pressed his lips to Rayna's palm. He had never been so bold, but he'd turned his face without thinking, as though it was the most natural thing in the world. If Rayna hadn't been affected, he might regret it, but the little hitch in her breath was the sign he needed to know he hadn't screwed up. What was it about this female that had his cock stirring, even if it was a twinge? Those he had been interested in previously were all human, so could it be because she was a shifter? Ace had been around other Gryphons his whole life, and none of them caused a stir in his Gryphon.

Instead of standing in the kitchen questioning why, he turned out the lights, locked the doors, and retreated to his room. Ace paused outside Rayna's door, listening. The shuffle of bedding was faint, indicating she was already in bed. He continued to his room and closed the door. As he went through his nighttime routine, Ace decided he wasn't going to question his body's reaction to Rayna. Everyone's sexual experiences were different, even those like him who were demi. He had been on many forums over the years searching for answers to his sexuality. It took some longer than others to get to the point where they wanted sex. Some felt the connection quickly when they and their person clicked. His Gryphon already said Rayna's Cheetah

131

was onboard, so did that mean the human was as well?

Ace climbed under the covers and slid one arm behind his head, staring at the ceiling. He had a job to do tomorrow, and then he was going to focus on spending as much time with Rayna as possible. They still had to figure out what was going on with her boss and David Spencer, but in the meantime, he was going to focus on his pretty Cheetah shifter.

When the clock rolled over to five a.m., Ace got up and dressed. He had a couple of hours ride ahead of him, and he was ready to get it over with. He set the coffee pot to come on at six and left a note for Rayna. He'd prefer to tell her goodbye, but he didn't want to wake her.

Where Haven was west of New Troy, Oasis was southeast. The ride wasn't a bad one with all the backroads he could take, but he wanted to get there and get back quickly, so Ace took highways as much as possible. When he was half a mile away, he parked his bike next to Viper's. Ace climbed off his Harley, searching the area for his fellow Hound. He checked his phone for a message, but there wasn't one.

He waited a half hour, and when Viper still didn't show, Ace stripped, stowing his clothes in his carry pouch, then shifted to his Eagle. He wasn't going to storm the castle without knowing whether Abraham was there. Maybe Viper had found

Abraham alone and decided to voice him. Ace flew over the compound several times, not seeing either male. He landed on top of the chapel, waiting and watching. People came and went, including Ruth, but Abraham was nowhere to be seen. Ace followed Ruth to the larger house at the back of the community. There was a guard stationed at each door, and the one at the front didn't speak to Ruth as she passed him.

"Where have you been?" Ruth asked someone inside.

"Hiding, same as your husband."

"If you hadn't got yourself arrested, he wouldn't need to hide. You had one job."

"And I did that job. For ten fucking years, I played both sides, and for what? I'm done being the good little sheep. Abraham has lost control of not one but two of the compounds. It won't be long until Oasis is also out of his hands."

"Is that what you think?" a male asked. *"I'm still in control, and you'd do well to remember that."*

Abraham was there. Where the hell was Viper?

"You're fooling yourself if you think you have things under control. And you'd do well to remember what I'm capable of. I no longer care about you or your shitty cult. You will *leave Rhiannon alone."*

"Watch your mouth, David," Ruth scolded.

"No, Mother. I will no longer do his bidding. I wasted ten years of my life behind The Ministry's walls, thinking Rhiannon was safe only to find out Josiah used

my baby for his own gain."

"And now where is she? With those heathen bikers. If you'd done what you were supposed to, she never would have run off."

"I did what I was supposed to. I married someone I didn't love. I elevated Haven's financial status. I provided weapons. And for what? To lose my daughter as well as my job with the GIA? I'm warning you now, Abraham. Leave Rhi alone, or the Feds will be the least of your worries."

"Are you threatening me?"

"Fucking right I am."

Ace flew to the ground at the side of the house, shifted to his skin, and dressed quickly. He skirted the side of the house, ducking back to keep from being spotted by the guard at the front door.

"Guard!" Abraham demanded. Ace peeked around once more to see the male entering the house. Ace crept closer and looked in the window. The guard and David were in a standoff, both with handguns pointed at the other. If he could get in there before they fired shots, he could voice them all. Ace eased his way up the steps, but his Gryphon growled, stopping him from going farther. Ace glanced over his shoulder to find the guard from the back of the house bearing down on him with a pistol.

"Who are you and what are you doing here? And where are your shoes?"

Ace thumbed behind him. "Gotta meeting with

134

Abraham." Lowering his voice, he instructed, "Put down the weapon, and get on your knees." The guard complied. Luckily, everyone in the house was so consumed with the chaos that they hadn't heard Ace's exchange. He turned and stepped up to the open door. David and the guard were both yelling at the other to drop their gun.

"Shoot him!" Abraham commanded.

Ruth yelled, "No," and rushed the guard. Both weapons fired multiple times. Ruth and the guard went down just as Ace ducked outside. He grunted when a stray bullet tore through the window, hitting him. He went to his knees, one hand grabbing his chest. Sticky liquid coated his fingers, and when he looked down, his hand was covered in blood. Fuck.

"What have you done?" Abraham yelled. "Get the fucking doctor."

Good idea. Ace needed one, but he couldn't hang around and count on these ass-wipes to take care of him. He struggled to his feet and stumbled down the few steps to the ground. The guard on his knees stared at Ace.

"Grab your gun and come help me," Ace ordered. The guard did as he was told. When he got to Ace, he wrapped an arm around Ace's waist, and Ace stumbled around the side of the house, heading back to his bike. Another gunshot went off, and Ace stumbled again. The guard tightened his grip but

135

didn't say anything. If Ace could shift, he might be able to start the healing process, but he needed to get to his phone.

After what seemed like an hour, they reached his bike. "Open the pack on the right and get my phone." When the guard had it, Ace said, "Call Sutton."

"I don't know how," the guard admitted.

"Fuck." Ace was close to passing out. He tapped the screen, bringing it to life, and angled it toward his face. He pushed the call icon, and it brought up his call log. Ace tried to tap Sutton's name, but he hit it too hard. The phone slipped from the guard's grasp, falling to the ground, as everything went black.

Rayna

THE AROMA OF coffee wafted through the air, and Rayna rubbed her eyes. She listened for any sign of Asher in the house, but all was quiet. Dammit. She wanted to see him before he left for Oasis. After stretching, Rayna climbed off the bed, made it up, then changed into shorts and a tee after brushing her teeth and twisting her hair into a messy bun to keep it off her neck while working outside. She padded down the hallway to the kitchen, glad the coffee was already brewed. A piece of paper sat on the counter next to the machine.

Rayna,

Sorry to leave without saying anything, but I didn't want to wake you. Enjoy your morning, and don't work too hard on the garden before I get back. See you soon, A

Asher's flowing, cursive penmanship was unexpected. Most men Rayna knew printed their words. If they didn't, it was barely legible. She brought the paper to her mouth and kissed it. Then she giggled like a teenager. Placing the note aside, she fixed a cup of coffee in an insulated mug, went to the pantry for one of the boxes of cereal Asher had bought her, then took both outside, settling on the same chair she'd used the night before. Rayna sipped her coffee and munched on fruity bits, enjoying the peacefulness. Asher's house was in a large neighborhood, yet it was quieter than Haven, which was situated out in the middle of nowhere. While she was glad to have met Glory and Lisa Ann, Rayna didn't miss the compound at all. She was thrilled Glory was away from the cult and had a new family who adored her. Rayna worried about Lisa Ann and wondered how the older woman was faring without Rayna or Glory to keep her company. Lisa Ann had been at Haven many years, but for some reason, had never been chosen as a wife. Rayna counted the other female lucky.

Rayna wasn't used to downtime. Having the chance to enjoy coffee on the patio and just be was something she could get used to. At Haven, she had a job to do every morning. With the FBI, she rarely had the opportunity to do nothing. Even on her days off, she poured over cases or chased down leads. When she did take vacation, she went to see her Gran. Now, though, sitting in Asher's backyard, Rayna imagined this being her life – not going to the office or chasing down criminals. Not answering to her boss. Rising each morning with nothing to do except have breakfast with Asher and then work in the yard. It was only her second morning at his home, and she already felt as though she belonged there. It wasn't like she was taking advantage of his hospitality by mooching off him. Rayna had plenty of money, and if she needed to, she could hide away somewhere else.

Even if things didn't work out with the hottie biker, Rayna could have the solitude. The peace. She could buy a house with a few acres and plant her own garden. Or she could move to Arizona to be with her grandmother. She had options, and the longer she stayed away from her job, the more she liked the idea of retiring.

A few cars drove down Asher's street, and

Rayna ignored them until a door slammed close by. She went inside and strode to the living room, peering out the window. Branson was unloading bags from the back of his truck.

Rayna stepped onto the porch to greet him. "Good morning, Branson."

"Hey, Rayna. Where do you want this?"

"Around back. Here, let me help."

"You can help by opening the gate. Ace would have my hide if I let you carry these."

Rayna stuffed her hands onto her hips. "Excuse me? Are you saying he thinks I'm weak?"

Branson grinned. "No, ma'am. None of our females are weak, but we prefer to do the heavy lifting."

"Well, I guess that's okay then." Rayna led the way around the side of the house and opened the gate. She pointed to the spot where she wanted the bags.

After he placed the first load on the ground, Branson studied the turned earth. "You know, we have plenty of room at Providence House for a garden, and it might be something the residents would like to learn. I'm not asking you to take on the task now, but maybe next spring, you could teach Lynette and me what to do. It's a good skill to have and be able to pass along."

Rayna was both shocked and touched that he would ask her to help. "I would love that." Helping at Providence would give her the opportunity to get to know Lynette better. Rayna had Vanessa, but her bestie was often busy with her kids and salon, so having another friend would be a blessing.

Branson finished hauling the bags and took his leave. Rayna got busy extending the garden. She stopped long enough to fix a sandwich, then she added the compost to the turned soil. She had just finished when a motorcycle roared down the street. Rayna's stomach dipped with excitement. Her Cheetah wanted free to play with Asher's Lion.

We'll do that later.

Rayna turned when the gate opened, only it wasn't Asher.

Chapter Eleven

Rayna

RIPLEY'S FATHER FROZE upon seeing Rayna. She stood and wiped the dirt from her hands. "Hi. I'm Rayna Bellamy. You're Conrad, right? Ripley's father?"

"I am. Have we met?"

"No, but I saw you Saturday night at Haven."

Conrad squinted at her. "You were at Haven?"

"Yes, Sir. It's a long story."

"I see. Is Asher home? He didn't answer his phone."

"No, Sir. He's off doing something for Sutton."

"Oh. I came by to see if he wanted to have lunch with my ma— wife and me." He closed the distance between them, eyeing the turned soil. "Have you known Asher long?"

"No. We met Saturday night."

"And you decided he needed a garden?" Conrad grinned, pointing at the ground.

"I was bored." She shrugged. "I spent the last

four months knitting, so I don't want to see yarn for, oh, about a year. Asher gave me free rein to do something while he's working. I can't cook, so I thought I would grow vegetables he can use."

"That's mighty kind of you, especially since you just met."

Rayna could tell Conrad was confused.

"Would you like something to drink? I'm not sure when Asher'll be back. He went to Oasis."

"You know about Oasis?"

"I do. I also know how you and Regina treat Asher like a son. And can I just tell you I am thrilled Glory has you in her life now?"

"We're thrilled too. How do you know Glory?"

"She and I were cabinmates. Only while I was there, everyone knew me as Melinda. I was undercover for the FBI."

Conrad took a step back. "If you hurt Asher—"

"Relax, Conrad. I would never hurt him. He's my mate, but I'm not sure he's onboard with the idea just yet."

"Your mate?" Conrad sniffed the air. "You're not... like us."

"Nope. I'm a King Cheetah shifter."

Conrad ran a hand across his dark hair. "I think I'll take that drink now."

"Come on in. I can't do any more in the garden until I go get the plants, and I was hoping Asher would go with me to pick them out." Rayna strolled past the male and into the house. She stopped at the sink to wash her hands. "What would you like? There's beer in the fridge, but there's also plenty of liquor in the den."

"Are you living here?" Conrad asked, helping himself to a beer.

"For now." Rayna poured herself a glass of water, then propped her hip against the counter while she explained her situation. "My partner knows I'm no longer at Haven, but he's the only one. I haven't told him where I am, though."

"Do you not trust him? Your partner?"

"I do, but I don't trust that the company won't have eyes on him. He's been looking into our boss and Spencer, and that could have thrown up red flags."

They chatted a bit more while Conrad finished his beer. After tossing it in the recycle bin, he said, "Well, I'll get out of your hair. Please tell Asher I stopped by. Since Ripley and Glory are busy with her family, Regina and I have time on our hands. We'd love to see him. Maybe take him out to eat. You're welcome too."

"I appreciate that, and I'll tell him." Rayna walked Conrad to the front door, beeped the alarm, then reset it once he was gone. With nothing left to do outside until she got the plants, Rayna took a shower. Once dressed, she retreated to the living room and turned on the TV. Her mind drifted to

Asher, praying he was okay. He hadn't said how long he would be gone, but the longer he was, the more she worried. If Oasis was like Haven, the guards had guns, and even though he was a shifter, Asher wasn't impervious to bullets.

She had watched several episodes of one of her shows when the doorbell rang. Rayna rose and looked out the window. A pretty brunette was holding a package. Having researched all the Lazlos, she recognized the female.

Rayna turned off the alarm and opened the door. "Hi. Lucy, right?"

"Yeah, and you must be Rayna." Lucy held out her hand, and Rayna grasped it.

"Please, come in." Rayna widened the door after releasing Lucy's hand so she could step inside. "Asher isn't here right now. He left earlier to deal with Abraham Goodman. Would you like something to drink?"

"I appreciate the offer, but I just stopped by to drop off this." Lucy handed the package to Rayna.

"What is it?" She shook it. The package was light so definitely not a computer.

"It's a prosthetic. Ace asked me to make one so you can move about without being recognized. I didn't have time to produce a voice modulator." Rayna opened the package and pulled out the mask and a couple of wigs. "Ace mentioned your pretty hair, so I thought you might like options to further camouflage yourself. Let's go in the bathroom, and I'll show you how to put it on."

Fifteen minutes later, Rayna was a new person. At least on the outside. "That's amazing." She had opted for the blonde wig, and she couldn't believe the person staring back at her.

"If I have time, I can make them where the hair is part of the prosthetic, but Ace only asked for this last night."

"No, this is perfect. Thank you."

"My pleasure. I hate to run, but—" Lucy's phone rang. She pulled it out of her back pocket. "Hey, Pops."

"Have you been to see Rayna?"

"Yes. I'm here now."

"Is Ace there?"

"No. I thought you sent him to Oasis."

"Ask Rayna if she's heard from him today."

Rayna shook her head. "No. He left before I got up. What's going on?"

Lucy narrowed her eyes. "How did you know what he asked?"

"Shifter hearing, but that's not important. What's going on?"

"You're a shifter?" Lucy asked.

"Yes, a King Cheetah, but again, not what we need to focus on. Where the fuck is Asher, and who is Pops?"

"My grandfather, Sutton."

Rayna grabbed Lucy's phone. "Sutton? Rayna. Asher left while it was still dark out this morning. He was supposed to meet Viper at Oasis."

"Yes, he was, but I can't reach either of them on their phones. Viper's mate hasn't heard from him, and if Ace isn't home..."

Rayna strode from the bathroom with the phone wedged between her ear and shoulder. "Tell me how to get to Oasis. I'll go look for him myself." She opened the drawer where she'd stowed her pistol and ID, removing both.

"Whoa," Lucy said. "Why do you have a gun?"

"I'm a federal agent. Asher knows this. I was undercover at Haven. It's a long story. One I don't have time to get into. What I need to do is go find my fucking mate."

"Rayna, calm down. I've already sent more Hounds to Oasis," Sutton commanded, pissing Rayna off.

"If your mate was missing, would you be calm? Either one of you?"

Lucy winced. "No. Pops, send the coordinates to my phone. Tamian and I will drive Rayna to Oasis."

"Dammit— Hang on. King's calling."

Rayna handed the phone to Lucy and went to the closet and pulled out a suit. If she was going in as an agent, she needed to look the part. But that meant not wearing the prosthetic. Fuck it. She

146

wasn't taking it off.

"Rayna?" Sutton came back on the line.

"It's me. Rayna's changing clothes," Lucy answered.

"King's at Oasis. Both bikes are there, but he didn't find either male. What he did find was a shitshow. Abraham was raving about how Spencer got into a shootout with a guard. Ruth jumped in front of David and was killed, then Spencer killed the guard too before running off."

"Maybe Asher and Viper shifted and are waiting until the chaos settles?" Rayna offered.

"If that were the case, one of them would have called. Rayna, I know you want to go find Ace, but let the Hounds look first."

"No. He's my mate. If the others haven't found him by now, they aren't going to. My Cheetah can talk to his Gryphon."

"Did you two complete the bond?" Lucy asked.

"Not yet, but our beasts still communicate. Sutton, either you send the coordinates, or I'll figure it out on my own. It'll be faster if you help me."

"Fuck," he muttered. *"Sending them now."*

"Have you called Ripley?" If they were as close as Asher said, Ripley would want to know what was going on.

"No. He and Glory have enough on their plate with her family. Lucy—"

"We'll be careful, Pops. I promise."

"Rory's going to skin me alive."

"No, she won't. I'll keep you posted." Lucy disconnected and blew out a breath.

"Lucy?" a male voice called out.

"Be right there." To Rayna, Lucy said, "Let's do this."

Rayna followed Lucy down the hall. A gorgeous male stood by the front door with his arms crossed over his chest, scowling. Lucy approached her mate, pulled his head down, and kissed him soundly. Tamian gripped Lucy's hips, pressing his forehead to hers once their lips parted. "Come on, Papa. We need to get Rayna to Oasis. There was a shootout, and Ace and Viper are missing."

Rayna wondered if the endearment was a kink thing or... No, when she reached out with her shifter senses, she detected the faint heartbeat alongside Lucy's. She hadn't noticed the small bump beneath Lucy's tee, but now it was evident. Rayna was happy for the couple, if not somewhat wistful. She set the alarm and locked the door behind them, then followed along to their SUV and climbed in the back seat.

Lucy's phone pinged, and she studied it a few seconds, then tapped the address into the car's GPS. Once they were on the road, Lucy turned sideways. "I've never heard of a Cheetah shifter. Are there many like you?"

"Not that I'm aware of. My mom, grandmother, and I are King Cheetahs. My grandfather was a regular Cheetah shifter. His family was spread over the world, but there weren't many of them. My grandmother was an only child, and her parents passed away before my mom was born."

"And your father?"

"Human. Has no idea I exist."

"Do Cheetahs have fated mates?"

"My grandmother says yes, but my mother didn't believe her, or maybe she did and just didn't want one. My Cat and Asher's Gryphon have decided we're mates."

Lucy cocked her head to the side. "You don't agree?"

Rayna tried to smile, but her heart was breaking not knowing where or how Asher was. "Considering I've known him four days and I'm ready to tear Oasis apart? Yes, I agree. I appreciate you siding with me since Sutton's your grandfather."

"Like I said, Tam and I understand. When we first met, I was working for the GIA, and my boss at the time hid me away in a basement lab to finish work someone else had started. We were able to mind speak even though we were barely acquainted, so the fact that your beasts can communicate makes sense to me. You mentioned you were undercover at Haven. Will you tell us about that?"

"Of course." Rayna explained everything that

happened from the time David Spencer was arrested up until then, including how Bishop and Henry were investigating both Spencer and her boss.

"No wonder Pops wanted me back here to help Bishop. With him and Henry tag-teaming the shit going on with Sultan and the mob..." Lucy scrubbed a hand down her face. "David is no joke, and if he's killing people, he has nothing left to lose. The man is even more unhinged than before, and that's saying a lot."

"Asher told me how David took control of Ryker's car when he was after Rhiannon the first time. That's next-level skills."

"It is. I can't do that." Turning to Tamian, Lucy said, "We might need to call on Lachlan Rokesby."

"Who's that?" Rayna asked.

"A brilliant Gargoyle who once worked against Tamian's Clan. I hate to ask him for help, but to protect Rhiannon, I will."

Tamian shifted in his seat. "Lachlan redeemed himself, Sweetheart. If Rafael can forgive him, that's good enough for me."

"Yeah, you're right."

"Let me call Xavier. Carter is working on their new house, and he should know how to get ahold of Hunter."

Rayna didn't know who all these people were, but it didn't matter. Yes, she was involved because

150

of her boss, but this mess with David affected the Hounds even more than it did Rayna.

Tamian pushed the Bluetooth button on the steering wheel and said, "Call X."

After a few rings, a deep voice answered, "Hello, Son."

"Hi, Dad. Lucy and I are in the thick of it again, and we could use Lachlan's help. Will you ask Carter to reach out to Hunter and have them call us?"

"Shit, Tam. If you're asking for Lachlan's help, I'd say you're neck deep. What's going on?"

"We're crunched for time, so please speak with Carter, then I'll fill you in. There's no telling where the two males are."

"Yeah, I'll call him now. Sit tight." The call disconnected, and Tamian blew out a breath.

"You know X is going to offer to help," Lucy said.

"He will, and I might take him up on it. If David's shooting folks, we're better equipped than the Gryphons to go after him. Plus, he and Stefan helped hide Rhiannon the first time David was after her, so they're aware of his desperation."

Lucy turned back to face Rayna. "Did Asher tell you much about Gargoyles?"

"No. He only mentioned you and Tamian are mates."

"Male Gargoyles have skin that's impenetrable.

They also have wings. The only way to kill them is either beheading or a couple of rare poisons. If David were to shoot one of them, it would only piss them off."

"Just ask Gregor," Tamian quipped.

Lucy rolled her eyes, grinning. "Tamian's sister, Tessa, shot her mate when they first got together, knowing it wouldn't hurt him. It's a running joke in the family."

"Is she crazy?" Rayna slapped a hand over her mouth. "Sorry," she muttered, but Tamian and Lucy both laughed.

"A little wild, yes. She's one of the fiercest females I've ever met, but she's also a lot of fun."

The in-car audio announced an incoming call. "Hey, Dad," Tamian answered.

"Carter contacted Hunter. He and Lachlan are in Greece. Lachlan is going to call you to see if he can help from where he is or if he needs to fly back to the States. Now, tell me what's going on." Once Tamian finished filling his father in, Xavier offered to help, just as they expected.

"I'd appreciate the help, Xavier. Rhiannon has a new baby, and she doesn't need David causing any more trouble than he already has," Lucy said. "Right now, we're headed to Oasis to see if we can locate the missing Hounds. Rayna and Asher haven't completed the bond, but they are mates, and she says her Cheetah was communicating with

Asher's Gryphon before he disappeared."

"I don't like you and Rayna heading into a situation where guns are being used, Lucy, especially with you carrying my grandson."

"Granddaughter," Lucy corrected.

"We'll see," Xavier joked. "Seriously, though. Why are you—?"

"I'm not putting myself in the line of fire. Rayna's a trained FBI agent. I'm just along for moral support."

The onboard system beeped again. "Dad, there's another call coming through. Hopefully, it's Lachlan. Call your buddies and get them ready, just in case."

"Will do, Son."

Tamian switched over to the new caller. "This is Tamian."

"St. Claire, it's Lachlan. Carter said you're in need of my services. Tell me how I can help."

CHAPTER TWELVE

Ace

ACE ALWAYS FIGURED when he crossed over it would be when he was much older than fifty-two. He imagined being dead would be a state of nothingness. Instead, he was floating along with all his memories intact. He had lived an honest life with few regrets. *Rayna.* Ah yes. Ace wished he'd had more time with his Cheetah. He knew in his heart she was the one who would have waited for him. His Gryphon had already claimed her, proving the pretty agent would have been there with him until the end.

"We've got to get out of here," a man said.

"And go where, Silas?" a woman asked. "We've lived here for twenty-five years. There's nothing for us on the outside."

"And if the police show up? What then, Claudia? We can go to my brother's. He'll take us in."

"And how do you suppose we get there?"

"I'll take the van. If anyone asks, I'll say I'm going on a supply run."

"And what about him? Or all the others who might need a doctor if we leave? You can't just leave this man, Silas."

Maybe he'd gotten the afterlife all wrong. If so, where were his parents? And why did he feel as though an elephant was sitting on his chest? It was then he noticed the faint beeping. It was a patient monitor. But if he had died...

We didn't die. They saved us.

Oh. But who was "they"?

The guard took us to the infirmary at the compound.

They have a doctor who can do surgery?

It appears so.

But why? Why save me?

We know not everyone at these compounds is bad.

The door slammed open. "Silas, I've been— Who is that?"

"We don't know, Brother Abraham. One of the guards brought him to us," Silas said. "He had been shot."

"Which guard? Never mind. I was also shot. Stitch me up."

"Yes, Sir."

"Silas, I'm afraid Oasis isn't the safe haven I created all those years ago. Ruth is dead, and her

155

son is responsible. Once I'm patched up, I'll be leaving, and I suggest you take Claudia somewhere else."

"What about our members?" Claudia asked.

"Henrick has led our people in my absence before. He can do it again."

"I'm going to numb the area after I clean it, then I'll apply the stitches."

"Fine," Abraham muttered.

"Where will you go?" Silas asked as he worked.

"South. I've prepared a place in the event something like this happened."

"Could we come with you?" Claudia asked.

"We have somewhere to go. No need in asking that of our leader," Silas chided the woman. "Hand me the needle and sutures."

Ace struggled to stay awake, and he managed a little longer. After Abraham was fixed up, the doctor said goodbye to him, wishing him well, then he and Claudia argued about staying there. In the end, Silas won. They didn't take any of the medical supplies, leaving them for whoever ran the clinic next. Silas checked on Ace's wound one last time before he and Claudia left. Ace needed to get out of there, but he could barely hang on to consciousness. Someone would find him there, but would they be as kind as Silas? Hopefully, the drugs he'd been given would run their course quickly so he could remain awake longer than a few minutes at a time.

He'd never been this vulnerable.

Rayna's coming for us.

How do you know?

Her Cheetah told me.

That was good, except there were guards with guns. Spencer was still out there, and…

Rayna

INSTEAD OF DRIVING directly to the compound, they met with King where Asher and Viper had parked their bikes. After introductions were made, King filled them in.

"Spencer is nowhere to be found, and we still haven't located Ace and Viper. About thirty minutes ago, Abraham left the compound after giving instructions to someone named Henrick to take over again. He also told the man to bury Ruth and the guard who were killed. Fury is following him since it doesn't sound like he's coming back."

"Uh, is that possibly Viper?" Rayna asked, pointing at a naked man stumbling toward them, his left arm tucked against his stomach.

King whipped around, putting himself between

Rayna and the male. "Viper. Shit, Brother. What happened to you?"

"Some teenage fucker thought it would be fun to shoot at an eagle. He clipped my wing. I've been shifting back and forth until I had the strength to walk back. Why are you all here, and where's Ace, and who's this?" he asked, pointing at Rayna.

"We don't know where Ace is. We're here because neither of you checked in, and Sutton couldn't reach you."

"As for me, I'm Rayna Bellamy, Ace's mate."

Viper snarled at her. "Since when does Ace have a mate, especially one who looks like a Fed?"

"It's recent," she quipped. "I am an agent, but I'm supposed to be undercover at Haven. Some shit went down with my boss and David Spencer; therefore, he doesn't know I am here instead of there. If question time is over, I'd like to go find Asher."

Viper waved a hand in the air, as if telling her to go ahead. She overlooked his rudeness since he was injured. Viper pulled some clothes out of his saddle bag, and King helped him since his arm was useless. Then, while King, Lucy, and Tamian discussed how best to get inside, Rayna stepped away from the group.

Can you reach Asher's Gryphon?

Let me try.

Rayna remained quiet, and after a few seconds,

her Cheetah's words brought her to her knees.

He was shot, almost died. He's in the clinic.

"Rayna?" Lucy knelt beside her. "What's wrong?"

"Asher was shot. He's in the clinic." To King, she asked, "Do you have any idea where that is?"

"No, but we can ask once we get inside."

Tamian stepped behind Lucy, placing his hands on her shoulders. "Rayna, I know you want to help Ace, and the best way you can do that is to stay alive. Let me go in after him. Bullets won't stop me."

"No, but what if they shoot Asher again?"

"I won't let that happen. I promise."

Lucy grabbed Rayna's hands. "Please let Tamian do this. He can protect Ace. I'll call Pops and have him get the doctor on standby."

"What if he can't travel? His Gryphon said he almost died," Rayna whispered.

Tamian ran a hand down Lucy's back before stepping away. "There should be a doctor on the premises. I'll find him." Tamian didn't wait for a response. He took off running at a speed that shouldn't be possible. Rayna wasn't sure her Cheetah could catch him.

"What if we're too—"

"No," Lucy stopped her. "We're going to think positive. Have your Cheetah tell Asher's Gryphon that Tamian's on the way and to hang on."

Rayna nodded. After her Cheetah relayed the

159

message, Rayna prayed to her goddess, asking for Tamian to be successful and for Asher to be okay. They had too many years ahead of them for him to be taken away from her now. She wouldn't be like her mother. She would love Asher with everything she had in her. She would turn in her resignation so she could spend all her time with him. They would go to Arizona so her grandmother could see how special Asher was.

Lucy rose and went to the SUV where she dug out her phone. "Hey, Pops. We found Viper. Or, he found us. He's wounded, but it's not life-threatening. According to Rayna's Cheetah, Asher was shot and almost died, but he's in the compound's clinic. We don't know how bad he is. Tamian's gone after him. If he can travel, we'll need Rev on standby. We'll also need someone to retrieve their bikes."

"I can ride," Viper said, but when Lucy arched a brow at him, the male held his hands up. "Fine."

Lucy finished the call and shoved the phone in her back pocket. "Let's get your arm cleaned up," she told Viper. The male didn't argue. He followed Lucy to the SUV where she retrieved a first-aid kit.

King, who had been mostly quiet, sidled up to Rayna. "So, you're a Cheetah shifter? I didn't know those existed."

"I'm a King Cheetah, to be exact. We're even rarer than regular Cheetahs. As far as I know, there are three of us. My grandmother, my mother, and me. My grandfather was a regular Cheetah."

"And your father? Is he a shifter?"

"Nope. Human." Rayna pushed to her feet and moved to stand beside King so she could talk to him while keeping her eye on the direction Tamian had gone.

"Why were you undercover at Haven? That would make sense if you were a male, no offense."

"None taken. And you're right. I think it was to get me out of the way. I interviewed David Spencer extensively, and I think my questions were hitting too close to home with my boss. I was supposed to be at Haven no more than a couple of months, but I was there almost four. When Sutton and the Hounds came in to rescue Glory, I took the opportunity to leave. Then Branson overheard me on the phone with my partner asking for a ride. I called him Sir jokingly, but that was a red flag for Branson. When he told Asher, he decided to follow me. We had a long talk, and here we are."

"Ace is one of the best Hounds I know. I'm glad he found his mate."

"Do you have a mate?"

King's smile said it all. Still, he confirmed he did. "I do. My Heather and I have been together almost fifty years."

"She's also a Gryphon?"

"She is. But even if she weren't, I would still love

her dearly. She's got the softest heart while being a fierce companion. We—"

"Rayna, Tamian has Ace," Lucy interrupted.

"I don't see them."

Lucy tapped her temple. "He told me in here. He said someone operated on Asher, and he's hooked to an I.V., but when Tamian asked for the doctor, no one knew where he or the nurse were. Things are a bit chaotic in there, but Tamian handled it. He wants us to drive the SUV into the compound so we can load Asher up. It's not ideal, but it'll be quicker than waiting on an ambulance and having to wipe the EMTs' memories."

"What about the guards? Won't they shoot at us?"

"No. Tamian voiced all the guards, and they're sitting in the chapel like good little sheep."

"Then let's go!" Rayna jogged to the vehicle and climbed into the passenger seat. Lucy got in on the driver's side, and King and Viper sat in back. When they were underway, Rayna said, "I thought voicing was a Gryphon thing."

"It is, but Tamian's special. He was created from the Original line of Gargoyles."

"Created?" Rayna didn't understand.

"You've heard of Jonas Montague?"

"Sure. He cloned the first baby."

Lucy grinned. "Tamian was that baby."

"No freaking way. I've never met a clone. Not

that I know of, anyway."

"They're just like anyone else. There are two mates in Tamian's Clan who are also clones. One didn't know it until she was an adult, but Trevor, he always knew. His story is sad, really. He was created because his older brother had a heart defect."

"So, he was considered spare parts? That's awful."

"They're each other's champion now." Lucy pulled up to the gate, which was already open. As she eased through, there were no men standing guard. Lucy continued as though she knew where she was going. She ended up at the back of the compound where Tamian was standing outside a square, block building. Rayna jumped out of the vehicle before Lucy put it in park and rushed toward the building.

"How is he?"

Tamian smiled softly. "Not bad considering. He's in and out of consciousness."

Rayna pushed open the door, not stopping until she was beside her mate. Her Cheetah howled upon seeing Asher bandaged and pale with an I.V. in his hand. Whoever operated hadn't removed his jeans or boots, but he was naked from the waist up. She brushed her fingers through his hair as she studied the ink on his chest. "I'm here, Asher. I'm going to take care of you. I promise."

"Rayna?" His eyelids fluttered.

"Yes, it's me." Rayna did her best to smile, but it was hard, knowing she'd almost lost him.

"Y-you're not Rayna," Asher whispered.

"I—" It was then she remembered the mask and wig. "It is me, Asher. Lucy brought the prosthetic you asked for."

"Am I dreaming?"

"No, Gorgeous. Maybe a little groggy from whatever is in your I.V., but I promise I'm real."

"Okay."

Tamian entered the building with King behind him. "Rayna, the door isn't wide enough to push the bed through, so I'm going to carry Ace, and I need you to hold the I.V. bag. King is going to take the mattress and put it in the back of my SUV."

"Got it." Rayna removed the bag from the stand, then Tamian carefully lifted Asher into his arms. King slid the mattress off the bed and carried it outside with Tamian and Rayna following. The back seats had been folded down to accommodate Asher. Once King had the mattress situated, Tamian handed Asher off to the male, then took the bag from Rayna until she could climb in beside her mate. She retook the bag from him.

"My phone," Asher husked.

"Where is it?"

"Bike. I think."

"I'll get it," King offered. He was back after a

couple of minutes, handing the device to Rayna. "It was on the ground covered in blood and dirt, so I cleaned it off."

Tamian had run off while King was looking for Asher's phone, and when he returned, he had the metal bar from the I.V. stand, which he bent to hook over the "oh shit" handle above the door. Tamian helped Viper climb in, so Rayna squeezed in behind Asher to make room for the biker.

"What about King?" Rayna asked as soon as Tamian and Lucy were buckled in.

"He's hanging back to wait on Fury. Depending on where Abraham ended up, Sutton might have them take the man down," Lucy explained.

"He's the least of our worries," Rayna said, scooting around so Asher's head was on her lap. "Spencer's still out there."

"Lachlan Rokesby agreed to help eliminate Spencer," Tamian said. "If anyone can find Rhiannon's father, it'll be him"

Rayna prayed he was right. She knew nothing about this Gargoyle, but if Lucy's family trusted him, Rayna would do the same.

Asher grew restless the longer they were on the road. The I.V. bag was nearly empty, so whatever was in it, probably pain medicine, was wearing off. The few times he opened his eyes, Asher gave Rayna a sleepy smile. He didn't talk, but his chest rumbled a few times. Her Cheetah assured Rayna that Asher wasn't in too much pain, and that he enjoyed her hands in his hair, so she kept up the rubs and gentle scratches. Viper seemed mesmerized by the motion as his eyes never left her hand. Rayna wondered if the male was thinking about his own mate.

Instead of going to a hospital once they arrived in New Troy, they drove to a clinic. A male they called Rev, along with his mate, Bethany, met them at the back door with a gurney. Rev helped Viper climb out of the back, then took his place. Rev briefly checked Asher over before instructing Rayna to remove the I.V. bag from the handle. Since the bag was empty, Rev rested it on Asher's chest before lifting him off Rayna's lap. Her legs were asleep, so she gingerly lowered herself to the ground, dancing around as she waited on the pins and needles to dissipate. Once she could walk, she followed everyone inside.

Bethany ushered Viper into one room while Rev wheeled Asher into another. Rayna remained by the door, not wanting to get in the way, but Rev motioned her forward. "If that were me lying there, I'd want my mate close."

A soft gasp came from the bed, and when Rayna looked at Asher, his eyes were wide. She winked at him, then closed the distance between them and ran a hand along his hair, leaving it there until Rev needed her to step back so he could run an ultrasound. Asher's eyes never left hers. She could see the question there, but she wanted to wait until they were alone to talk about being mates.

Rev placed a hand on Asher's shoulder. "Everything looks good, Brother. It was a through and through. The bullet missed anything vital. It did nick one of your ribs, but whoever operated did a good job. Are you in pain?"

Asher finally looked away. "Yes, but I'd rather deal with the pain than not be able to stay awake."

"Let me know if you change your mind." Rev removed the catheter from the back of Asher's hand and disposed of it along with the fluid bag. He placed electrodes on Asher's chest to monitor his vitals and flipped a few switches on the machine. "I'm going to step out and check on Viper. If you need me, send your mate down the hall."

Asher's eyes flicked to Rayna as Rev left them alone. "My mate?"

Rayna sat on the side of the bed and gently took his hand. "If you'll have me."

"Why..." Asher coughed, and Rayna offered him a sip of water from the cup Rev had left on the side table. After he got his fill, he asked, "Why would you want me, though?"

Rayna retook Asher's hand. "Why wouldn't I? You're the sweetest male I've ever met. I know you're demi, and I'm willing to wait however long it takes for you to have romantic feelings for me."

"I… It probably won't take as long as you're thinking. I… fuck, this is embarrassing."

Rayna brushed her hand across his hair. "You can tell me anything."

"I've already had, uh, stirrings, if you get my meaning." The blush on his cheeks was adorable.

"That's wonderful, Asher. For now, though, I don't want you to worry about that. I want you to focus on healing. We have the rest of our lives to get to know each other. You might find you don't want me after a while."

"Can… Will you take off the mask? For now? I'd like to see the real you."

Rayna removed the wig first, then carefully peeled the prosthetic away from her face. She placed them on a chair, then turned toward her mate, smiling. "Better?"

"Much. As for not wanting you, I don't see that happening."

Rayna leaned down and pressed her lips to Asher's forehead, lingering a few seconds.

Lucy and Tamian entered the room, interrupting them. "Hey, Asher. How are you feeling?" Lucy asked.

"Like I was shot," he deadpanned. To Tamian, he said, "Thanks for getting me out of there."

"No problem. Can you tell us what happened?"

"I got to Oasis and couldn't find Viper, so after waiting half an hour, I decided to fly over. I saw

Ruth leaving the chapel, so I followed her to the main house. Abraham and David were already there, and they began arguing. David told Abraham he was done with all things Ministry and threatened him about going after Rhiannon. When Abraham called for his guard, I shifted back to my skin and got dressed, thinking I could voice them all before things got out of hand. I was too late."

Rayna's Cheetah bristled when Asher told how he was shot by a stray bullet. "I voiced the guard outside, and he helped me back to my bike, but before I could call for help, I passed out. I overheard the doctor telling Abraham a guard brought me to the clinic. Silas, the doctor, and his wife, Claudia, left immediately after patching Abraham up. Oh, Abraham said he had somewhere already set up down South in case something like that happened."

"Fury followed Abraham, so we should know where his new place is soon," Lucy explained. "Tamian called a Gargoyle named Lachlan who's as good or better than David with computers. I know Pops asked me to come help, but honestly, this is more than I can handle."

"You should put him in touch with Bishop. He and Henry are looking into Rayna's boss. They can compare notes so Lachlan isn't starting from scratch."

"Yeah, I'll do that. Do you need anything? Either of you?"

Asher's eyes were drooping, so Rayna answered for them. "No, thank you. Asher needs to rest, and I'm not going anywhere."

"Sounds good. Rev and Bethany will take care of you. Don't hesitate to call, though, if you need somewhere to hide out. You can come stay with Tamian and me."

"Thank you both for everything."

"That's what family does." Lucy winked at Rayna, then wrapped her hand around Tamian's bicep and led him to the door.

"Family. I like that," she whispered.

Chapter Thirteen

Ace

EITHER ACE WAS still floating from the pain meds, or he was the luckiest bastard alive. After a handful of days, Rayna was claiming him, and she was willing to wait for his romantic feelings to catch up to hers. Ace never understood why all his previous attempts at a relationship failed. Until now. He had to go through the heartache to get to his perfect mate. And Rayna was perfect. He knew he needed to rest, but he wanted to remain alert so they could talk. That was the main reason he didn't want any pain medicine.

"Ripley's dad stopped by earlier to invite you to lunch. I had just finished getting the rest of the dirt turned, so I showed him the garden spot, then he and I chatted."

"You chatted, or he interrogated you?"

Rayna scrunched her nose. "A little of both. It was evident he cares for you. Before he left, he invited both of us to join him and Regina for a meal."

"That's good. Like I said before, they basically adopted me, so I'm glad you got along."

"We did. I'm happy for Glory, having someone like him as a father figure considering the one she had growing up. I'm looking forward to hanging out with her outside of Haven. I really like her."

"I'm happy she and Rip got together. They both deserve to have someone special."

So do we.

Ace agreed with his Gryphon. He had prayed for a mate, and now, here she was.

"I agree. Maybe once you're all healed up, we can invite them over to hang out. From what Rev said, you're in good shape considering. We'll get you home, and you can rest on the patio while I do the planting. You can supervise from the lounge chair."

"That sounds like an excellent idea," Sutton said, entering the room.

"Hey, Boss." Ace tried to sit up, but Rayna's hand on his shoulder stopped him.

"Let me." She pushed the button on the side of the bed, raising the back.

Sutton stepped closer to the bed. "How are you feeling?"

"Not too bad. Honestly, I thought that was the end for me, and if their guard hadn't gotten me to the clinic, I probably would have bled out."

"Thank Zeus for that. Lucy already told me the rest, so you don't need to rehash it. Fury found Abraham's newest location. It's smaller than the others, and there are no guards with guns. It looks like he's starting from scratch. When you overheard his new compound was south, he didn't mean *the* South. It's only about four hours away. I instructed Fury to voice him, which he did, so we shouldn't have any more trouble out of him. Fury convinced him to go to the local FBI office and admit to everything he ever had a hand in that wasn't legal."

"Did Fury ask if Abraham told anyone about Rhiannon's gift? Because if he did, she'll still be a target."

Sutton cut his eyes toward Rayna, and Ace got it. Rayna was new, but if they were going to be mates, Sutton needed to know he could trust her. "Rayna's one of us now."

"Is that right?" Sutton asked, his eyes dancing with mirth.

Rayna faced Sutton. "Yes. Asher and I haven't had a chance to talk about the future with everything going on, but as soon as we track down David Spencer and ascertain whether my boss is on the take, I'm resigning from the agency. I have a nice nest egg, so I don't need to work, but I do like to keep busy. If there's anything I can do to help the Hounds, I'll be glad to do so."

"For now, just take care of Ace. Fury did ask

Abraham about Rhi, and he said neither he nor Ruth told anyone about her abilities. He also admitted there were a few outlying compounds, and we now have all their locations. At least those on this side of the country. Abraham admitted he answered to a man named Isaac Brown, who is the leader over all of The Ministry in the states."

Ace eased his head back onto the pillow. "At least we can now manage the ones around here."

"And I have plenty of other Hounds to do that. Your job is to get well and spend time with your female. Ripper and Glory are planning a trip to Florida to take Glory's sisters to their grandmother's. In the meantime, Regina will need someone to dote on, so if you need help with anything, maybe reach out to her."

"Yeah, Con stopped by the house earlier and invited Rayna and me out to eat. I guess I should call them and let them know what happened. Then again, if I do that, Regina will tell Ripley, and I don't want him to put off his trip."

Sutton patted Ace's leg. "If he knows you are on the mend with someone taking care of you, he'll be fine. But he's your brother, so do whatever you think is best. I'll leave you now so you can rest. If you need a ride home, let me know."

"Thanks, Boss."

Once the door closed, Rayna resumed brushing her fingers through Ace's hair. "When I researched the Lazlos, I couldn't wrap my head around the fact that Sutton was old enough to be a father to Ryker and the others. Now that I know he's a shifter, it makes sense."

"He's actually a great-grandfather. He and Rory have three sets of twin daughters down in Texas who are in their eighties. Rory was satisfied with all girls, but Sutton wanted a boy. He got five of them."

Rayna sighed wistfully. "I can't imagine having such a large family. I always wanted a sibling. Don't get me wrong; I love my grandmother, and she made my life fun, but it wasn't the same as having someone my age to play with."

"You'll have that with the Hounds. We might not all be related by blood, but we are a family. With Ripley and Glory, you'll get Regina and Conrad, so be ready to be adopted by them. You've met Kerrigan, and the other Lazlo mates are friendly as well. Rhiannon is probably the sweetest human I've ever met. And little Daisy is just precious." Ace wanted to know how Rayna felt about having kids, but he was afraid to ask. Then again, if they were going to be mates, it was important he knew where she stood. "I love kids. I bought the house I'm in hoping to fill it with a family one day. And since I didn't think I'd find a mate, I started looking into adoption."

"Really? Asher, that's wonderful. You'll make an amazing father."

"I appreciate you saying that, but if we're going to be mates, how do you feel about being a mother?"

Rayna pressed her hand to his cheek. "Hopefully, we'll have children of our own someday, but that doesn't mean you can't adopt a child or children who need a home now. Asher, I'm all in. My Cheetah knows you're our mate, but if we try this and you decide I'm not who you want, I'll still be your friend. It won't be easy, but I want you in my life however I can have you, and if that means being the cool aunt to your adopted kids, I'll happily play the part."

That was when Ace knew what his Gryphon had been telling him – Rayna Bellamy was theirs. Someone willing to put her own feelings aside for his? "Instead of being the cool aunt, how about being the cool mom? I can't promise being with me will be easy in the beginning, but I'll get there. I know that in my heart, Rayna."

"And I know in my heart being with you will be the easiest thing I've ever done in my life. We're meant for one another. Maybe my goddess knew you'd be at Haven, and she had a hand in my going undercover even though it didn't make sense at the time. Whatever the reason, I'm now glad I was there. I say we take it a day at a time. We'll get you home where you can recover. I'll plant the garden, and... Can Regina cook? I don't want you trying to feed us, and goddess knows we don't want me in the kitchen. Maybe she can prepare some casseroles to freeze that I can pop in the oven. Surely, I won't screw those up. If not, I could always ask Gran to come stay with us for a week or so."

"If you want your grandmother with us, I'm good with that, but yes, Regina is an excellent cook. Conrad isn't bad either. Besides, I shouldn't be laid up too long. Once Rev says it's okay, I'll shift to help the healing process."

"Then let's ask Regina for help. Not that I don't want Gran here, but if that were to happen, she'd stay with us, whereas Regina will just come by for a little while."

It took Ace a few seconds to understand the implications of her grandmother staying with them. She would be there twenty-four seven, not giving them alone time. Not that they would be having sex anytime soon, but it would be easier to be intimate in other ways – snuggling in bed, cuddling on the sofa – if they weren't entertaining the older woman.

"Regina it is."

Rayna stretched out beside him on the bed, insisting he get some rest. It didn't take long for him to fall asleep, secure in the knowledge he had someone in his life who wouldn't leave him because of his issues. When he woke, Ace was alone with only the beep of the monitor keeping him company. His chest and back ached something fierce, and he pulled the sheet down to look at the damage, but there was a bandage covering the exit wound. If the scar messed up his ink, he'd be pissed. No, he was already angry. David fucking Spencer. Not only had the male killed a guard but his own mother. Sure, it was an accident, but still, Ace couldn't imagine how that would affect someone. Someone already unhinged. Was it because he'd lost Rhiannon? If so, that was his own fault. Ace couldn't imagine having a child and allowing him or her to be used for profit.

Parents were supposed to protect their children. Love them unconditionally. They didn't ask to be brought into a cruel world. Was Ace doing a disservice to any future kids he and Rayna had by doing the same thing? Adoption was taking those already in the world and setting them up with a family. Things were shitty, no doubt about that, but if no one had kids, civilization would cease to exist. At least if he and Rayna had children, they would be loved and sheltered. Taught how to make life better for those around them.

Rayna had that love with her grandmother since her mom had been selfish. Ace had it with his parents until they passed away. He did his best to honor their memories by being kind and protecting those who couldn't protect themselves. Now he had love from Ripley's parents, and he would continue to be the best Gryphon he could. He and Rayna would pass on that same love to children, whether adopted or biological.

His stomach rumbled from hunger. He had no idea what time it was since the room didn't have windows. He reached out with his senses, listening to see who was close by. Rayna's soft laughter was joined by Conrad's deep voice. Ace smiled, glad his loved ones were close by and getting along. He wanted Rayna to know a father's love since she'd never had that. She and Glory were lucky to have Con in their lives. Ace's own dad had been one in a million, and Conrad Davidson was equally as wonderful.

"He's been asleep a while. I only got up because I had to pee," Rayna said. His sweet female. Ace turned his eyes toward the door, waiting to see her face. It didn't take long until she entered the room followed by Rip's father.

"Oh, you're awake," she cooed, rushing to his side. "How's your pain? You want me to get Rev in here?"

"What time is it?" he asked instead.

"Going on ten."

Conrad stood with his arms crossed over his chest. "You didn't answer the question, Son. How's your pain?"

"On a scale of one to ten, about a seven. But I can handle it."

"You can, but you don't have to." Conrad turned and left the room.

Ace squeezed Rayna's hand. "Hi."

"Hi, Gorgeous. Sorry I wasn't here when you woke."

Ace lifted her hand to his lips and kissed the back of it. "You need to look after yourself. I heard you say you only got up to pee. You need to eat."

Rayna shrugged one shoulder. "I was comfy next to you."

"Ace? Ready for some pain meds?" Rev asked.

"I'd rather have food. And Rayna needs to eat."

"Bethany left sandwiches, pasta salad, and fruit in the breakroom fridge. There's also soup broth to heat up for you. If you hold that down, then you can try something heavier. I don't think you'll have an issue since you're a shifter, but it's better to be safe than have you puking."

"I'll go heat the soup for you." Rayna pressed a kiss to his forehead, then left the room with Rev following.

Ace watched her go, and when Con cleared his throat, Ace asked, "What?"

"It's good to see you smitten, Son."

"It's good to be smitten. I never thought I'd get this, especially with someone like Rayna."

"She's something else, all right. We had a nice talk at your house earlier, and it was clear then she was all in. I especially like how she planted a garden for you since she can't cook. She's willing to contribute to the relationship in other ways. And being an FBI agent means she's tough. Add in that she's a shifter? Nothing against human mates, but this way you don't have to worry about her lifespan."

Once again, Ace thought about the serum Lucy and Jonas Montague were working on. Not that he would need it for Rayna, but the other Hounds with human mates like Ripley could possibly have extended years with their partners.

Rayna returned carrying a tray and placed it on the rolling cart. She adjusted the height, then moved it over Ace so he could reach the bowl of broth.

"Where's yours?"

"I'm going to fix me a plate. Be right back." Rayna ran a finger down his cheek before leaving again.

"She's crazy about you," Con said.

"Which is crazy in itself. We've only known each other a few days."

"That's the beauty of meeting the right person. When you know, you know."

"Yeah." Ace lifted a spoonful of broth and sipped it. It was surprisingly flavorful instead of the bland crap he'd expected. He crushed the crackers Rayna had added to the tray over the soup, mixing it together. He'd finished the bowl by the time she returned.

When Rev came back, he had some toast and another bowl of broth. It wasn't the sandwich and pasta Rayna was eating, but it was something on his stomach. By the time he downed the second bowl, he was full.

Conrad promised to return whenever Rev released Ace to escort him and Rayna home before saying goodnight. Rev checked Ace's bandages, then he too left them alone, only he went to his office where he was spending the night. Rayna kicked off her shoes, lowered the bed, and climbed on next to him. There was no TV in the room, so they snuggled and recounted their own versions of the day. With his mate by his side, Ace slipped into a dreamless sleep.

Chapter Fourteen

Rayna

ASHER WAS READY to go home the next morning, but Rev wanted to keep him at least one more night, shifter healing or not. Conrad and Regina came to visit, helping keep Asher's spirits up. They filled Asher in on what Ripley and Glory were going through with Glory's mother after Rayna explained about the prosthetic and wig they found in the chair.

When Regina offered to take Rayna to Asher's so she could shower and change clothes, Asher convinced her to go. Ripley's mother was a hoot, dressed the same way Rayna preferred in cut-off denim shorts and a rock band tee. Her arms were covered in ink. If Rayna didn't know she was a Gryphon, she would assume Regina was a cool, young woman in her forties. She sure didn't act like Colette. Regina was loving as well as funny. Then Rayna remembered Regina was the one who killed Glory's father as well as Thomas, and she had an even deeper appreciation for the female. Glory deserved to have a fierce mother figure.

Rayna trusted Regina, so she explained her situation from going undercover, to leaving Haven, to hiding out with Asher, and everything happening with Spencer and her boss. When they arrived at Asher's house, Rayna rushed through her shower, not wanting to be away from the clinic too long. When she pulled clothes out of the drawer, she picked up the burner Seth had given her and powered it on. By the time Rayna was dressed, the phone showed several missed messages. Instead of reading them then, she shoved the phone in her pocket since she figured he was calling to catch up. After slipping into her shoes and tying them, she made her way to the living room, where she grabbed one of Asher's books in case he wanted to read later.

As Regina drove back to the clinic, Rayna read Seth's texts.

Seth: *We have a problem. Grissom wants me to bring you in from Haven.*

So much for speaking in code. Rayna checked the time on the message. It was from yesterday morning at 8:22. The next one was about an hour later.

Seth: *Grissom is sending me to get you, and Perkins is going with me.*

"Shit."

"What's wrong?" Regina asked.

"The deputy director sent my partner to Haven to pick me up."

"And you aren't there. I thought your partner knew this."

"He does, but he's the one who suggested I pretend to still be undercover, thus the burner phone."

"What are you going to do?"

"There's not much I can do considering that was early yesterday morning. I'm going to text Seth and see what went down."

Va.nessa: *I just now saw your texts. My friend is in the hospital, and I've been there since yesterday. What happened?"*

Rayna didn't expect an immediate reply, but her phone rang. "Hey, Seth."

There was a brief pause, then a voice she never expected said, "Agent Bellamy?"

Fuck! What was he doing answering Seth's phone? "Uh, yes, Sir. Where's Seth?" Rayna covered the phone and told Regina to pull over.

"He's working a case. Would you care to tell me why you're texting your partner on a burner phone stating you were with a friend in the hospital when you're supposed to be undercover at Haven?"

Regina pulled into a drugstore parking lot, put the car in park, and raised an eyebrow.

Rayna had no idea what Seth had told their boss

when she wasn't found at Haven. "Is Seth okay?"

"You need to worry about yourself, Agent Bellamy. Why aren't you at Haven?"

"I was supposed to be there no longer than two months. The reasons for me being undercover there didn't make sense in the first place since we all know how women are treated within The Ministry. When I had an opportunity to leave, I took it. Then I found out David Spencer is no longer in FBI custody, and that didn't make sense either, so I remained undercover, only I was doing so outside the compound. David Spencer is still a threat to his daughter, and—"

"You and your partner seem to have differing stories, Agent. I want you in the office at oh-eight hundred tomorrow, or you'll be written up for insubordination."

Regina grabbed the phone and whispered, "What's your partner's name?"

"Seth McCauley."

Regina put the phone to her ear. When she spoke, her voice took on that strange quality when voicing someone. "You will believe the story Agent McCauley told you. You will forget you spoke to Rayna." She disconnected before giving Grissom time to respond.

"Thank you. The IT techs can still see my text message, but at least they don't know— Shit." Rayna disassembled the phone, removing the battery.

"Can they trace a burner? Is that why you removed the battery?"

"Probably. If I toss it, they may still be able to track it to New Troy."

"Don't panic. I have an idea. I saw it in a movie, but it might work."

Rayna grinned despite the situation. "Yeah? What's your idea?"

"We'll send the phone somewhere else." Regina flipped a U-turn and drove to the nearest bank where she took several hundred dollars out of the ATM. "Shit, I don't know where the truck stop is." Regina pulled into a spot at the bank and opened her phone, handing it to Rayna. She searched the internet while Regina got back on the road. They pulled into the truck stop twenty minutes later, and Regina parked in front of the building. "I'll be right back." She grabbed the phone Rayna had reassembled and got out, only Rayna didn't want her going alone, so she followed.

Regina caught the eye of several truck drivers, but the female strode up to the closest one. "Excuse me, but I was hoping you could help a girl out."

The burly man narrowed his eyes. "I'm a happily married man, young lady."

Regina gasped. "I'm not a lot lizard, thank you very much." She held out the phone. "I'm trying to hide from my ex-boyfriend, but I'm afraid he can trace my phone. He's a cop. Would you be willing to take my phone with you and toss it when you're out of town? I'll pay you three hundred bucks for your trouble."

"Hell, I'll do that for free." He held out his hand, and Regina handed the device over.

"You'll toss the phone when you get out of town, and you won't remember this conversation," she said, her Gryphon's voice echoing around the man.

After he repeated her words, he got in his truck. Regina grabbed Rayna's hand, hauling her back to the car.

"Holy shit," Rayna husked between laughs. "He thought you were a hooker."

Regina flipped her braid over her shoulder. "Maybe we don't tell Con that part."

Rayna made an X across her chest. "Promise."

"Now what?" Regina started the car after putting on her seatbelt.

"Now, I'm going to call Seth's wife, Vanessa. Can I borrow your phone, since mine's..." Rayna thumbed over her shoulder. Regina unlocked her phone and passed it over. Rayna dialed the salon's number, expecting the receptionist to answer.

"Blue Rhapsody Salon and Day Spa, Vanessa speaking."

"Vanessa, it's R—"

"Well, hello Rachelle. How are you? Good,

good. Are you ready for your touch-up?"

"Uh, yes? Is there any way I can come see you today?" Rayna asked, deepening her voice.

"No, I'm afraid I'm fully booked today. I might can get you in next week. Let me check my appointment book." The sound of footsteps came through the phone. "Let's see, I have Tuesday at ten or two. Would one of those work for you? Okay. I'll put you down for two. See you then." With that, the call went dead. Rayna pressed Regina's phone against her forehead.

"What was that about?" Regina asked.

"That was my best friend being stealthy."

"Which means someone was there listening in, or her phone is tapped."

"Yep. I'll have to go see her in person. If I wear the prosthetic Lucy gave me, I should be able to do so with Grissom being none the wiser."

Regina tapped the steering wheel. "Or I could go. Scope out the shop and see if anyone is there. I could pass her a note if there is."

"I don't want you on the FBI's radar."

"Meh, you let me worry about that. I've had more action this week than I've seen in years. It's kind of exciting."

"That's right. You were in the loft with Glory at Haven."

"You know about that?"

"I was there, watching as everything unfolded.

189

Asher also told me how you took care of Glory's father too."

"Damn. I need to have a talk with my son about spilling my secrets," Regina chided.

"I promise I won't tell anyone."

"I know you won't, Rayna. If I didn't trust you, I wouldn't let you anywhere near Asher. He's special to me."

"And to me, considering he's my mate. Let's get back to the clinic and regroup. I want to check on Ash before we head out of town."

"Where exactly is Vanessa's salon?"

"New Latham. Not too far."

When they got back to the clinic, Sutton was there with his mate, Rory. Like Regina, Rory appeared young, when in fact, she was a great-grandmother. Rayna had only allowed herself to think about having children. She'd never considered living long enough to have grandkids. She couldn't wait, especially knowing how much Asher wanted children.

Asher squeezed Rayna's hand. "You were gone a while."

Rayna blew out a breath. "Yeah. I decided to check the burner to see if I had a message from Seth." Rayna explained the texts and the deputy director answering Seth's phone.

"Do you think Seth's in trouble?" Asher asked.

"I do because I called Vanessa, and she

pretended I was a customer as though someone were listening in."

"That doesn't explain why you were gone so long." Asher didn't sound upset, just curious.

"Well, we had an adventure of sorts," Regina admitted.

Conrad tugged his mate's braid. "What did you do?"

Regina grinned at him, then told everyone about going to the truck stop.

"Does Vanessa have security cameras in her salon?" Sutton asked.

"She does, inside and out."

"What's the address?"

"I'm not sure of the street number, but it's Blue Rhapsody Salon and Day Spa on Rutledge Street in New Latham."

The elder Hound pulled out his phone. "Hey, Lucy. I need you to hack the security cameras at Blue Rhapsody Salon and Day Spa. It's owned by Seth McCauley's wife, Vanessa, in New Latham." He then explained why. "Call me back."

Regina crossed her arms over her chest. "Well, that's not as fun as going there to snoop."

Conrad pulled her back against his chest. "I think you've had enough excitement this week."

Asher tugged on Rayna's hand. "I have to wonder what Seth told the deputy director, since he said your stories were different."

"That's why I called Vanessa, so she could find out. Even though Regina voiced him, I need to know what Seth's story was in case I run into Grissom. At some point I'm going to have to show up at the office, especially if Seth's in trouble."

Sutton's phone rang. "Go ahead, Lucy."

"There are currently no agents in the salon, but earlier, two men dressed in suits entered the building. One of them, the older one, spoke to who I'm assuming is Vanessa because she was furious. There isn't audio, but her face and hand gestures indicated she was not happy with whatever the man said. She took a phone call, then walked to the front desk, so I'm assuming that's when Rayna called. Afterward, she pointed to the front door, and both agents exited. The older man got in a car and drove off, while the other is parked out front, watching the building."

"What the hell is going on?" Rayna muttered. "I need to find Seth."

"It's too dangerous," Asher argued.

"Lucy, have you heard from Lachlan?" Sutton asked.

"Not yet, but he's searching for Spencer and anything linking him to Agent Hanson."

"Ask him to include the deputy director to his inquiries."

"Will do." The call disconnected, and Sutton stared at Asher.

"No," Asher told his boss.

"I didn't say anything," Sutton countered.

"No, but you didn't have to."

"What am I missing?" Rayna asked.

"He wants you to go back to your job, and I don't like it." Asher sighed, scrubbing his free hand down his face.

"I have the prosthetic. They won't know it's me."

"And I can go with her," Regina offered. "They don't know my face. Rayna and I can be two women out for a spa day."

Asher's hand tightened against Rayna's. "And if the salon is wired? Lucy didn't mention what the younger agent was doing while the older one was arguing with Vanessa."

Regina wasn't going to be deterred. "Then I'll ask him when we get there. If he says he bugged the place, I'll voice him to remove it. If not, I'll also voice him to ignore everyone coming in and out of the shop."

Asher looked to Conrad, who tightened his arms around Regina's stomach. "You know what she's like, Son. Ripley couldn't stop her from going after Amos any more than you can stop her from helping your mate. It's the momma Lion in her."

Regina pushed away from Conrad's embrace, sliding her arm around Rayna's shoulder. "Damn straight. No one fucks with my kids."

Wow. So this was what it was like having a mother who gave a shit. One who had your back. Rayna could get used to it.

"I could go for a spa date," Rory added, surprising Rayna. The female had been quiet up until that point.

Instead of getting upset, Sutton smiled at his mate. "It has been a minute since you took time for yourself."

"Oh, for Zeus's sake," Asher fussed. "I'm not winning this argument, am I?"

"Better to learn this lesson early on, Son," Conrad told him. "Besides. They're all shifters. One is a trained agent, and the other two can voice their way out of a sticky situation."

"I thought I could voice *my* way out of a situation too and look where it got me."

"And once we capture David Spencer, I'll be taking a piece of his hide for it," Rory said, her own momma Lion coming to the front. Literally. Her face morphed into her feline briefly before reverting to human.

"If it makes you feel better, I'll follow them and hang out down the street," Conrad offered.

"No. They can handle themselves." Asher tugged Rayna down so she was sitting on the bed. "Please be careful."

"I promise." Rayna leaned down and gave him a chaste kiss.

"Don't forget your mask," Asher said.

"I won't." She kissed him again, then retrieved the prosthetic and wig. She entered the small restroom, donning both. Rayna walked back to where the females were waiting. "Ready?"

Regina and Rory kissed their mates, and Regina clapped. "Let's do this."

CHAPTER FIFTEEN

Rayna

RAYNA WAS WORRIED about Seth and Vanessa, but she was also excited. It had been months since she was in the field, and spending that time at Haven had been hell. While this wasn't a case, it was similar. During the drive, Rory called Lucy and told her what the three of them were up to, asking her to monitor the security cameras. In other words, delete the evidence of Regina speaking to the agent.

Rayna had missed seeing Vanessa while undercover, and listening to Rory and Regina chat about their lives made the ache greater. Regina and Conrad were looking at houses in New Troy now that Ripley and Glory were mates. They were keeping their home in Florida as a vacation house.

"Asher already asked if he could use the house in New Boca, so once this mess is over, maybe the two of you can take a vacation," Regina said.

"I'd love that. I've never been to Florida."

"It's secluded enough that you can shift without

being seen."

"Now that's an awesome benefit. Asher and I shifted to our cats when I first got to his house, and it was wonderful even if we couldn't do more than stretch out in the living room. My Cheetah was ready to throttle me while we were at Haven. I rarely go four days without taking to my fur, much less four months."

"Not being able to shift aside, I don't see how you managed to remain there for months without throwing down with the men. Those fuckers are nuts," Rory said.

"That they are. But I reminded myself I was doing it for Rhiannon, even though I knew that wasn't true. We, as in the FBI, were aware how the men treated women, so why my boss thought going undercover would help was a mystery. When I left Haven and met up with my partner, we both assumed I was sent away so that there was one less set of eyes on what my boss was up to. I hate that Josiah kidnapped Glory, but it did give me the opportunity to get the hell out of there. It was fascinating seeing Sutton voice the congregation and watching how everyone's eyes just sort of glazed over."

Rory turned in her seat to look at Rayna, who was sitting in the back. "What do you mean?"

"For whatever reason, voicing doesn't work on me. It took me a few minutes to realize what Sutton was doing, but I overheard Ripley tell Glory the Hounds had voiced the guards, so I put two and two together. Asher tried it on me when he followed me to the house where I was staying. It's a strange sensation, I'll give you that."

Rory angled her head, studying Rayna. "It must be because you're a shifter." She turned back around when the GPS alerted them that they were close. Rayna could have given Regina directions, but it was easier to let the computer do so. Rayna clocked the Fed sitting across the street, and she pointed him out before Regina parked in the lot at the side of the building.

"Hang on. Let me text Lucy that we're here." Rory tapped her phone, and when it pinged a few seconds later, she said, "Okay. We're good to go."

The trio got out of Regina's car. Rayna and Rory waited at the side of the building while Regina jogged across the street. She knocked on the window, and the agent rolled it down.

"Did you put any type of device in Vanessa McCauley's salon that can listen in on conversations or watch who comes and goes?"

"No."

"Are the phones tapped?"

"Yes."

"You will forget this conversation, and you will not pay attention to who comes in and out of the building. Got it?"

"Got it."

"Oh, do you have any cameras on your person or vehicle monitoring the building?"

"No."

"Carry on."

Regina crossed back over, and they entered the salon together. Vanessa, who normally was booked solid every day, was sitting at the front desk, staring out the window. She glanced up when the bell rang.

"Welcome to Blue Rhapsody." Her jovial invitation was muted, and Rayna wanted to punch someone.

"Hey, Vanessa. I'm Rachelle. We spoke earlier on the phone? This is what I would like my hair to look like." Rayna slid a note across the desk that she'd written during the drive. Vanessa frowned, but after she read Rayna's words, she slumped back in her chair, staring at Rayna. "Grissom answered Seth's phone earlier. Do you know anything about that?"

Vanessa's eyes watered as she looked over her shoulder.

"Is someone here?" Rory asked.

"No. Grissom left, and the other agent has been sitting across the street ever since. He came in here demanding to know where Seth is. What the fuck is going on, Ray?"

"That's what I'm trying to figure out. Have you heard from Seth today?"

"No." She swiped the tears off her face. "He told me he had a case and was following a lead, and that was yesterday morning when he left for the office. I haven't seen or talked to him since, and that's what I told Grissom."

"Dammit. Seth texted yesterday morning that Grissom ordered him to pick me up at the place I was undercover, and he sent Perkins with Seth. I didn't get the messages until today, or we could have gotten our stories straight. When Grissom answered, I told him I was still undercover, just doing so away from the cult. Goddess, this is a mess."

"The cult? What the hell, Rayna?"

"Yeah, fun times, but I was doing my job. I was probably safer there than out on the streets since women are expected to keep their heads down and be silent."

"Why don't you just go back to the office? Wouldn't that be the easiest way to find out what's going on?"

"Probably, but Seth's the one who didn't want me there."

"Why wouldn't he?" Vanessa leaned her head back, staring at the ceiling. "Ray..." When she lowered her eyes, they were once again filled with tears. "Something's not right." She glanced at Regina and Rory.

"I should have introduced you. This is Regina

Davidson and Rory Lazlo. They're good friends with Asher, my boyfriend."

"Since when do you have a boyfriend? You didn't find him in this cult, did you? I mean, you didn't have one before then."

"It's new, and you'll meet Asher when the time is right, which isn't now. Now, we need to figure out what's going on at the office."

"Then *go* to the fucking office, Ray. I can't lose Seth." Vanessa sucked in a breath. "Sorry."

"Nothing to be sorry for, but why would you think you're losing him?"

"He's been... off. Ever since you went undercover, he's been gone more than usual. When he is home, he's distant."

"Nessa, I hate to ask, but are you having money issues? Or were you in the past?"

"No. We've always lived modestly. You know that. The salon is busier than ever, and Seth makes... you know what he makes." Vanessa leaned forward, frowning. "Why did you ask that?"

"Whatever's going on at the office, money is changing hands. A GIA agent was brought in for trying to kidnap his adult daughter. One who is scary good with computers and making shitloads of money. When I left Haven, Seth told me that agent had been released, and we think Hanson is colluding with the man."

"Then why ask about Seth? You should know

better than anyone that my husband is an honest man, Ray. He would never take a bribe or whatever it is you think Hanson did."

"I know, but people get desperate. That's why I asked about your situation. Seth would do anything for you and the kids. Anything."

Vanessa stood, placing her hands on the desk, and scowled. "Not that. Never that. He would find an honest way if we were having issues. He'd ask Delia or his parents before he ever did something illegal. I can't believe you."

"I'm sorry. Truly sorry. I'll figure out what's going on. If you do hear from him... Shit." Rayna turned to Regina. "My phone."

Regina stepped forward. "Write down my phone number. You can reach Rayna through me." She then dropped her voice. "You will not share this number with anyone. Not even Seth."

After Vanessa took down the digits, Rayna rounded the desk and pulled her best friend into a tight embrace. "I'll find him, Nessa. I'll do whatever I have to so he comes home safe." Vanessa hugged her back, but it was lacking.

"Are you really going back to the office?" Regina asked once they were in her car.

"I don't see any other way to find out what's going on. Unless... Maybe before I do that, I'll stake out the office. If I don't see Seth, then I'll follow Grissom and see if he's up to no good."

"Ooh, we need snacks," Regina crowed. "I've never been on a stakeout." She started the car and drove back the way they came. "Wait. Where's your office located?"

"Albany," Rayna admitted, although she wasn't sure getting Regina and Rory more involved was a good idea.

"What's close by? Anywhere we can park without looking conspicuous?"

"There's a sports complex across the street. With it being summer, there are baseball games during the day, so the place is busy."

"Excellent. Do they have concession stands?" Regina was excited about food.

"I have no idea, but I would assume so. Listen, maybe I should do this alone. I don't want Sutton and Conrad mad at me."

"Pfft. I'm going to call Lucy," Rory said. She tapped on her phone, and when Lucy answered, Rory said, "Hey, Little Dove. Vanessa hasn't heard from Seth since yesterday morning, so we're going to sit across from the field office. If we don't find Seth, we're going to follow Grissom if we see him."

"Have you informed Pops of your clandestine outing?"

"Not yet because I don't want a pack of Hounds showing up and blowing our cover."

Lucy snorted. *"You're my hero, you know that?"*

"That's sweet, but we both know you're the

hero of our family."

Lucy ignored her grandmother's praise. *"I was able to track Grissom from Vanessa's salon through town, but I lost him on the freeway. There aren't many CCTV cameras close to the FBI field office, but I'm still looking for his car. I'll call you back if I find it somewhere other than close to Albany."*

"Thanks, Little Dove. Love you."

"Love you too, Rory."

Rayna couldn't help but smile at the love between the two. It made her miss her own grandmother more than she already did. Maybe once she and Asher settled down together, she could convince Gran to move to New Troy. Then again, Gran loved the hot weather out west. Rayna would have to convince Ash to take lots of vacations instead.

The drive to Albany only took twenty minutes, and Rayna directed Regina to the sports complex. After parking, the trio piled out and walked around, searching for a concession stand. They loaded up on hot dogs, chips, and sodas, then returned to the ball field closest to the road between the fields and the office. Sitting on the third-base-side bleachers, they could see both entrances to the building. The females were decades older than Rayna, but you'd never know it by the way they carried on. While Rayna kept her eyes on the building across the street, Regina told her how Glory found out Ripley was a Gryphon. "Ripley was beside himself, because the first female he thought was his mate freaked out when he revealed his shifter side. But he didn't need to worry. Glory was more worried about Rip being naked in front of Con and me when he shifted to his skin."

"What's going on with them now? Ash said they were dealing with Marjorie not wanting to go to Florida."

"She decided this morning she's going back to Haven, but the good news is she's allowing the two younger sisters to go live with their grandmother."

"I can't imagine anyone living at the compound willingly. Four months was more than enough for me."

"According to Glory, Marjorie has always lived a pious life with her husband taking care of her. She has no life skills outside the home. They convinced her Amos wouldn't be returning, but at Haven, Marjorie can just do whatever job they give her and sing praises to her God. Honestly, I'm glad she's going back. That way, Glory can focus on the future, and her grandmother can dote on her younger sisters. Hope, the older sister who's married, and her husband, Scott, are also moving to Florida to help look after Splendor and Majesty."

Rayna chewed her bite of hotdog, then washed it down with Coke. "I really like Glory. She's such a sweetheart. I'm hoping we can be friends, especially since our mates are besties."

"I have no doubt you will be. She is a wonderful young lady."

"Did you really buy her a piano?"

"We did. You've heard her sing, right? That girl is destined for greatness with a voice like hers, and the way she can listen to a song a couple of times, then play it without sheet music is unbelievable."

"Asher mentioned her singing skills, but she never sang around me. Not even when we were in chapel. She and I would sit together, but we both mouthed random words instead of singing. It was her way of thumbing her nose at whoever was leading chapel that day, and I worship my goddess, so I wasn't interested in paying tribute to a deity I don't believe in."

Rory pointed across the street. "Someone's coming out of the building."

Rayna focused, using her Cheetah's enhanced vision. "That's Bill Jessup."

"Do you know all the agents who work out of this office?" Regina asked.

"No, but I'm only searching for two, so it doesn't really matter."

"That makes sense. Do you enjoy your job?"

"I did for a long time. It was Vanessa who convinced me to become an agent. She and I went to college together, and when I couldn't decide on a major, she had Seth speak to me about the agency.

It was better than nothing." Rayna shrugged one shoulder. "But I'm turning in my notice soon."

Rory looked around Regina. "What do you want to do after you retire?"

"Love on Asher," she admitted. "I don't need the money. I have plenty in savings and investments, so I plan on focusing on him for the time being."

"What about that man?" Regina pointed this time.

"That's Grissom. Let's go." Rayna jumped from the top of the bleachers, landing stealthily on her feet. The other two females walked down the seats and met her at the bottom. They dumped their unfinished food in a trash can as they jogged to the car. By the time they were at the exit to the complex, Grissom was pulling out onto McCarty Avenue. Regina let him get several car lengths ahead before following. He drove across town to the ritziest hotel and parked in the lot.

Rayna was itching to follow the man. "I could use a drink," she said to her partners in crime.

"Oh, good idea." Regina parked a few rows over. The trio made their way inside the hotel and chose a high-top table close to the door of the bar. While waiting on their drinks, Rory texted Lucy, asking if she could hack the cameras. Regina's phone vibrated where it was sitting on the table.

Glancing at it, she grinned. "Con is checking in."

After reading the message, Regina rolled her eyes, typed out a response, then eyed Rayna.

"What?"

"Asher is getting agitated."

"And that makes you happy?"

The server brought their drinks, and once he walked away, Regina sipped her margarita. "Not happy, but it's good to see him so invested in your well-being."

"Yes but—"

"Rayna, I've known Asher a long time, and I've never seen him invested in anyone other than the Hounds and their mates and kids."

Rayna knew the reason for that, but she wouldn't betray his trust, even with someone he considered a mother figure. "I don't want him agitated. Please have Con tell him we'll be back soon. I want to talk to him about this situation."

"Won't *that* agitate him?"

"Not when I explain what I must do. He knows it's my job and that I'm capable."

Regina leaned closer, placing her hand on Rayna's wrist, and lowering her voice. "Sweetheart, take it from me. No matter how capable you are or what you have hiding inside, our males are always going to be protective. It's in their nature. Sure, Con and Sutton didn't stop Rory and me from coming with you, but that's because they've learned it does no good to argue. Do you think Ripley wanted me getting my hands dirty when it came to Amos? No, he didn't. He even asked his father to step in, but Con didn't. He knew it was my right to get my pound of flesh, if you will, for what he and William did to my son and Glory. Or tried to do. Now, if I'd said I was going after Amos alone, Con would have intervened. Not by stopping me, but he'd have gone with me and had my back. Asher's laid up and going to be a few days while he heals, and that will be what upsets him. Not that you aren't capable, but that he can't be there to help."

"I get that, but Seth isn't only my partner. He's a good friend. My best friend's husband. If I wait two days for Ash to get better, that's forty-eight hours Seth might not have."

Rory's phone vibrated, interrupting their conversation. "Lucy was able to look at the hotel's security feed. Grissom has been alone each time he entered the hotel."

Rayna tapped the table. "Please ask her to get his room number."

"What are you thinking?" Regina asked as Rory did what Rayna requested.

"I'm thinking we go upstairs, and when Grissom opens the door, you can use your voodoo on him. Ask him where Seth is."

Regina rubbed her hands together. "I can do that."

Rory looked around. "We could also hire a

prostitute and record her knocking on his door."

"You are devious. Let's save that until we know if he's guilty of anything other than doing his job."

When Rory's phone lit up, she tapped the screen, then told them what Lucy had found. "He's in 1407."

Regina got the server's attention. The trio downed their drinks while waiting to pay the tab, then they were out of the bar, headed to the elevators.

CHAPTER SIXTEEN

Ace

ACE FORCED HIMSELF to stay awake since Conrad had remained to keep him company. If it had been anyone else, he might have asked them to leave so he could rest. And by rest he meant stare at the door, waiting for Rayna to return. "Was that Regina?" he asked the male man-spreading in a hard chair beside the bed with his arms crossed over his chest now that he'd put his phone away.

"Yes. They're at the hotel where Grissom is staying."

"Doing what exactly?"

"Having a drink while Lucy hacks the computers."

Ace huffed. "How do you do it?"

"Pretend that I'm okay with my mate out playing Jane Bond with your female?"

Asher's mouth quirked in a quasi-smile, but it was short-lived. "Yes."

"Knowing that Sutton followed them helps, but

211

I learned a long time ago that Gina is her own being. She's strong and intelligent. I trust her. Does she sometimes do things I'd rather she didn't? Yep. But I wouldn't want a weaker female. One who couldn't think for herself. It doesn't mean I don't need to protect her in here." Con tapped his temple, then his heart. "Just like when she wanted her shot at Amos, and Ripley argued with me. I didn't want her getting her claws bloody, but who am I to say no to a momma wanting revenge for her kids? You have to know she's just as protective of you and Rayna as she is of Ripley and Glory. Yes, Rayna is a trained agent, but that doesn't matter to Gina. Since you couldn't go with her, Regina did so on your behalf. Besides, our Gryphons check in with each other often. If there were a problem, I'd know it."

"But you were texting her," Ace accused.

Conrad leaned forward, propping his elbows on his knees. "I was getting an ETA for you, Son. You look like you're ready to jump out of the bed and go after your mate."

"And?" Ace hated being a whiny bitch, but damn, he wanted Rayna back where it was safe.

Con grinned. "Gina said soon. Why don't you tell me how the two of you met."

"I thought you already talked to Rayna about that."

"I did, but I'd like your take on it."

Ace knew the male was distracting him, but he

launched into his side of the last few days anyway. What he didn't share was about being demi. Not that he thought Con would judge him. He just didn't feel it was necessary to share that when Rayna considered them mates. That was another thing he was trying to get used to besides sitting in bed, unable to help. Why hadn't she told him he was her fated mate?

Because you needed time to get to know her. She didn't want to put pressure on you.

Her comment about how she would be his friend if things didn't work out now made sense. She wanted him in her life however she could get him. Rayna was going to get all of him, heart, soul, and eventually body. Too bad he'd been shot, or the body might have come sooner than later.

"Asher?" Con called his name.

"What?"

"I lost you."

"Sorry. Just thinking about Rayna."

Regina's voice carried down the hallway, and Ace perked up. Rayna was first through the door, followed by Con's mate. Rayna walked directly to his bed and sat down, tossing the mask and wig off to the side before lifting his hand to her mouth. She kissed his knuckles before placing his hand on her lap. Her mood was off.

"What's wrong?"

Regina took a seat on Con's lap as Rayna

recapped everything that happened. "Once we had Grissom's room number, Regina was going to voice him regarding Seth, but he wasn't there. Lucy tapped into the security cameras, but there was no sign of him getting off the elevator on his floor. It took her a bit, but she figured out why. The cameras in the hotel had been set on a loop, and we all know who has that ability."

"Spencer," Ace said. "But if he's helping Grissom, does that mean both the deputy director and Hanson are on the take?"

"That's the question of the hour," Regina added. "That and where the hell did he go?"

"We couldn't check every room of the hotel. We did knock on the doors surrounding his room, and he wasn't in any of them." Rayna rocked her head from side to side, popping her neck. "I had an idea, but you're not going to like it."

"What's your idea?" Ace braced himself.

"Spencer was held at the correctional facility up in New Ray Brook. I want to drive up there and ask questions."

That wasn't as bad as Ace had been expecting. He wouldn't tell Rayna not to go even though he wanted to shelter her from her bosses. "To what end?"

"Mainly to see if Seth is there. If Grissom stashed him somewhere, it's possible he made it appear Seth was being detained."

"That kind of shit goes on within your organization?" Conrad asked.

"Not often, but it does happen. I need to rule it out before I go into the office." Rayna toyed with Ace's fingers. "I want nothing more than to go home and take care of you when Rev gives the all-clear."

"But you need to do this for Seth and Vanessa. I get it, Ray. If it were Ripper who was missing, I'd do whatever it took to find him."

"Goddess, this sucks."

"It does, and I may not have known you long, but I understand this is something you need to do. You're a trained agent with an impeccable record, so go find your partner. Con and Regina will make sure I get home and settled."

"Damn right we will," Regina said.

Rayna studied Ace's face. He smiled even though he wasn't happy. She leaned down and pressed her lips to his while running her fingers through his hair. "As soon as I find Seth and make sure he's okay, I'm turning in my resignation. I can't help find Spencer, and if one or more of the bosses are involved with him? That's above my paygrade anyway."

"Then go find Seth and come back to me safely. We have a garden to plant and stars to gaze at."

"I'm going to stop off at your house for my suits, so don't worry if you see some of my things gone."

"I have several burner phones in the drawer by

the refrigerator. Grab one before you leave."

"I will. Thank you."

"Do you want me to drive you?" Regina asked.

"Just to Asher's. I'll call for a ride back to my place."

"Be safe," Ace said, not wanting to let her go.

"Always." Rayna lifted his hand, pressing it to her cheek, then kissed his palm. She rose from the bed, grabbed the prosthetic and wig, then she and Regina left once again. Ace had never felt as useless as he did in that moment.

"Do you want me to follow her?" Con offered.

"No. I have to trust Zeus and her goddess to watch after her. I don't think I'd be given my mate after all these years to lose her this quickly." Ace sent up a prayer asking his god to keep his female safe.

Rayna

IT FELT STRANGE entering her home after being gone for so long. The house was stuffy, so Rayna cracked a few windows to let the air circulate while she took her toiletries to her bathroom and unpacked them.

She hadn't brought her casual clothes from Asher's since she planned on going back soon. She hung up her suits and tossed her low heels onto the floor instead of placing them in the rack. Her service weapon and holster were next, but she didn't put the gun in the lockbox since she was leaving again soon.

Rayna went to the bathroom and dabbed on a little makeup before twisting her hair into a low bun. She swapped her shorts and tee for a button-up and one of her pantsuits. She hated pantyhose, so she opted for the nylon footies that weren't much better. After putting on her shoulder holster, she checked her weapon before sliding it home. She grabbed her jacket, shoved her feet in the ugly shoes, and retreated to the living room where she'd left her purse. The new burner phone was already loaded with several numbers including those of Regina, Conrad, Lucy, and Asher. She found her work phone where it was charging on the kitchen counter. How long could a phone stay plugged in? It had been months, but when she tapped the screen, it loaded normally. She didn't carry a purse while she was working. Instead, she had a slim wallet that fit in her back pocket, which held her driver's license and one credit card. She grabbed both phones and her keys, then locked up behind her. Once she stepped into the garage, her Cheetah growled.

What's wrong?

Someone's been in here.

Rayna pulled her weapon from the holster. *Are they still here?*

No. But it smells like Seth.

Yeah, he was supposed to be here to start my car once a week.

Her Cheetah grumbled, but Rayna ignored her. Once she was behind the wheel, she pushed the button, and it started right up. While working, she drove a company vehicle, but she didn't plan on being employed much longer, so she didn't go by the office to swap.

The drive to Ray Brook normally took two and a half hours, but Rayna stopped at a drive-thru for chicken nuggets and fries. When she arrived at the facility, she went through the standard security protocol. Once inside, she made her way to the desk of Special Agent Carl Sartain whom she worked with when interrogating Spencer.

"Agent Bellamy, it's been a minute," he said in greeting.

"That it has." Rayna lowered her voice. "Have you seen Seth?"

Carl leaned back in his chair and clasped his hands behind his head. "Not since David Spencer was transferred. Is Seth no longer your partner?"

"He is." Rayna had always trusted Carl, but now she didn't know whether she should confide in him. Taking a big chance, she shared, "But there are strange things going on in our office, like the deputy director answering Seth's phone and refusing to tell me where he is."

"That's fucked up. Do you think McCauley's in trouble?"

"I do. I went undercover, and when I... took myself out of the situation, Seth warned me to stay away from the office. He was looking into something, and it could be that he found proof of wrongdoing." Rayna couldn't come right out and accuse their boss.

Careful. He smells... hostile.

"Wait, you said transferred. Seth told me Grissom made a deal with the GIA to release Spencer."

"Then he lied to you. McCauley's paperwork showed he was moving Spencer to a high-security facility."

"Seth's paperwork?"

"Yes. He was the one who picked Spencer up."

"Fuck," Rayna muttered. "Spencer was not taken to another facility. If he was, he escaped because yesterday he showed up at one of The Ministry's compounds and got in a shootout with a guard. Spencer's mother and the guard are dead, and an innocent bystander was struck by a stray bullet. Now Spencer is missing, and my partner could be as well. His wife hasn't heard from him since yesterday morning."

"There are protocols in place for transfers. If he didn't show up within the designated timeframe, someone would have been notified."

"Unless the paperwork was never filed. Do you know which facility he was supposed to go to?"

"Canaan in Pennsylvania. Hang on." Carl leaned forward and tapped his keyboard. "Sonofabitch." Carl ran a hand down his face. "There's no record of the transfer."

"Spencer *is* one of the best hackers out there."

Carl spread his hands. "What if the paperwork was a false trail, and Seth took Spencer to meet with a GIA agent?"

"Then he would have told me that's what happened." *Wouldn't he?*

"Rayna, you know your partner better than anyone."

"I do, and that's why I will not for one second believe he had anything to do with Spencer not being where he was supposed to be."

Carl's eyes flashed with something akin to disbelief. It could have been pity, but he masked it quickly. "Where's Hanson in all of this?"

"According to Seth, he sent an inner office memo saying he was going out of town. Grissom stopped by the office Monday asking for Hanson's whereabouts. There are too many things that don't add up about all of this." She wouldn't admit to Carl that the Hounds were doing their own research in the background. Speaking of, she wondered if Bishop or Lachlan had made any progress.

"I agree. What are you going to do now?"

Rayna sighed. "Go to the office and confront Grissom."

Carl stood and walked around his desk, leaning his hip on the edge. "Do you honestly think that's a good idea?"

"No, but it's the only one I have."

"I have a buddy that works in your office. I'll give him a call and see if he's noticed anything odd."

"I appreciate it. Take care, Carl."

"You be safe out there, Rayna. Let me know if you find your partner."

Rayna turned and gave him a two-fingered salute as she walked away. When she got in her car, she checked the burner for any messages.

Lucy: *I finally pieced together what happened with cameras from different businesses. Grissom entered the hotel, then immediately left out a side door. He got into a vehicle belonging to a Chris Perkins. They traveled east. I alerted Lachlan to help track them because they got on the interstate.*

Rayna: *I'm leaving Ray Brook now. Can I call?*

Lucy: *Yes*

Rayna connected the phone to the Bluetooth and dialed the female.

"Hey, Rayna. What did you find out?"

Rayna recounted her conversation with Carl. "I don't get why Seth would lie to me."

"Maybe he's protecting you. Until you know otherwise, keep trusting him. I'm going to try to retrace his steps. Vanessa said he left home yesterday morning, so I'll search the cameras around town and see what I come up with."

"Thanks, Lucy."

Rayna disconnected, then headed home. Her thoughts spiraled, swirled, danced, and twisted between Asher, Seth, and her boss. Why would Seth tell her Spencer had been turned loose when he was the one who was involved in the transfer? No, the transfer was bogus. Paperwork to cover his ass while he moved Spencer. But move him where? And why lie to Rayna unless he were involved in something he shouldn't be?

Needing to hear Asher's voice, she called her mate. After asking how he felt, she repeated her conversation with Carl.

"I still think until you know otherwise, you trust your partner. You have good instincts, Rayna."

"Thank you, Asher. I'm going home to change clothes, but I'll see you soon."

"I can't wait."

By the time Rayna got to her house, she knew what to do. She parked in the garage and as soon as she opened the car door, her Cheetah growled.

What's wrong now?

I think you should look around. Something feels off.

Since her Cheetah had better instincts than Rayna did in her skin, she searched her house room by room, but nothing was out of place. The doors were intact, as were the locks. None of the windows were broken. Seth and Vanessa were the only ones with keys and the code. Still, she did a cursory glance for tracking devices. Not finding any, she blew out a breath and dropped down on the sofa. What the fuck? Why would Seth break in without leaving a note? *Because he didn't think she would notice if the alarm wasn't tripped.*

Rayna went through her house once more, this time, searching more thoroughly for anything hidden. She looked in all the air vents. She checked the bottom of her furniture, removing cushions. She stripped her bed after pulling the frame away from the wall. Rayna checked behind every piece of artwork. She then went to the garage and looked around. After a cursory glance, she turned to go back inside when she noticed her shovel. It was hanging on the rack but in the wrong spot. Taking the tool with her, Rayna moved through the house and out the back door, searching her yard for signs of turned soil. She didn't see any, but what she did notice was a large flower pot in the wrong spot.

Rayna moved the pot to the side, and there she

found disturbed earth. She carefully dug, not sure what she would find. Buried about six inches down was a gallon-sized freezer bag. She dug it out using only the shovel, not wanting to get her fingerprints on the plastic. Inside was a thumb drive, a stack of photos, and some folded papers. Rayna ran inside and grabbed a paper towel, which she used to lift the plastic bag, taking it to her kitchen. She then replaced the dirt and put the flower pot back where she'd found it so if Seth were to come back, he wouldn't immediately know something was amiss.

Rayna went to the garage and retrieved a pair of latex gloves from the kit in her trunk. She also grabbed the burner phone from the console. She opened the camera app and took a photo of the sealed bag. Rayna wanted to know what was on the thumb drive, but she wasn't going to risk turning on her computer to do so. She reached for the folded papers, but one of the photos caught her attention. Using a gloved fingertip, Rayna spread them out.

"Holy shit." She studied them all before taking a photo of each one. She then unfolded the documents, read them over, and took a picture of them as well. After restacking the photos into a pile, she shoved them, the documents, and the thumb drive back inside the plastic bag. She then retrieved another Ziploc bag from her pantry and inserted the evidence bag inside it to keep it safe.

Rayna rushed through the house and began

packing while calling Lucy on her burner.

"Hey, Rayna."

"Lucy, I don't know what the fuck's going on, but someone, and I'm pretty sure it was Seth, buried something in my backyard. There are documents, photos, and a thumb drive. I'm not about to put the drive in my computer, but oh my goddess…"

"Breathe, Rayna."

"I took a picture of everything on my burner. I'm going to text everything to you after I encrypt it."

"Why don't you bring that stuff to my house? We can look at the thumb drive on my computer."

"Yeah. I'd appreciate that. Shoot me your address. You live in New Troy, right?"

"I do."

"I'm going to pack, but I should be there within an hour."

"See you then."

Rayna sent the encrypted text, then packed everything she would need for at least a month because she wasn't coming back to her house for at least that long.

CHAPTER SEVENTEEN

Rayna

RAYNA KEPT HER eyes peeled for wildlife as she drove the back way toward New Troy. Thinking she should at least text Asher and let him know she wasn't immediately coming to the clinic, she reached out to tap the icon on her display when headlights shined behind her. They brightened, and Rayna slowed down. The car sped up, moving into the oncoming lane. Rayna slowed even more. Big mistake. The other vehicle rammed into her rear quarter panel. Rayna was a skilled driver, but her car fishtailed a few times before the other vehicle rammed into hers again. The force of the impact had her rear tires sliding toward the shoulder. The other car continued pushing until Rayna was in the weeds, then wedged against a tree. By the time she regained her bearings, her door was flung open, and a strong hand grabbed her left wrist. The seatbelt held her in place as she struggled against her attacker.

"Let go of me!" Her claws popped out on her right hand, and she raked her sharp nails across the attached arm.

"You fucking bitch!" a familiar voice shouted, his grip faltering.

Rayna disengaged the seatbelt, but as soon as she was free, the man struck again with his uninjured hand, punching her in the temple. Fuck. Her head throbbed, and her vision dimmed. The man once again pulled her left arm, and Rayna grabbed for purchase, missing the steering wheel, and her claws dug along the door's interior. The male's grip was strong. Since she didn't want her shoulder to be dislocated, Rayna allowed herself to be dragged from the car.

Drawing on her beast's abilities, Rayna twisted, landing on her feet. Perkins had a gun trained on her, but she was fast enough to claw him a second time on the wounded arm holding his pistol. Perkins screamed, releasing her wrist and dropping his weapon. Rayna didn't give him time to retaliate. She popped a front kick into his stomach, sending him flying. She retracted her claws, picked up his gun, and moved toward him, but another voice stopped her in her tracks.

"Stop right there, Agent Bellamy."

Rayna raised both hands in the air, finger on the trigger guard, and turned. Grissom stood on the far side of his vehicle, shielded. His service pistol was aimed at her chest.

"Sir? What's going on?" Rayna allowed her voice to tremble.

"What the fuck are you?" Grissom asked.

"Shoot her!" Perkins yelled. "Look at what she did to me!" Rayna didn't have to look to know his arm was torn apart, dripping blood.

"I'm an agent, Sir. A confused one. Why are you after me? I've been undercover at Haven. I was coming back to work in the morning like you instructed."

"What did you do to Perkins?"

"I didn't do anything." Rayna glanced over her shoulder. "He must have cut his arm on the car."

"Where's your partner?"

"I don't know. You told me he was on a case. I haven't spoken to him."

Tell Asher's Gryphon we need Tamian. Now.

On it.

"Don't lie to me." Grissom raised his gun. Her past life didn't flash before her eyes. What did, though, were the future years she wouldn't have with Asher if Grissom shot her in the head.

"No!" Rayna screamed, eyes wide as she stared behind her boss. Grissom turned to look behind him at her frightened outburst. *Dumbass.* Rayna lowered Perkins's gun, shooting Grissom in the shoulder before diving to the ground. She commando-crawled until she could see under his car, then shot him in the foot. His high-pitched curses scared the birds nesting in the nearby trees. Rayna rose to a crouch and turned to be sure Perkins hadn't moved. He hadn't, but he was glaring at her.

"You'll pay for this, bitch."

Using her shifter strength, she bent her legs, then leapt atop Grissom's car, landing on silent feet like the cat she was. "Toss your weapon," she demanded. Grissom did as instructed, although reluctantly.

"What are you?" he asked again.

Ignoring the question, she jumped to the ground beside her boss. "On your stomach." When Grissom complied, Rayna searched him for another weapon. Finding none, she stood with the gun trained on him while keeping Perkins in her sight. "Get up," she commanded. Perkins was slow to move, but he did as she bade. "Strip."

"I'm not getting naked for you. You're not my type." Rayna aimed at his feet and fired off a round a few inches from his toes. "I won't ask again."

"Fuck. All right." When Perkins was down to his underwear, she stopped him. "Turn around, hands where I can see them, and walk backwards toward me. Slowly." When he was ten feet away, she commanded, "Stop. Don't move." Keeping both men in her field of vision, Rayna sidestepped to the driver's side door and popped the trunk. Thankful to find a field kit, she grabbed enough cable ties to secure them both. Once they were properly restrained, she removed the kit from the trunk and made them both get inside. That took a little persuading, but when she aimed at their heads, they complied while threatening and cursing her parentage. She slammed the lid, then leaned against the car, staring into the darkness.

Now what? Fuck. She was thankful it was late and no cars had passed by. She had to get off the road. There was nothing she could do about her car, so she got into Grissom's vehicle and started the engine. When the men began shouting, Rayna wished she'd taped their mouths. Half a mile down the road, Rayna noticed a faded sign for an old quarry. She turned and drove the short distance to the abandoned entrance. The long-forgotten gate hung crookedly. Rayna put the car in park, got out, and with her shifter strength, was able to move the gate enough to drive through it. She continued past an old trailer that had been used as the office and parked behind it. Turning off the engine, Rayna got out and reached for her phone.

"Shit." She'd left it in her car. Rayna had two choices. One, she could go back and get it, or two, she could trust her Cheetah to speak to Asher's Gryphon and get word to Tamian. Rayna didn't trust Grissom and Perkins not to get out of the trunk, so door number two it was.

Ace

ACE TWISTED THE phone in his hand. He was sitting in the chair instead of reclining on the bed. He had walked down the hallway to see Viper earlier, but the Hound had gone home with his mate. Regina and Conrad finally left when Ace kicked them out, telling them to go home and get some rest. He had the book Rayna brought him, but after reading the same paragraph several times, he gave up. Now, here he was, bored out of his skull, waiting on his phone to ring. When it did, it made him jump.

"Hello?"

"Hey, Asher. It's Lucy. Have you heard from Rayna?"

"Not since she was on her way home from Ray Brook. Why?"

"Okay, I don't want you to panic, but she was supposed to be on her way to my house. Now I can't get her on the phone. Before she left her place, she sent me photos of some items she found buried in her backyard. She thinks Seth left them there since her house wasn't broken into and the alarm wasn't tripped. Only Seth and Vanessa have the code to get into her house."

"What kind of items?" Ace pushed to his feet and ignored the twinge of pain in his chest.

"Photos of Frederick Hanson. Someone had slit his throat. There were also some documents, mostly bank statements, and she had a thumb drive she was bringing to me. I've tried to find her on cameras between her house and here, but there's no sign of her car."

"Shit. I need some clothes. I—"

"And this is you panicking," Lucy deadpanned.

"Of course I'm fucking panicking, Lucy. Rayna's my mate. Rev!" Ace yelled. The Hound came running down the hallway.

"What are you—?"

"I need clothes. Rayna's missing, and I need to go."

"You don't have a car, Brother, and if she's missing, where are you going to look for her?"

"I don't know, but I have to get out of here. I'm not sitting on my ass doing nothing." Ace put the phone to his ear. "Lucy, keep searching. I'll be to your house as soon as I get a ride and a fucking shirt. Screw the shirt. I just need a ride."

Rev put a hand on Ace's good arm. "I'll drive you to Lucy's myself."

"We'll be there in twenty, Lucy."

"See you then." Ace punched the screen and turned to Rev. "Let's go."

"Hang on, Cowboy. You might not want a shirt, but you're fucking well getting one." He walked to a cabinet and pulled out Ace's boots. "Do you need help with these?"

"No. I can manage." At least he hoped he could. Ace took the boots, sat down in the chair, and sucked in a breath. "Would I not heal quicker if I shifted?" He'd already asked, so Rev's negative response wasn't unexpected.

"No. Not with where the bullet hit your rib. That'll take time. Get your boots on while I grab a shirt." Rev rushed out of the room, and Ace struggled with his footwear. By the time Rev returned, Ace was sweating, but he didn't care. He could endure a little pain. He'd endure any amount of discomfort if it meant getting out of the clinic and going to help find Rayna.

Rev held out a button-up, and Ace slid his arms in. "Let's go." He followed the Hound down the hallway and out the back door to where his truck was parked. Ace climbed in the passenger seat, gripping his phone like a lifeline. He placed it on his lap long enough to button the shirt, then he stared at his phone, begging it to ring.

"What happened?" Rev asked as soon as they were on their way.

Rev was already up to speed with everything going on with the Feds and David Spencer, so Ace filled him in on what he'd learned in the last few hours. "Rayna went to the Ray Brook facility earlier to see if Grissom had stashed Seth there. He hadn't, but the agent showed Rayna the paperwork where Spencer was being transferred to a high-security facility, which was contradictory to Seth telling her that Spencer was being released. Seth was the one who took possession of Spencer. Then, when Rayna got home, she somehow found documents and photos buried in her backyard. She's positive Seth placed them there since only he and his wife have the alarm code to her house, and there was nothing indicating someone had broken in. Plus, her Cheetah sensed he had been in the garage. The photos showed someone had slit her immediate boss's throat, and the documents were bank statements. There was also a thumb drive, but Rayna didn't want to access it on her laptop, so she was taking it to Lucy. She hasn't shown up, and Rayna's not answering her phone."

"Where does Rayna live?"

"New Latham, which is less than fifteen minutes from Troy. Shit, I don't know her address."

"I'm sure Lucy can get that for you, but I thought we were going to Lucy's house."

"Maybe something happened at Rayna's, and she can't answer her phone." Ace called Lucy's number. When she answered, he said, "Can you give me Rayna's address? I want to stop by there to make sure something didn't happen."

"Tamian already did a drive-by. He's been riding around searching for her car… Hang on, he's calling. I'm going to put you on hold." The line went silent, and Ace drummed his fingers on his thigh.

Rayna needs Tamian.

Ace bristled. Why would his mate need the Gargoyle? *Where is she?*

"Are you still there?" Lucy asked.

"Yes, but my Gryphon was speaking to Rayna's Cheetah, and it said she needs Tamian."

"He found Rayna's car. From the looks of it, someone pushed her off the road with their vehicle, and there was a scuffle."

"A scuffle? Like blood or…?"

"Like claw marks on the door as if her Cheetah came out to play. There is minimal blood, so it's possible she attacked the other person. There're no shredded clothes, meaning she didn't fully shift, but there are a set of men's clothes on the ground for some reason. Her burner phone was in the car, so I can't track her that way."

"Lucy, why would Rayna ask for Tamian?"

"Maybe because whoever took her has a gun? She knows he's impervious to bullets."

"Oh, that makes sense. Where is her car? We'll head that way."

"It's on Bullock Road, west of 87. I'll send you the exact coordinates. Tamian will be waiting."

Ace disconnected and scrubbed a hand down

his face. *Does her Cheetah know where they are or who they're with?*

Yes. It's her boss, Grissom. But Rayna's in control.

If she's in control, why does she need Tamian's help?

He's a Gargoyle.

And?

That's all she said.

Lucy's text came through, and after plugging in the coordinates, Ace gave Rev directions to the tree-lined road. Rev's headlights shined on Tamian who was leaning against his SUV with its emergency flashers on, tapping on his phone. When they parked in front of his vehicle, he glanced up, continued typing, then put the phone in his back pocket. Rev told Ace to stay put, then came around to help him out of the truck.

Tamian inclined his head. "Ace, Rev."

"Show me the blood," Ace demanded.

Tamian walked to the side of Rayna's car and pointed at the ground with the toe of his boot. His Gryphon threatened to come out, and the air swirled around them in a miniature cyclone.

"Ace, control your beast," Rev commanded while holding his hands in front of his face.

Ace took a deep breath, berating his animal to calm the fuck down. When it complied, Ace gingerly knelt, dipping his fingers in the sticky substance. He brought it to his nose, and after inhaling, let out a sigh of relief. "It's not hers." He braced himself against the car and stood. "Rayna's Cheetah is asking for you. It said Rayna is with the deputy director, but she's in control."

Tamian didn't seemed surprised. "Does her Cheetah know where they are?"

"My beast hasn't said. Let me ask." Ace waited for his Gryphon to reach out again.

She's waiting at an old sand quarry not far from here. She hid the evidence bag in the trunk and needs Tamian to bring it to her.

Frustrated, Ace relayed the message, then asked, "Why you?"

Tamian's stoicism softened. "You are supposed to be resting in the clinic. Besides that, she knows bullets won't hurt me, and I can also voice humans like a Gryphon can. We had this conversation during our drive to Oasis." Tamian walked to Rayna's car and pushed the trunk release button. With the back end being damaged, the Gargoyle had to pry the trunk lid open to retrieve the plastic bag she'd hidden there.

Ace pulled out his phone and opened the map app. "She's here," he said, showing Tamian.

The Gargoyle hummed. "Not far then. I would tell you to go home and let me handle this, but I won't patronize you. Do you want to ride with me or follow behind?"

"You should ride with Tamian," Rev said. "I'm

237

going to call Sutton to have someone come tow Rayna's car to the clubhouse. We don't need humans asking questions about the claw marks. I'll stay here and wait on the truck."

"Thanks Rev."

"You got it, Brother. And do try to take it easy if possible. You are still healing. Come on." He motioned his head toward Tamian's vehicle. Ace didn't bother fussing. Instead, he let his friend help him into the cab, which honestly, was much appreciated.

The quarry was less than a mile away, and when they approached the gate, Ace opened his senses, searching for trouble. Tamian continued through the entrance, following the gravel road until they reached a dilapidated trailer. Rayna was nowhere he could see, but Tamian drove around behind the metal building. Thank Zeus one of them had their emotions under control.

Ace had never seen a more beautiful sight when his mate came into view. Rayna was leaning against a car, holding a gun. When she noticed Ace, her eyes widened. She shoved the firearm into the back of her pants as she strolled toward Tamian's vehicle.

"What are you doing here?" she asked as he opened the door. Rayna crowded Ace, not letting him get out.

"Came to assist you."

Rayna rolled her eyes, but then she grinned up

at him. "I'd have done the same thing." Looking past Ace, she said, "Hey, Tamian."

"Rayna. I brought the evidence packet. Where is Grissom?"

She waved behind her. "He and Perkins are in the trunk. They may need medical attention." Rayna placed a hand on Ace's thigh. "The reason I asked for you is because you're a Gargoyle, and both Grissom and Perkins had firearms."

"Why didn't you take them to the field office?" Ace asked.

"Because I don't know who to trust. Plus, I want to see what's on the thumb drive first."

The two men were shouting about bleeding out and needing a hospital. Ace asked, "Did you shoot them?"

"Grissom, yes, but nowhere critical. I did claw Perkins, so one of you will need to voice him and convince him he cut his arm trying to drag me out of the car."

Ace narrowed his eyes. "Did he hurt you? Is that the real reason your Cheetah reached out to my Gryphon?"

"I wasn't sure how I was getting out of being confronted by two agents with guns. If I were human, I probably wouldn't be standing here, but I'm fine. Now that you're both here, can we take the thumb drive to Lucy and see what's on it?"

"What are you going to do with those two?" Ace

inclined his head toward the other vehicle.

"Can we take them to the clinic and have Rev patch them up after you voice them? I don't want them losing too much blood."

"Rev's waiting at your car for one of the Hounds to bring a tow truck. We didn't want someone to happen upon it and see the gash marks in the door."

"Oh, that's awesome. While you're voicing Grissom, maybe you could encourage him to pay for the damages since he's the asshole who ran me off the road."

"You're not going to tell... Who are you going to give the evidence to if you don't know who to trust?" Ace asked.

"I'll probably go to Stanton Milsap, the director."

"Once we see what's on the thumb drive, we can pass it off to Lachlan. He can do a deep dive to uncover who all is involved," Tamian said. "Do you want me to drive the two captives and meet with Rev while you two head to our house? Or would you rather get back to the clinic?"

"That's up to Asher."

"I don't want to go back to the clinic."

"Then Lucy's it is, but I need to get my bags out of my car before it's towed." Rayna patted Ace's leg before closing the door and heading around to the other side. She removed the weapon from the back of her pants and handed it over to Tamian before climbing in. Once seated, she leaned over and pressed a kiss to Ace's cheek. "You really feel up to this?"

"Yes, ma'am." And he did. Ace would much rather be with Rayna, enduring a little pain, than sitting in the clinic wondering what she was doing.

Rayna reached over and squeezed Ace's hand. "I'm glad you're with me."

Ace entwined their fingers. He was glad too.

CHAPTER EIGHTEEN

Ace

ACE WAS HANGING out in an overstuffed armchair in Lucy's living room while she and Rayna sat side-by-side on the sofa, looking at the information on the thumb drive.

"I emailed copies of everything to Lachlan so he can research the accounts. All except for one. One of the accounts is in little Daisy's name listing Rhi as the executor until Daisy is twenty-one."

"Which means Spencer is behind the money. No surprise there," Rayna said.

"What about the other accounts?" Ace asked.

"They're in Frederick Hanson's name. But why kill him if he was also on the take?"

"Maybe he wasn't. What if he figured out Grissom was in bed with The Ministry? It could be why Hanson was acting cagey and stopped allowing me to interrogate Spencer."

"Look at this." Lucy pointed to the screen. Rayna studied whatever Lucy had pointed out. "Do you recognize him?"

"Yes. That's Chris Perkins. Where is this?"

"The Hotel Marquis. Hang on. Let me rewind it." After a few seconds, Rayna pointed at the screen. "That's Hanson, so he obviously didn't go out of town." To Ace she described what they were looking at. "This video shows Hanson entering the hotel and less than five minutes later, Perkins walks in. I'd lay odds Perkins killed him."

Lucy hummed. "But did he take the photos?"

"Maybe someone paid him to kill Hanson and the photos were proof."

"Then how did Seth end up with them?" Lucy returned her focus to the laptop. "Uh, Rayna? This is a message addressed to you." She tapped the keyboard, then a male's voice sounded from the small speaker.

"Agent Bellamy, I hope your time at Haven wasn't too terrible, but I needed to get you away from the office so you wouldn't get caught in the crossfire. From what I could tell by our time together, you're a good agent, unlike Grissom."

Rayna reached over and stopped the message. "Holy shit. That's Spencer." She then restarted the message.

"I'm entrusting you with the evidence I've collected over the past couple of years in case something happens to me before the GIA can meet with your director. I've also sent copies of everything to my boss at the GIA along with my resignation. Being undercover, playing spy for

243

so long, let's just say I'm tired, Agent Bellamy. Tired of living all the lies. Tired of having my daughter think the worst of me. Tired of pretending to be someone I'm not. I don't expect you to believe me, not after everything that's happened, but it's the truth.

"*Ten years is a long time to be undercover. In doing so, I lost myself. The man I was when my wife, Daisy, was alive. When Rhi was my little girl and ran to me with open arms and a smile. I realize now I didn't handle things with her and the biker as I should have, but she was my last link to her mother, and I didn't want to lose her. I lost her anyway.*

"*Hopefully, by the time you find this package, my boss will have spoken with the director, and Grissom will be behind bars where he belongs. If not, this is my way of ensuring someone trustworthy will see to it that Grissom gets what he deserves. I know I don't have the right, but I have a favor to ask of you. Please tell Rhiannon I'm sorry for everything, and she is now free of me. Take care, Agent Bellamy. You're a rare breed in this crazy world.*"

Rayna stood and began pacing. "This still doesn't explain where Seth is. He's the one who hid the evidence in my yard, which means he and Spencer had to have met up at some point."

"If Agent Sartain wasn't lying, then Seth had access to Spencer when he was supposed to have transferred him," Lucy offered.

Rayna stopped beside Ace's chair and ran her fingers through his hair. "True, but he wouldn't disappear without a word to Vanessa."

"Did you ask Grissom where Seth is?" Ace asked.

Rayna smacked her forehead. "No."

"I'll tell Tamian to ask him," Lucy said while typing on her keyboard. Her phone rang, and she put it on speaker. "Go ahead, Lachlan."

"I've traced the accounts in Hanson's name back to their origins. We know Spencer was funneling money to The Ministry, and the funds in the accounts listing Hanson as the owner came from the same source. The thing is, they weren't originally in his name. They were in Grant Grissom's name up until about ten months ago."

"So, Hanson either convinced Spencer to transfer the money to him, or he had someone else do it?" Lucy asked.

"Neither. I located a different hacker who made the change and convinced him to tell the truth, or he'd never see the light of day again. Grissom had the male set up a shell corporation hidden within several others and move a small portion of the money to accounts in Hanson's name."

Rayna sat on the chair arm, reaching down for Ace's hand, lacing their fingers. "Then why kill Hanson if he was sharing the wealth?"

"I don't think he was sharing it. I think he was setting Hanson up. Spencer most likely realized what was happening and warned Hanson during their private talks. Your partner did say the two men met behind closed doors, and Hanson could have provided a computer for Spencer."

Rayna slid off the chair arm and began pacing again. "Okay, so maybe Hanson organized Spencer's supposed transfer, and he trusted Seth to do so?"

"But that was months ago," Ace said.

"That's not all," Lachlan said. "The amount of money in these shell corporations is in the millions. More than a deputy director would make in a lifetime. He must be into some highly illegal shit."

"Hang on," Lucy interrupted. "Tamian asked Grissom where Seth is, and he admitted he locked him up at Ray Brook."

Rayna stopped pacing, her hands clenched. "Then why did Grissom interrogate Vanessa as to Seth's whereabouts?"

"He was covering his tracks," Ace said. "And possibly looking for you since he had an agent sitting outside the salon."

Rayna blew out a breath. "Lucy, please have Tamian ask Grissom if Agent Sartain knew this."

Lucy gazed into the middle distance. When she refocused on Rayna, she nodded. "He did."

"That lying sack of shit. I'm going to gut him."

"She's feisty. I like her," Lachlan said.

Ace wanted to go to his mate, so he did. He groaned as he rose, grabbing Rayna's attention. When she opened her mouth to protest, he held out his hand. "I'm fine." Fine was relative, but he wouldn't sit there doing nothing while she was upset. "We'll get Seth out of there, and then we'll find out his role in all this."

Lucy stood and stretched, rubbing her belly. "Yes, we will. I've tasked Tamian with asking Grissom certain questions, like who was involved, what their end game was, and why he imprisoned Seth. We have Spencer's message, but we don't have the male. Just because he said he was playing a double agent doesn't mean he's innocent and gets to walk away from his sins."

"What message?" Lachlan asked.

While Lucy recounted Spencer's words, Ace pulled Rayna into his good side and hugged her gently while inhaling her hair. He'd been so scared of losing her, and injured or not, there was no way he was letting her go back to Ray Brook alone. The easiest way to get Seth out of there would be to call Agent Sartain and voice him, and he told Rayna as such. "We can have him escort Seth to us."

"We'll need somewhere isolated because I wasn't kidding about ripping Sartain a new one."

"I have just the place," Lucy said. "And it won't be the first time the Hounds have taken care of business there."

"Yeah? Where's that?" Rayna asked.

Lucy tapped the floor with her bare toes. "Downstairs. My adopted father had a lab down there, which I had gutted once I found out the types of experiments he was conducting when he was alive. It's where Glory's father was 'handled' as well as the male who tried kidnapping Rhiannon after she escaped Haven. It's soundproofed, and there's a drain in the floor, which is handy for cleaning up messes."

"If the GIA wasn't going to the director with his proof, I'd bring Grissom here and gut him as well," Rayna seethed.

"That's an option," Lucy said. "Let Spencer's boss go to the director. It'll just look like Grissom took his money in the shell corporation and disappeared. Excuse me for a moment. I've gotta pee."

Rayna turned her face up to Ace. "What would you do? I know we've talked about certain people who don't deserve to live, but does whatever Grissom is guilty of warrant a death sentence?"

"We don't know the extent of his crimes." Ace brushed a stray strand of hair off his mate's face. "I think we should bring him here and interrogate him. Reserve judgment for after you have your answers." Rayna rested her forehead against Ace's chest, and he pressed his cheek to her hair.

Lucy returned to the living room. "I'm back, Lachlan."

"If Spencer really is turning over proof of Grissom's wrongdoings to the director, you can guarantee he's covered his own tracks. That or he had permission from someone higher up in the GIA to do what he did. You don't stay undercover that long if it isn't sanctioned. The government isn't going to allow an agent to disappear for eleven years without knowing where they are."

"He did say he was turning in his resignation." Lucy plopped down on the sofa and stretched her legs out. "And we know he has the means to disappear."

Rayna turned so her back was plastered against Ace's chest. "I hope he was telling the truth when he said he wouldn't bother Rhiannon."

Ace wrapped an arm around her waist. "He set up an account in Daisy's name, which means he's been watching Rhi all this time. I'm not a trained agent, but he sounded resigned in his message to you."

Rayna trailed her fingertips across Ace's arm. "Not only has he lost Rhiannon, but he killed his mother. It was an accident, but that's not something you get over quickly."

Rayna's words jogged Ace's memory. "Something he said doesn't make sense. When Spencer was confronting Abraham, he told his mother he'd lost both Rhi and his job. If that's the case, why would he say he's resigning?"

"To make himself look better? To keep me from going after him?"

Lucy adjusted the pillow at her back, then resettled, looking at Rayna. "What's the plan? Are we bringing the agents here for interrogation time?"

"I think that's the easiest way to get the truth out of everyone, Seth included. And I said I wanted to gut Grissom, but I'm not a killer. I think we should voice them to tell the truth and record their confessions. We'll add that to the evidence Spencer already has."

Lucy smiled softly. "I'm glad that's your decision. Unless he admits to killing animals and babies, then I'll slice him open myself. I'll tell Tam to bring Grissom and Perkins tonight if Rev is finished patching them up. Since it's late, we should probably have Sartain take Seth to a neutral location early tomorrow and ask one of the Hounds to bring them here in an SUV. Sound good?" When Ace and Rayna agreed, Lucy continued, "Thanks for the assistance, Lachlan. I'll give you a call after we question the agents."

"You're welcome. Talk soon."

Lucy sat up and rubbed her belly. "The princess needs sustenance. Are either of you hungry?"

Rayna's stomach rumbled, and Ace chuckled. "I think that's a yes. It'll be good to eat something solid. I know Rev means well, but I'm a Gryphon, and soup doesn't cut it."

Rayna led Ace back to the armchair. "You still need to rest, though. You hang out here, and I'll help Lucy." When Ace arched a skeptical brow, Rayna playfully slapped his arm. "I can wash and cut veggies." She turned to Lucy. "I can't cook, and he knows that."

Lucy looped her arm through Rayna's. "Excellent. I'll throw some burgers on the grill, and you can put some French fries in the air fryer."

Ace was thankful to be sitting. Yes, he was a Gryphon, but nicked ribs were no joke, even for a shifter. He leaned his head back and closed his eyes. He thanked Zeus for keeping Rayna safe, and he asked for guidance in moving forward with their relationship. Just because Rayna was his mate, that didn't mean things would be smooth sailing. Yes, he'd felt flickers of arousal, but she was a beautiful female and could have anyone. Someone without hangups. She told him she would be patient, but that wasn't fair to her.

You *aren't being fair to* **her.** *She already cares about you. We have a long life ahead of us, and waiting a few weeks or months isn't going to matter.*

Ace sighed. There was no arguing with his beast. Not that he wanted to. He hated conflict, especially with the other part of himself. Laughter rang out from the kitchen, and Ace smiled. Rayna had a best friend in Vanessa, but it was good to have more than one friend. Lucy would make an excellent one, as would Glory once she and Ripley

251

settled things with Glory's family. Thinking of Rip, Ace pulled out his phone and texted his best friend.

Me: *Just checking in. How's it going with everything?*

It took a few minutes, but Rip messaged back.

Ripley: *Not bad. Marjorie went back to Haven yesterday, and Glory and I brought her sisters and Scott to her grandmother's today.*

Me: *That's great. Call me when you get back.*

Ripley: *Will do.*

There was no doubt his friend would rip Ace a new one for not telling him about being shot, but Ace knew the male wouldn't stay mad long. That was part of being someone's ride or die. Ace wondered if Vanessa was that for Rayna, or if the following day, finding out Seth's truth would cause an irreparable rift between them because Ace had a feeling Seth wasn't as innocent as Rayna believed.

When the food was ready, Ace joined the females in the kitchen where they ate at the smaller table instead of in the dining room. Ace had enjoyed many meals with Lucy and her family. He couldn't wait until he and Rayna gathered with the other Hounds for not only meals but rides as well. He and Ripley could take their mates out on couples rides too.

Instead of heading to Ace's house for the night, Lucy convinced them to stay with her and Tamian.

The Gargoyle had delivered Grissom and Perkins, both of whom were tucked safely in the basement. And by tucked, he meant they were strapped to chairs. Rev had patched up both agents, and neither had any idea of the shitstorm coming for them the next morning. But that was a problem for tomorrow.

When it was time for bed, Lucy told them to choose any of the rooms upstairs in the west wing. Rayna followed Ace, and when he stopped at one of the doors, she gestured to the room. "Do you mind if I sleep in here with you? If this isn't okay, I'll choose one of the other rooms," she offered.

"This is perfect," he lied. It had been years since Ace shared a bed with someone, and the last time had ended in heartbreak for him. As with every partner who lasted more than a few dates, he explained to Ellory that he was demi. She said she understood. They were together less than two months when she asked to spend the night. Against his better judgment, he agreed. When Ellory came to bed in a see-through negligee, he knew how the night would turn out. He gave her an orgasm with his hand and mouth, but Ellory still tried seducing Ace. When his dick didn't get hard after almost an hour of her coaxing, she climbed off the bed and said, "This isn't going to work for me. I have needs, Asher." He didn't bother arguing. He simply turned over, putting his back to the door, and waited for her to leave.

Since Ace hadn't planned on spending the night away from the clinic, he wasn't prepared, but Lucy supplied a new toothbrush and a pair of Tamian's sweatpants. He used Rayna's toothpaste, but he didn't bother showering since he didn't want to get his bandages wet. When it was her time in the bathroom, Rayna made sure Ace was comfortable, kissed his cheek, and said, "If you need me during the night, just shake me." He thought that odd until Rayna exited the en suite in her fur. She climbed on the bed and settled at his feet.

Huh.

Ace was both grateful and disappointed. Grateful there would be no tense moments when he didn't touch her intimately. Disappointed for the same reason. They had held hands. Given chaste kisses. Spoken about the future. No, this was for the best, especially since they weren't alone. Ace closed his eyes, and purring from Rayna's Cheetah lulled him to sleep.

Chapter Nineteen

Rayna

RAYNA JUMPED OFF the bed and padded into the bathroom to shift and dress for the day. It had been months since she slept so well. Yes, she would have rather been in her skin so she and Asher could talk, but his discomfort at her sleeping in the same room had been tangible. After nosing the door closed, she returned to her skin, stretching her arms overhead. She showered and dressed in a clean T-shirt and shorts, then returned to the room where Asher was sitting against the headboard, his inked chest on display. Rayna studied the tattoos briefly before meeting his eyes.

"Good morning." She sat next to his hip, keeping her hands on her lap.

"Morning. Sleep well?" Asher asked in his sexy, just-awake voice.

"Like a kitten," she joked. "I'm going in search of coffee so you can get dressed." She stood, leaned over, and brushed a kiss to his temple. When she

255

turned to go, Asher snagged her wrist.

"You didn't have to shift last night, but I appreciate the gesture. Maybe tonight…"

"Whatever you need, Ash. I never want you to be uncomfortable around me." Rayna turned her hand so she could hold his. "We have the rest of our lives together, and as for intimacy, we'll get there when you're ready. I'm used to taking care of those needs myself, and I have no problem continuing to do so. Until then, we'll get to know one another in other ways, yeah?"

"How did I get so lucky?" he whispered.

"By being a wonderful male." Rayna lifted Asher's ink-covered hand and kissed it. With a wink, she released him, then padded across the room, closing the door behind her. Once downstairs, she found Lucy and Tamian in the kitchen. Lucy was seated on her mate's lap, and the two were sitting silently, just being. That was the type of intimacy she craved with Asher. She had no doubt sex would be fulfilling if not hot, but it was the connection she wanted more than anything.

Lucy smiled. "Coffee's on, and I've got pancake batter ready to go. Is Ace awake?"

"Yes. He's getting dressed."

A timer beeped, and Lucy slid off her mate's lap. Tamian rose, pressed a kiss to her temple, then guided her back to the chair. He grabbed a potholder and pulled a pan of bacon out of the oven.

Lucy slung one arm over the back of her chair as she ogled her mate. Rayna couldn't blame the female. The Gargoyle was almost as fine as Asher. "Lachlan came through with Sartain's cell phone number, so he's downstairs tied up with Grissom and Perkins. Seth is in the game room. Tamian voiced him to remain where he was until further notice."

"Damn, I can't believe I didn't hear you bring them inside." Rayna added creamer to her cup before taking a seat at the table.

Tamian scooped the bacon off the pan onto a paper-towel covered plate. "We brought them in through a tunnel at the back of the house. It leads to the basement. I called Sartain at four-thirty and convinced him to retrieve Seth. He told Seth he was taking him to a less secure location, which wasn't a lie."

"Wow. Secret tunnels and a defunct lab. And you grew up here?" Rayna asked Lucy.

"I did. Although at the time, I had no idea about the tunnel, and the lab wasn't creepy whenever I was learning alongside Lucius. If I'd had any knowledge of the things he was working on when I wasn't down there, I might have run screaming."

Rayna had so many questions, but she didn't want to be rude. Her skin prickled, and she turned toward the doorway just as Asher ambled into the kitchen. He wasn't walking as stiffly as he had been the night before. Rayna set her mug on the counter and poured him a cup, handing over the undoctored java with a smile.

Lucy got busy with pancakes, and Tamian scrambled a dozen eggs. Once everything was plated, the two couples enjoyed their breakfast while discussing next steps. They decided to interrogate Seth separately, so once the table was cleared, Tamian disappeared momentarily. When he returned, Seth was following. Tamian gestured for him to take a seat at the table.

Seth froze when he saw her. "Rayna? What are you doing here?"

"We'll get to that. Coffee?" Rayna offered.

"You don't look surprised to see me," he said, crossing his arms over his chest.

"Because I'm not." Rayna strode to the counter and poured him a cup before placing it at the seat in front of him. She sat down and gestured to the chair.

Sighing, he sat and pulled the mug toward him. "Why am I here?"

Rayna took a sip of her own brew, then asked, "Would you rather I left you where you were?"

"How did you manage that?" Seth asked, his tone accusing.

Rayna angled her head toward the couple watching them silently. "I made some new friends when I left Haven. The reason you're here is so we can find out the truth once and for all, starting with your part in David Spencer being released."

"I don't know what—"

"You will tell the truth," Tamian interrupted. His command was similar to when the Hounds voiced someone, although it didn't make Rayna shiver.

"Did you let Spencer go?" Rayna asked.

"Yes."

"Why?"

When Seth hesitated, Rayna raised her eyebrows. "Because Hanson made a deal with the GIA. Spencer was undercover, and they needed their agent back to put Grissom away."

"So you lied to me from the very beginning?"

"It was to protect you," he pleaded.

Rayna hummed. "Spencer was undercover with The Ministry, so how was he supposed to help with Grissom?"

"He was allowed to come and go as he pleased. He had an apartment where he was set up to work away from the GIA office."

"What was Grissom doing that the GIA wanted him taken down?"

Seth reached for his mug and took a sip. "By the numbers on those accounts, it wasn't anything good."

Rayna tapped her short nails on the table. There were so many questions she needed answered, but she went with, "Why did you tell me Grissom was responsible for Spencer being released?"

"I didn't want you involved in any of this, Ray. It's why I convinced Hanson to leave you at Haven." Seth's shoulders sagged, then he looked at her. "When I arrested Spencer, he was adamant he was innocent of everything except kidnapping his daughter. He admitted taking her to keep her safe from her thug boyfriend. His words, not mine. He admitted to being undercover for the GIA, but since I wasn't high enough in the chain of command, he wouldn't say more than that. When he convinced Hanson to speak to his boss, they came to an agreement on getting Spencer released. It was Spencer who suggested sending you to Haven to get you out of the way, and Hanson agreed. And before you ask, Hanson told me all this."

"Why leave me there? If Hanson was going to release Spencer, I would have gone onto another case."

"Maybe, but you also sat in on the interrogations and asked all the right questions. The deal between Hanson and the GIA happened before you went to Haven, and Spencer didn't want you getting caught in the mess with Grissom. He knew going up against Grissom would be dangerous for those of us who worked under him. Spencer admired you, Ray. He even told Hanson he was going to have his boss try and recruit you to the GIA but not before Grissom was taken down."

"I find that hard to believe. You and I both know how convincing Spencer is. I think I was too close to finding out that he was playing both sides, and he wanted me out of the way. Those bank accounts with Grissom's name on them? The money came from Spencer."

"No, Grissom was being paid off by Yesu Chin."

"The mafia don?"

"Yes. It's the reason Chin never went to jail."

"Who told you that, Spencer?"

Seth flopped back against his chair, squeezing his eyes closed, and Rayna had her answer. "Like I said, he's very convincing. Why did Grissom toss you in Ray Brook?"

"I assume it was because Hanson couldn't handle being tortured and gave me up. He knew Spencer had evidence of what Grissom was up to. He gave one copy to his boss, and I had the other one."

"The one you buried in my backyard?"

"How the hell did you find it? Spencer made sure the cameras were turned off at your house."

"She has her own computer specialist," Lucy lied before Rayna could come up with a plausible tale.

Seth frowned at Rayna, but she moved on before he could ask who. "Why did you bury the evidence instead of passing it on to Milsap?"

A fine sheen dotted Seth's forehead and upper

lip. "As insurance. Spencer said he sent one copy to his boss, but he wanted another copy hidden in case things didn't go according to plan."

"It seems like you and Spencer worked closely together. How did you get away with that when you should have been working on other cases?"

"Hanson approved it. He made sure I didn't have any other cases. It wasn't easy for Hanson to go about his days as though we weren't aware that our boss was a criminal."

"And Spencer didn't help with that if he told you Grissom was covering for Chin. So when you told me you tried to look at the files on Spencer but they were locked down, that was also a lie?"

"I'm sorry, Ray. I truly thought it was best you didn't know what was going on."

Rayna didn't believe him, even though Tamian had voiced him, and that sucked. "Who took those photos?"

Seth swallowed hard. "I did. Hanson called and said he was being followed, and he was afraid it was Grissom or someone he was paying. He told me where he was going and if I didn't hear back from him within an hour to send in the cavalry. I waited, and when he didn't call, I texted Spencer to see if he could get eyes on the hotel. He did. He saw Perkins follow Hanson, so he looped the cameras so I could get in and out without Grissom knowing."

"Wow. You have Spencer on speed dial. How

quaint," Rayna deadpanned. "Weren't you afraid to go in there? If you knew Hanson was dead, did you not think Perkins might be lying in wait for you?"

"Spencer was monitoring the situation. He knew Perkins had left the area."

"Did you call the police? Or the director?" Lucy asked.

"I called the director and told him I thought Hanson was in trouble. I didn't let on I knew he was already dead. He asked why I bypassed Grissom and called him instead, and I admitted it was because Grissom was a dirty agent and that I had proof. Granted, I waited until I printed the photos and added them to the evidence bag and took it to your house for safekeeping before calling him."

"Did you tell him where the evidence came from?" Tamian asked.

"I said I was working with the GIA but not David Spencer specifically. Milsap was supposed to send a team down from DC to assist me in bringing Grissom in for questioning, but Perkins got to me first. The trip to get you out of Haven was bogus. Now I'm out of the loop and have no idea where Grissom is."

"Why didn't Perkins kill you instead of tossing you in Ray Brook?" Rayna asked.

"Because Grissom wanted the evidence. He threatened Vanessa and the kids, but I told him if something happened to them or me, I had safeguards in place."

"But even if you gave up your copy, Spencer is still out there with the originals."

Seth shrugged. "True, but Grissom is a decorated agent. Maybe he believes his word would carry enough weight against a hacker who can fabricate evidence."

Tamian stood. "The good news is we know where your boss is. He, Perkins, and Sartain are downstairs. We have video equipment set up to take their confessions. You'll do the interview to make it official. Then, you'll call Spencer's boss at the GIA. You and he can hand deliver all three agents along with the evidence and their confessions to your director."

"What?" Seth plunked his mug onto the table, coffee sloshing over the side. "How did you manage to get the three of them here? And why include Sartain?"

Rayna stood and grabbed a paper towel to wipe up the mess. "I went to Ray Brook looking for you and had a conversation with Sartain who said he hadn't seen you. He must have called Grissom as soon as I left. I was on my way here last night after finding your buried treasure when Grissom and Perkins ran me off the road. I got into an altercation with Perkins, and Grissom pulled a gun on me. I managed to distract him long enough to wing his shoulder. After subduing them both, I called my friends to assist, and here we are."

"Holy shit, Ray. You could have been killed."

"I could have, yes, but they were so sure two against one put the odds in their favor. They bet on the wrong side."

Seth rubbed the back of his neck. "What makes you think they'll tell the truth? Grissom will argue the documents and photos are fake."

Lucy pointed at her closed laptop on the table in front of her. "I have video evidence including timestamps of Hanson then Perkins entering The Marquis hotel. You, yourself, took the photos, which you'll say you're handing over to both the director of the FBI and the head of the GIA. We also have documentation showing Grissom working with a hacker who is not Spencer to form a shell corporation where all the money he's been taking is hidden except for the small sum he had transferred to an account in Hanson's name. You show them the evidence, and they'll point fingers at one another."

"I want to look at all this" — Seth waved a hand toward the laptop — "before I present it to them so I know exactly what's on there. Rayna, have you seen this proof?"

"I have," she hedged. She hadn't put eyes to the information Lachlan sent them, but she trusted Lucy. "After you look it over, please call Vanessa and let her know you're okay before doing the interview. She's worried sick."

"Good idea," Lucy said. "That'll give Tamian time to go downstairs and make sure the video equipment is ready to go."

"I don't have a phone," Seth reminded her. Asher removed his from his back pocket, tapped in the security code, then slid it across the table. "Thanks, uh, Asher, isn't it?"

When Asher arched a brow, Rayna moved to stand behind him. "Yes, this is Asher McMurray."

"You look mighty cozy there, Ray," Seth joked, even though he was frowning.

"I am. Now call your wife so she'll stop worrying." Rayna grabbed Asher's hand, tugging on it. He stood, and she led him into the dining room where Lucy had gone. "I take it Tamian isn't checking video equipment?"

"No. He's voicing them to behave and tell the truth when Seth gets down there. He'll have to remove some of Seth's memories after this is over like where we live and how we managed to get him out of Ray Brook."

"Yeah, I'm fine with that. I'm pissed he lied to me this whole time, but I'm relieved he wasn't colluding with Grissom. It would have broken Vanessa's heart if Seth had been on the take."

Asher brushed his hand down Rayna's arm, then linked their fingers. "Yours too."

"Yeah. We've been partners and friends a long time."

266

"Are we ready?" Tamian asked when he entered the room.

"Just waiting for Seth to finish up a call with his wife," Lucy explained.

"I'm here." Seth stared at Rayna and Asher's clasped hands, but she didn't pull away. Her partner would have to get used to their affection. "Do you have a suit to put on for the interview?" he asked Rayna.

"I'm going to sit this one out." Rayna released Asher's hand and stepped closer to her partner. "Considering Hanson's dead and Grissom's going to jail, I'll tell you now. I'm resigning. I'll type up a formal resignation letter for whomever the director puts in charge."

"Rayna, no. You're one of the best agents we have. Don't throw away your career for..." Seth glanced at Asher, and that pissed her off even more.

"I was a great agent, but after being sent to Haven for months, it gave me time to reassess how I want to spend my future. I'm not throwing away anything. I'm moving forward with my life. You know I don't need the money, and now that I have Asher, I don't want to put myself in the line of fire if I don't have to. Last night was a close call. One I'd prefer to never endure again."

"But you just met him. Or is there something more you haven't told me?"

"We did meet recently, but that doesn't mean

what we have isn't serious. Now, there's somewhere Asher and I need to be." Rayna turned and held out her hand to her mate. "Let's go home." Before they were out of the room, Rayna remembered something she wanted to ask. "Seth, if Spencer was working against Grissom, why did he manipulate the cameras at the hotel so Grissom could get away without being seen?"

"What are you talking about?"

"I followed Grissom from the office to the hotel where he was staying. The computer specialist who was helping me figured out his room number, but when I went to confront him, he wasn't there. When they searched further, the camera feed had been set on a loop so it didn't show Grissom going out a side door immediately after entering the hotel and getting into Perkins's car."

"If he had a hacker putting together shell corporations, he could have asked him to manipulate the cameras."

"Yeah, you're right. I still have a hard time trusting Spencer. Well, I'll let you get on with it." Rayna tugged Asher toward the front door, but she stopped before opening it. As soon as Seth walked away with Tamian, Rayna led Asher back to the living room where she guided him to the same chair he'd sat in the evening before. "Hang out here for a few minutes. I want to make a copy of the thumb drive, plus I need to grab my bags from upstairs."

"Why don't I get your bags while you talk to Lucy? My rib's a little sore, but I'm a Gryphon, Rayna. I'm tougher than I look."

Rayna grinned while wrapping her arms around Asher's neck. "You look pretty damn tough."

Asher grasped her hips, his fingers skimming bare skin beneath her T-shirt. He lowered his face to hers, pressing their lips together. It wasn't passionate, but it was full of something akin to love, and she relished it. When he leaned back, his eyes were shiny. "I'm so thankful for you," he whispered. "Now go find Lucy." Asher squeezed her waist before walking away. Rayna touched her lips as she watched him go. When he was out of sight, she went back to the kitchen where Lucy was preparing a cup of tea. "If you don't mind, I'd like a copy of the thumb drive. I want to give it to Rhiannon so she can hear her father's words."

"I can do that. I also just realized you don't have a vehicle here. You can borrow one of mine."

"Oh, that's kind, but we can call for a ride."

"Nonsense. Your car is out of commission, so you can use mine until yours is fixed or you get a new one. Tamian didn't say how much damage yours incurred, but if it needed to be towed, I'd say it's extensive."

Rayna wouldn't hesitate to accept such a gracious gift from Vanessa, and that's what this was

269

– a favor from a new friend. "Thank you. I would appreciate that."

By the time Asher returned with Rayna's things, Lucy had made a copy of the thumb drive. "I made two. One has all the evidence, and this one only has the voice recording plus the bank account information for Daisy's trust fund. I'm sure David will send the originals to Rhi at some point, but at least she'll know what he did for her daughter." She held out a key fob. "It's the black Benz. Keep it as long as you need it."

"Thanks again." Rayna gave the female a hug, then she and Asher made their way to the large garage. She pressed the button to open the trunk, where Asher tossed her bags. Once they were both seated and buckled in, she turned to her mate. "I could use a few quiet days before going to see Rhiannon, but I'm not sure I trust Spencer was telling the truth about leaving her alone."

"How about we head that way and get it over with and then spend a few quiet days alone? And yes, I feel up to it," he added sternly.

"I won't apologize for worrying about you, but I will stop nagging," she promised.

Asher's face softened. "You aren't nagging, and I apologize for being an ass. Thank you for worrying."

"No thanks needed. Now, tell me where I'm going."

CHAPTER TWENTY

Ace

ACE DIDN'T WANT to show up at Ryot's without calling first, so once they were on the road, he phoned the male. After telling him why they wanted to visit, Ryot cursed a blue streak, then said he would be waiting. By the time they arrived, the driveway was filled with bikes.

"Are they having a party?" Rayna asked.

"No. It's not unusual for the brothers to gather when something is going down though." Ace pointed at the bike with the painted-up sidecar. "I hope Mayhem brought the twins. They're a hoot."

The front door opened, and one of the twins ran outside. Ace knew by the mischievous grin it was Major. Marshall was more laid back. When the boy noticed Rayna, he froze and cocked his head to the side. "That's Major, and there's no telling what will come out of his mouth."

"I can't wait," Rayna said. When she opened the door, Major started bouncing.

"Who are you?" he asked.

"Major Lazlo," Natalia chided from the front porch.

Major whipped around and spread his little arms out. "But Lolly! I don't know her."

"No, but we talked about this. Manners—"

"Maketh the man. But I'm not a man, Lolly. I'm just a kid. And maketh is a stupid word."

Natalia rolled her eyes as she approached her son, gripping his neck, and giving a gentle shake. "He overheard that in a movie. I thought it was a teaching moment. Guess I was wrong." Releasing her grip, she held out her hand to Rayna. "I'm Natalia Lazlo, Maveryck's wife."

"Rayna Bellamy. Asher's—"

"She's my mate." Ace stepped up and wrapped an arm around Rayna. "Everyone here is family, and the kids know better than to share what we are."

"Are you like my daddo?" Major asked.

Rayna glanced at Ace, the question clear in her eyes. He nodded, so she told Major, "No. I'm a King Cheetah shifter."

"But you're a girl. Wouldn't that make you a queen?"

Rayna giggled. "You would think so, but that's just a different type of Cheetah. You know how there are different types of whales? Blue whales, killer whales, humpbacks, and so forth?"

Major nodded, then stepped forward with his little hand out. "Major Lazlo. Nice to meetcha."

Rayna shook his hand, still laughing. "Nice to meet you too."

"Come on in," Natalia said. "Ryker told us you were on your way. Something about Rhi's father?"

"Oh. Let me get the thumb drive." Rayna dipped back in the car for it. When she closed the door, Ace took her hand and led her toward Ryot's house. Ace pulled Rayna to a stop when he noticed Ryot standing on the porch, his arms crossed over his chest. He didn't look happy. He glared at Rayna. "Agent Bellamy." Ryker practically spit her title.

"Rayna, please. I'll be turning in my resignation soon, so—"

"So, say what you came here for, then you can go back to spying on others and leave us alone."

"Ryker," Rhiannon chided, coming around to stand in front of the large male. "Please forgive my mate. He can be a little gruff."

Ryker uncrossed his arms and put one around Rhi's shoulders. "I asked you to let me handle this."

"And I didn't listen. Please come inside," she offered.

Rayna didn't move, and Ace didn't either. He wasn't going to subject her to Ryker's wrath.

Ryker sighed. "Come on in." Rhi smiled up at him, patting his chest.

When they got to the front door, Major was

waiting. He put a finger over his lips and whispered, "Daisy's napping."

Natalia grinned at her son. "She is, but she's up in her room, so we don't have to whisper." She led them to the living room where all the Lazlo brothers were gathered with their mates and kids. Rhi was now sitting on the sofa with Ryker behind her.

Major whisper yelled, "She's a King Cheetah." He turned to Rayna. "Uh, I don't know what that looks like."

Maveryck grabbed his son and picked him up like a sack of potatoes. "We'll look it up later. How about you and Marsh take Mateo outside?"

"Okay, Daddo." Major giggled when Mav flipped him upside down and swung him by his feet before flipping him upright. Major and the other boys took off through the house.

When the back door closed, Ryker said, "I would make introductions, but Pop said you spied on our family, so I'm sure you know who everyone is."

Ace bristled. "Did Sutton also tell you Rayna was at Haven and overheard Glory admitting to taking out Josiah, but she conveniently forgot to mention that to her boss for Glory's sake? Did he mention that Rayna is my mate?"

Rhi reached up and threaded her fingers with Ryker's. "Again, forgive my mate. He's a little protective."

Rayna waved her off. "There's nothing to forgive, Rhiannon. I won't lie and say I didn't research the Hounds because I was ordered to after David mentioned what some of the Hounds do for a living. What I found was a strong family unit. An honorable one at that."

"Ace mentioned you have something you want to show me?"

Rayna held out the thumb drive. "It's a message from your father. I'm not sure how truthful he was being, but I'll let you be the judge. I won't interfere further with your family time. Asher and I will—"

Rhiannon stood and approached Rayna. "Stay. Please. You're Asher's mate, which makes you family."

When Ryker scoffed, Natalia turned on him. "Have you forgotten how Maveryck and I met? Or do you still hold that against me and not consider me part of this family?" Asher wasn't surprised at the Russian's outburst. She was one of the fiercest when it came to welcoming the other females into the fold.

Ryker scrubbed a hand down his face. "Of course you're family. Forgive me, Rayna. Like Rhi said, I'm a little protective." All of his brothers laughed out loud, garnering a stern glare from the eldest Lazlo. "Fine. I'm overprotective. Sue me."

Rhi took the thumb drive from Rayna. "You've listened to this?"

"I have. The message was to me, but he talked about you and your mom. Also, David set up a trust fund for your daughter. The information is on there too."

"I'm not taking his money. Does he think he can buy my love?"

"I don't think so. He didn't mention the money in his message, but... Well, I'll let you be the judge of his actions. For what it's worth, I know all about having a parent who sent money instead of being there for me."

"Did you keep the money?"

"My gran used very little of it to help raise me. The rest she invested. Now it gives me the opportunity to retire from a job I no longer enjoy and relax while Asher and I navigate our future." Rayna took Rhi's hands. "I can't imagine what you went through, Rhiannon, and I won't tell you that you should keep the money, but it is a large sum. If you don't want it for Daisy, I'm sure you can think of a worthy cause where it would be useful. It's not something you have to decide immediately. The longer it sits, the more interest it gains."

"How much is a large sum?" Mav asked. "Because I've got a set of twins who are growing out of their clothes too fast."

Kyllian smacked the back of his brother's head. "Behave."

Before Mav could retaliate, Daisy started

fussing, and four large males jumped to their feet, each vying to get to the baby first.

"Children," Quinn muttered, rubbing her belly, which was getting rather round. Ace wanted to watch Rayna as their child grew inside her tummy.

It was Kyllian who carried Daisy as the brothers returned downstairs after a few minutes. The brothers were grumbling, but Kyllian said, "I need practice. The rest of you don't."

"Speak for yourself," Hayden countered.

Kyllian narrowed his eyes at his younger brother. "Something you forgot to tell us, Havyk?"

Hayden rubbed the back of his neck, glancing at his mate. Sadie, who was curled up in an armchair, arched a dark brow. "Uh, we were going to wait until Sadie was further along, but yeah, we're pregnant."

The room erupted, startling little Daisy. Kyllian cradled her closer, covering her ear with his big hand. He rocked the baby back and forth as the younger boys came running inside.

Rayna stepped out of the fray, backing up against Ace's chest. He wrapped his arms around her and placed his chin on her shoulder. He was happy for his fellow Hound and Sadie, but it made the longing that much worse. Rayna leaned away and glanced up at him. "That'll be us one day. Right?"

Ace squeezed her a little tighter. "Yes."

"What's all the noise for?" Major asked while Marshall padded over to Kyllian. He reached up and took Daisy's tiny hand in his small one, rubbing his thumb over her fingers. Kyllian knelt, and Marshall pressed a sweet kiss to Daisy's forehead.

Mateo went to his mom when Sadie gestured for him. "Do you want to share the good news with your cousins?"

Mateo's eyes got big. "Can I? Really?"

Sadie ruffled her son's hair. "Really. It's time."

The adults got quiet, and Mateo patted Sadie's belly. "Mama's got a baby in her tummy. I'm going to be a big brother."

Major ran to his cousin, grabbed his hands, and began jumping up and down. Marshall sedately joined the boys, but their joy was infectious, and soon the trio was hopping as though they were in a mosh pit.

Kyllian rose, swaying Daisy, as he walked over to where Hayden was hugging his mate. "Do Mom and Pop know about this?"

Hayden pressed a kiss to Sadie's hair before saying, "You know mom can sniff out a baby within a hundred-mile radius, so I told her before she could come at me with her claws."

When Daisy scrunched up her face, Rhi took her from Kyllian before she got wound up. "Let's get you fed."

In all the excitement, Ace tugged Rayna toward

the door. "This is going to turn into a party, so how about we head home?"

"Do we need to say bye?" Rayna asked, smiling at the Lazlo clan.

"Nah. I'll call Hayden later." They made it to the car before the front door opened.

"Ace," Ryker called out. "Y'all don't have to leave." It was odd hearing the Texas twang slip into Ryker's speech.

"I'm ready to get home and get off my feet, and Rayna needs some downtime after the shootout."

"Shootout? What the fuck?" Ryker jogged down the steps to where Ace and Rayna were standing. "What happened?"

"I was headed to Lucy's last night with evidence against the deputy director when he and another agent ran me off the road. If I weren't a shifter, I probably wouldn't be alive." Rayna told him how she took down the two agents, then explained Tamian's assistance.

"Zeus, that's..." Ryker shook his head. "I'm glad you weren't hurt, or worse, and I'm really sorry about how I acted before."

"I get it. Listen, don't let Rhiannon listen to Spencer's message alone. I spent many hours interrogating the man, and he always came across as sincere. Unless he's a psychopath, he believes what he says."

"Is it that bad?"

"Depends on if Rhiannon believes him or not. If she does, it could offer closure."

"Yeah, okay. Thanks. We'll have a barbeque later after the two of you have time to rest up. Welcome to the family."

"Thank you, Ryker. I look forward to it."

Ace held open the driver's side door for his mate. Once she was seated, he closed it, then went around and got in. He was more than ready to be home alone with Rayna. He was looking forward to locking the door, turning off their phones, and just being. That couldn't happen until after he called Con and Regina or until Rayna turned in her notice. He was ready to see what the future held for them.

He should have known they wouldn't get downtime straight away. Conrad called when they were two blocks from the house. When he went to check on Ace that morning, Rev filled him in on the events of the previous night, and Con invited himself and Regina over to "take care of their kids." Ace couldn't be mad about that even though he wanted Rayna to himself.

Since the hotel where they were staying was closer to Ace's house than Ryker's, his pseudo parents beat them there. Ace and Rayna found the older couple on the patio. They didn't have a key to get inside, but they weren't afraid to walk through the gate to the backyard.

Regina jumped up and stopped in front of Ace

first, holding onto his upper arms as she looked him over. Then she did the same to Rayna before pulling her into a hug. Rayna embraced her back, and as the older Gryphon fussed over his mate, Ace took one of the patio chairs, letting them have their moment.

When she turned loose, Regina asked, "Are you hungry?"

"I could eat," Ace admitted. Lucy's pancakes had been delicious, but he was ready to eat again. Rayna concurred, so Regina went inside to busy herself in the kitchen. Rayna followed to help, and Ace didn't complain. Rayna had her grandmother, but he wouldn't begrudge her having the warmth of a mother's love and guidance as well.

"How are you doing, Son?"

Ace rolled his head toward Conrad. "Better. Rib is still tender, but I'm not nearly as sore as I was."

"I was referring to the near miss with Rayna and her boss last night."

Ace looked out over the yard, specifically at the ground Rayna had turned for their garden. It seemed a lifetime ago since they discussed what to plant. "I've never been so scared in my life. I just found her, and I almost lost her before we could complete the bond." Ace closed his eyes. He hadn't let himself dwell on what could have happened. Rayna was alive and well. She was tough yet gentle. Kind yet fierce. She was perfect.

"I don't think Zeus would be so unkind. He

281

wouldn't bring the perfect person to you only to take them away so quickly."

"Now I know how Ripley felt when Glory was taken. I texted Rip, and he sounded like he had his hands full."

"It was touch and go for a minute, but Marjorie and that bitch Helen went back to Haven yesterday, and Ripley took Glory and her family to Florida this morning."

"Good. I'm glad that's settled. Once they get back and I know they aren't using your house in New Boca, I want to take Rayna there for some downtime."

"What about her job?"

"She's resigning. I can't say I'm unhappy with her decision, especially after last night."

"I'm sure, and I agree. It'll give the two of you time to get to know one another when you aren't off searching for Ministry assholes."

Ace chuckled. "All the assholes are now accounted for on this side of the country. Unless Sutton gets involved on the West Coast, I'm out of a job. I'm calling it early retirement. Both Ray and I have plenty of money, and we've talked about starting a family. Whether biological or adoption, I think we'll focus on us for a bit, then give you and Regina grandkids."

Something crashed in the kitchen, then Regina let out a whoop.

Chapter Twenty-One

Ace

THE FOLLOWING WEEK was both a flurry of excitement and chilling at home. Once Regina got over the fact that Ace and Rayna had already spoken about children, the two couples enjoyed a nice lunch on the patio where they talked about Glory and how talented she was, Ace and Rayna's plans for the future, and Regina showed them photos of the houses she and Con were looking at. Ace was ecstatic they were moving closer. When he and Rayna had children, he wanted them to have grandparents, and the Davidsons were the perfect couple to dote on kids.

Even though Ace felt well enough to cook, Regina threw together a few meals they could freeze, then pop in the oven when they wanted them. She and Conrad left them alone to get started on giving her some grandkids – her words. Ace didn't share that it wouldn't happen as soon as

Regina wanted, but he also didn't say it wouldn't.

Sutton called Ace, asking if he and Rayna would consider moving and continuing their work taking down The Ministry, helping some Hounds who had taken over the task on the West Coast. Ace told his boss that he and Ray were looking forward to some down time and starting a family. Rayna typed up her letter of resignation and sent it to the director. He didn't respond with a counteroffer. He merely replied with his acceptance. Then again, he had his hands full with two agents who had confessed to all sorts of crimes. Grissom's were the worst including extortion, guns, and drugs, all of which went back several years. Perkins would go on trial for the murder of his fellow agent, Hanson. Sartain had done nothing wrong other than lie to Rayna about Seth being held at Ray Brook, but he'd done so on the orders of his boss. When that fact came out during Seth's interrogation, Tamian took the agent aside, voiced him to forget about everything that happened that morning, and convinced him that Seth had never been at his facility.

Lachlan found David Spencer, who moved to France, changing his name and purchasing a defunct vineyard. He left his wife, Marion, behind at Haven. When Lucy asked Rhiannon if she wanted the Hounds to seek David out and voice him to forget about her and Daisy, Rhi said no. She no longer cared what happened to her father, but

284

after listening to his message to Rayna, Rhi figured he'd lost enough when Rhi's mom died.

Ace accompanied Rayna to get seeds, and since his ribs were no longer aching, they planted their garden together. He and Rayna had progressed from chaste kisses to making out, and the one time Ace had gotten fully erect, Rayna gave him his first blowjob instead of expecting penetrative sex. That was the moment he fell in love with her. He thought he would pass out from how explosive his orgasm had been. He returned the favor by licking her clit while fingering her. Ace had watched plenty of porn over the years, and he knew how to please a partner without going all the way, so when his mate came apart from his efforts, he rode the high all night. *Soon*, he thought as he held his mate while she slept.

They met up with some of the Hounds for a group ride, and Rayna got to know the other mates. Ryker had the barbeque he'd mentioned, and Rayna got to meet Mac, Elijah, and Nikita. The twins kept everyone entertained with their cuteness, and Ace got to hold Daisy. Knowing he had a mate who could give him children settled something in Ace, and he no longer felt such a deep longing being around the baby girl. Rayna came back from the bathroom, and when she saw him with Daisy in his arms, her eyes lit up. Then she strolled over, bent down, and whispered, "You're going to make the best papa." His father had been a stellar role model, and if Ace modeled himself after the male, gave his child or children all his love, he thought he would be. Maybe not the best, but as close as he could get. He understood being different, so he would help his kids navigate the world while offering unconditional support. And he would do so with Rayna by his side.

The night after the barbeque, Rayna was lounging on the patio, and Ace had gone inside to whip up another batch of margaritas when his phone rang. As expected, Ripley was pissed when he found out what Ace had been through and hadn't told him. He and Glory were still in Florida when Rip called Ace to check in.

"You are on my shit list," Rip said after Ace answered.

"Rip—"

"Fucking hell, Ace. You're my best friend. My brother. Didn't you think I'd want to be there for you?"

"I knew you would, and that's why I didn't say anything. You had your hands full with Glory and her family."

"I could have at least offered moral support over the fucking phone. Zeus."

"I'm…" Ace blew out a breath. "How is Glory?"

"She's great. The sisters and Scott are settling in. I bought Hope and Scott a car, and we're looking at houses for them since Leona's place is too small for everyone. Glory and I spent a few days at my parents' place. We're headed back to her grandmother's to take care of a few things and then we'll be home."

"Good. Rayna's looking forward to seeing Glory again."

"You mean Melinda?" Ripley chuckled. "I told Glory the whole story, and she was both shocked yet excited. She really likes your female."

"The feeling is mutual. Rayna only has one good friend that I'm aware of, and Vanessa is busy with work and her kids when they're not visiting their grandparents. Rayna loved riding my Harley, so maybe we can take our mates out when you're back."

"I know Glory will want that."

"Also, we're both looking forward to hearing Glory play piano. Con couldn't stop talking about how talented she is."

"So fucking talented, Ace. Like, imagine Rhiannon singing Daisy a lullaby and multiply it by a hundred. On top of her singing, Glory can listen to any song, then after a few times running through it on the keys, she can play it perfectly. You'll see when we get back."

"I can't wait. I miss your ugly mug."

"I miss you too, Brother. So, uh, how is it with you being demi? Are you attracted to Rayna that way? Sorry if that's too intrusive."

"Like you said, you're my brother, and if I can't talk to you about my issues, who can I? And I'm getting there." More like he was already there, but that would be TMI. "Maybe it's because I'm her fated mate, but I knew she was something special the moment I met her. My Gryphon felt the connection immediately, and her Cheetah assured my beast everything would be okay. That Rayna could be patient. And she is. Rayna is so much more than I could have dreamed of."

"I'm so happy for you, and I look forward to getting together when we get back. And expect Glory to ask Rayna to see her Cheetah. My mate loves big cats." Rip chuckled, and Ace smiled. After they disconnected, he took the pitcher of drinks outside where his own cat was lounging on the patio in cut-off jeans and a thin, spaghetti strap camisole. Ace's dick approved of her bare skin that was deeply tanned from all her time spent outdoors.

Rayna turned to face him as he stepped outside. "Everything okay?"

Ace refilled her glass before pouring his own. "Yes. Ripley called. He and Glory will be home soon."

Rayna took the proffered glass. "How much grief did he give you for not calling him?"

Ace blanched. "Not too much."

"Right." After taking a sip, she set the glass on

the table next to her, returning her gaze to the dark sky.

Ace took his chair, but instead of looking at the stars, he stared at his mate. She must have felt his eyes on her because Rayna glanced over. "What?"

"I'm ready. I want us to claim each other." They'd talked about completing the bond without sex, but Ace had wanted to wait.

"Are you sure? We don't need to rush."

"I've waited fifty-two years, Ray. I want you."

Rayna rose, then climbed onto Ace's lap, straddling his legs. She ran a hand over his spiky hair and leaned down to kiss him. It was the first time his dick had come into contact with something other than his own hand or Rayna's mouth, and even through their clothes, it was electric. Rayna undulated her core, stoking the fire.

"Let's move this inside." Ace cradled Rayna to him and stood, carrying her to their bedroom. Rayna pressed open-mouth kisses to his neck, nipping his skin with her teeth. Ace shivered, ready for the bite that would tether them for eternity. When he reached their room, he lowered his mate to her feet. Ace thought he would be nervous, but he wasn't. He was ready. His dick was pressing against the zipper of his shorts, harder than ever.

Rayna lifted the camisole over her head, dropping it to the floor. Her nipples were pebbled, and Ace cupped her breasts, rolling the hard peaks between his thumb and forefinger. Rayna arched her back, pushing into his hands. Staring with hooded eyes, she unbuttoned his shorts and lowered the zipper, pushing the garment along with his briefs down his thighs. Ace shrugged them the rest of the way, kicking them off to the side. He removed his tee, then stood naked while Rayna divested herself of her own shorts and panties.

Stepping closer, Rayna ghosted her fingertips across the many tattoos on his chest before leaning in and licking a stripe from his sternum to his jaw. His cock jumped, the tip leaking. Rayna gripped his length and tugged with just the right amount of pressure. Ace grasped her wrist, stopping her. "I'm too close."

Rayna released him, then palmed his cheek. "Good."

"Good?"

"Mmm hmm. I like that you're so turned on." She folded the comforter down, then climbed on the bed, her ass wiggling. She glanced over her shoulder with a wink before lying in the middle with her head on a pillow. She crooked a finger at him, and Ace didn't hesitate to follow her command. He settled between her parted legs with his hands on her bent knees. Ace knew every inch of her skin, and now he was itching to know her from the inside out. Gripping his cock, he rubbed the tip over her clit, and Rayna writhed, her hands gripping the sheet.

"Asher, please."

He placed the tip at her slick opening and pushed inside. Ace bottomed out and held still, taking a deep breath to gain control. He was too close to coming, and he wanted their first time to last. Rayna hooked her feet around his ass, opening herself to him while tugging him closer. He leaned down, placing his hands on the bed beside her neck.

"Zeus, you're stunning." Ace rocked back and forth, the glide slick, as her channel hugged his length. "You feel so fucking good, Ray." He called on his Gryphon's strength and fortitude to keep his orgasm at bay long enough to satisfy his mate. Ace raised up and draped her knees over his arms, changing the angle of his thrusts. Rayna moved her hands to her breasts, squeezing and tugging on her nipples, moaning softly. Ace had never imagined sex with his mate. He never thought he would find them, but watching Rayna touch herself was better than any porn he'd perused over the years. Her moans were real, and her gaze was steady. Filled with heat and love.

"I'm close," she husked. "I want you to bite me, Asher. Bite me and make me completely yours." Her fangs elongated, and Ace had never seen a more enticing sight. He released his own sharp teeth and rocked into her body faster and harder when she urged him to do so.

"Ash!" Rayna's claws dug into his biceps as her core tightened around his cock. Rayna pulled herself up and sank her fangs into his shoulder. His orgasm was instantaneous, and he roared with the powerful release and her toxin coursing through his veins. When he was somewhat coherent, Ace returned the bite. Rayna's pussy tightened around his still hard cock, and she groaned around her fangs still in his shoulder. Ace retracted his fangs and lapped at her blood. His cock pulsed, shooting more of his seed deeper into her body. His head swam with dizziness as the toxin from her bite ignited every nerve cell. Rayna licked over the punctures, settling back against the pillow.

Ace lowered Rayna's legs, barely catching himself before he crushed her. "Holy, Zeus." He shook his head, praying his equilibrium returned.

Rayna pressed her palms to his cheeks. "Are you okay?"

"Yeah. Yes." Ace blinked several times, and his mate came into view. "That was... I'm not sure I have the words to describe it."

"You don't have to, my love. I felt it too."

My love.

Ace eased his spent dick from her core and rolled to his side, taking Rayna with him so they were facing. He brushed her hair back from her face, then kissed her softly. Tears filled his eyes, and he didn't try to stop them. Never had he felt as alive, as loved, as fulfilled as he did in that moment, and it was all due to the unbelievable female in his bed.

"I..." He cleared his throat. "I love you, Rayna Bellamy. You have made me the happiest male on the planet, and I will cherish you as long as we live. I vow to be the best mate to you and the best papa to any children we have."

Rayna pushed on his shoulder so he was lying on his back. She draped herself across his chest. "I love you too, Ash. So very much. I'm looking forward to every second of our lives together." Rayna kissed him, filling him with the love she vowed.

Ace lie awake with his mate asleep in his arms. He couldn't turn his brain off. Nor could he get his dick to go down. Now that his libido had awakened, it was raring to go with no provocation other than Rayna's scent in his nose. She awoke around three and climbed off the bed, padding naked to the bathroom. After the toilet flushed, the water in the sink ran for a bit, and when she returned a few minutes later, the combined smell of their orgasms was gone. She slid under the cover, snuggling back into his side.

"Hi." Rayna nuzzled his neck with her nose as she ran her fingers up his hard length. "Ready for round two, or do you want my mouth?"

How was this his life? Both sounded amazing, but he wanted something he'd seen in a video.

"I'd love for you to ride me."

Rayna straddled him, lowering down on his erection. Using her thigh muscles, she set a slow, sensual pace. She lifted his hands to her breasts, and Ace kneaded the tissue, rolling her hard peaks. His mate moved up and down, then rotated her hips in a figure eight. She kept her eyes glued to his, and whenever Ace groaned, Rayna took note of what pleased him and did it over and over. He lasted much longer than the first time, and when this orgasm hit, it wasn't as explosive, but it was just as mind-blowing. She found her release as well, and when they came down from their high, she suggested a shower. They silently washed each other, sharing gentle caresses and soft kisses. Ace was afraid to go to sleep. He just knew this was all a fantastical dream, and when he awoke, it wouldn't be real.

The next morning proved it was so very real when Rayna woke him with her mouth around his morning wood. When he offered to return the favor, she smiled and said she'd rather have coffee. When he frowned, Rayna laughed. "I always want you, Ash, but I'm sated for now." They dressed in shorts and T-shirts, then retreated to the kitchen where she sat on the counter sipping her morning go juice while Ace whipped up some breakfast. Every time he looked at Rayna, she giggled, and he chuckled along with her. He felt so much younger than his fifty-two years.

As they shared bacon, eggs, and biscuits at the kitchen island, Rayna wiped her mouth with a cloth napkin. "I was thinking..." She took a sip of coffee, and when she set the mug down, she reached for Ace's hand. "I think we should have the same last name for when we have children."

"Rayna McMurray? It does have a nice ring to it. Speaking of rings..." Ace stood, held up a finger, then disappeared for a few seconds. When he returned, he pulled her down from her stool, got down on one knee, and held out a black box. He opened the lid to reveal a band with alternating diamonds and onyx. "We've already tethered our shifter lives together with our mate bond, but I'd love nothing more than to officially make you my wife. Will you marry me?"

Rayna held out her left hand, and Ace slid the ring on her finger. "I would be honored."

Chapter Twenty-Two

Rayna

December

WHEN RAYNA AND Asher visited Fern in Arizona back in August, it took less than half an hour before her grandmother was ready to pack up and move to New York. Since she and Asher had purchased a new home not far from Glory and Ripley, Asher's house was sitting empty. They had planned to sell it, but once Fern decided to move, they'd gifted the house to her. Although she was older than Regina, Fern and Rip's mom got along too well. She and Rory had also struck up a tight friendship, comparing notes as the two eldest females of the bunch.

She and Asher along with Glory, Ripley, and Gran were at their new home, getting the house ready for Christmas. The males had gone out and cut down a tree from the woods on their property. Rayna shook her head at her grandmother as she leaned around Rayna to get a good look at Asher and Ripley. Fern Bellamy was just as in love with Ash as Rayna was, and the older woman wouldn't stop ogling the male. Glory giggled at Fern's antics, especially when she turned her eyes toward Ripley and let out a "hubba hubba" at his popping biceps as he carried in the large cedar tree.

The last few months had brought many changes to Rayna's life. While she and Vanessa were still close, Rayna now had more friends than she knew what to do with. When she resigned from the FBI, she had no idea how she would fill her days, but Rayna didn't have time to be bored. The Hounds rode often, sometimes in large groups, sometimes just a few couples. December temps had already dropped, but that didn't stop them from taking the bikes out often. She and Glory were tight, and Rayna spent many hours listening to her friend sing and play piano. Rayna and Rhi joined in whenever a large group was gathered.

At Ripley's birthday party in October, Glory announced she was pregnant, and Rayna couldn't be happier for the female. Rayna and Asher had been trying for their own little one, but so far it hadn't happened. They were married in a small ceremony in their new backyard. Gran and Ripley's parents, as well as a few of the Hounds and their mates were present. Rhiannon gifted Rayna with a stunning floral arrangement she'd made herself.

Marshall and Mateo carried their rings, while Major came behind tossing pink rose petals in the air, garnering laughs from the crowd. Glory sang acapella as Conrad escorted Rayna down the aisle toward Asher.

The ceremony was short yet sweet, and after, a party ensued as it often did when their group gathered. Regina and Fern provided the food. Kerrigan set up the bar, playing mixologist. Sadie and Hayden tag-teamed a stunning three-tier cake, which Hayden had airbrushed with lifelike renditions of Ace's Lion and Rayna's Cheetah. Lucy played DJ, running the songs from her laptop, which was connected to speakers Tamian had placed around the yard. The only downside to the day was not having Vanessa with her. Both kids had come down with a virus, giving it to Vanessa in turn. Seth, who had been promoted to assistant director, was home taking care of his family. Rayna had forgiven her former partner for lying because he was trying to protect her.

"Rayna, is this okay?" Asher asked, bringing her back to the present. He and Ripley had the tree in the stand set up in the corner of the room. Since they were in the middle of fifteen acres, there was no one around to see the tree through the front window, and Rayna wanted it where she and Ash could enjoy it while lounging on the sofa.

"Perfect." Rayna couldn't wait to decorate the

tree with the blue and silver baubles she and Gran had purchased Saturday when they'd spent the day together in New Latham. They first visited Vanessa for a mini spa day, then they had lunch at a new bistro. Afterward, they drove to Albany and bought enough decorations for both houses. Seth had dropped by the salon with the kids so they could visit with their Auntie Rayna. He asked her several times if she was certain she didn't want to come back to the FBI. As much as she missed working with her old partner, she was happy with her new life.

The front door opened, and Regina called out, "The party can start now."

Glory jumped to her feet and ran to her mother-in-law as though she hadn't seen her the day before. Rayna got it. Growing up with a mother like Marjorie, Glory hit paydirt when Rip's mom came into her life.

Gran was kicked back on the sofa, her socked feet on the coffee table, with a glass of wine in hand. She didn't bother to get up when Regina entered the room. Instead, Fern raised her glass in greeting.

"You started without me?" Regina chided.

"Yep. I figured you and that hot mate of yours might be delayed."

Glory giggled, and Regina elbowed her playfully. "Don't encourage her." Then she whispered in Glory's ear, "She's not wrong, though." Glory slapped a hand over her mouth, trying to smother her laugh. The older couple were still crazy in love, and Rayna knew she and Asher would be the same when they too were looking at being grandparents.

Rayna followed Regina into the kitchen and poured her a raspberry margarita. Asher had taught Ray how to mix the delicious drink since it was her favorite. Gran preferred wine over fruity drinks, and Glory was sipping ginger ale. Rayna was topping off her own glass when the doorbell rang. They weren't expecting anyone else, but it also wasn't unusual for one or more of the Lazlo couples to drop by. They usually called first, but Rayna didn't mind having more company. She and Regina returned to the den to find Sutton holding a toddler and Rory holding a little boy's hand.

When Asher and Ripley joined them, the little boy turned loose of Rory's hand and ran to Asher, who picked him up, no questions asked.

"Let me get his coat off," Rory said. Asher held the boy while Rory unzipped the small coat. Once it was off, the boy shoved a thumb in his mouth and laid his head on Asher's shoulder. Rayna's heart melted seeing her mate's inked hand stroking the boy's back.

"Who are they?" Rayna asked. Rory's eyes were wet, and she tried to blink back the tears but failed.

Pressing a kiss to the boy's head, Ace said, "This

is River, and that's his sister, Aria."

"Arson's kids?" Ripley asked.

Rory nodded, blowing out a breath while swiping at her face.

"What happened?" Ace whispered.

Sutton handed the little girl over to Regina when she held out her arms, then he walked over and tugged Rory to his chest. "I'd rather tell this when little ears aren't listening."

Gran stood and gently pried River from Asher's arms. "I think there are some cookies in the kitchen. Let's go see." Regina followed with Aria.

"Yesterday, Arson went to pick Cora up at work. When she didn't come out of the bank, he texted, but she didn't respond. After another ten minutes, he went in to see what was taking so long. The door was locked, and when he looked inside, he could see three armed men. One of them was pointing his weapon at Cora, so Arson busted out the glass. He was shot before he could get to her. When she tried to run to him, the bastard shot her too. Cora died instantly, and Arson... He was shot multiple times when his fangs and claws came out." Sutton closed his eyes and shook his head. "One was a head shot, so he didn't stand a chance. We got lucky that one of the cops was a Hound. He was able to voice everyone in the bank, and he called Bishop to have him wipe that part of the security video."

"Please tell me he killed the bastards," Ripley seethed.

"Two are dead, and one is in custody.

"Do they have family to take them in?" Rayna asked, looking toward the kitchen.

"No. Arson's parents have been gone a while, and Cora was raised by her aunt, but she's in her eighties and in an assisted living facility. Ace—"

"We'll take them," Asher blurted. Then he turned to Rayna, his eyes begging her to agree.

"If that's an option," Rayna added, "Absolutely."

Sutton smiled, but it was sad. "That's why we're here. Ace had mentioned adoption, and we'd rather they go to someone in the Hounds than be put in the system. Since they have no close relatives, Arson listed Rory and me as emergency contacts. The social worker said we can keep the kids until other arrangements are made, so we have time to get things squared away."

Asher turned to Rayna and held her face in his hands. "You sure about this?"

"Yes. Those babies need a home, and we have one."

Asher kissed her softly, then took her hand and led her into the kitchen. Regina held Aria out to Rayna, and she snuggled the little girl to her chest. She didn't know anything about raising kids, but with all the parents currently in the house, she and

302

Asher would have plenty of guidance. He sat next to River who was munching on a cookie. River held it out, and Asher took a nibble. The boy gave a tremulous smile.

"Momma and Papa are gone."

"I know, Buddy, and I'm so sorry. Rayna and I have this big ole house, and we would love it if you and Aria stayed here with us."

"Can I bring my toys?"

"You can bring anything you want. Your toys, clothes, pictures of your momma and papa. We can even bring your furniture."

"And sister's things too?"

"Yep."

River leaned against Asher, who wrapped his arm around the boy. Rayna's heart ached for the siblings.

Ripley stepped into the kitchen. "Dad, Sutton, Rory, and I are going to start gathering their things, if that's okay?"

Asher nodded. "Thanks, Brother."

"No thanks needed." Ripley eyed the little boy, and when he turned away, he wiped his face. Rayna got it. Losing parents at any age would be hard, but these two were just babies. Aria tugged on Rayna's hair, and she smiled down at who would soon be her daughter. Goddess, that sucked. She wanted to be a mother. Wanted to give a child what she didn't have from her own mother, but not this way. Rayna glanced at Gran, who nodded. She got it. She had taken in Rayna and loved her like her own. If Rayna was half the caregiver Fern had been, Aria and River would never know anything but unconditional love.

Things moved quickly after that day. The kids had gone to stay with Rory and Sutton while Rayna and Asher got their rooms ready. She and Asher spent as much time with the children as possible at the elder Lazlos' home. When the court date was set, the kids came to stay in their new home, and Rory spent the night in the guest room, just in case the children felt more at ease with her.

Rayna didn't know who facilitated the expediency, but the adoption was approved two days before Christmas. By then, the little ones were used to being in their new home. Aria, being eighteen months, didn't appear to understand what was happening, but little River who was four… He cried for his parents, had bad dreams, wet the bed, and had several meltdowns.

Asher was patient and loving. He was soft-spoken. He contacted a child psychologist to help navigate River's issues. Gran offered to move in for the time being so she could be another set of hands, and they took her up on it.

Christmas morning, Gran was up early, preparing breakfast, when Rayna came downstairs with Aria. "Good morning." Gran set down the spatula, and once Rayna had the little girl in her highchair, kissed her dark curls. Aria pounded on the tray, bouncing. Rayna walked to the pantry and grabbed the round oat cereal, placing a few in front of her daughter. *Her daughter.* Yep, that still hadn't sunk in yet. Instead of grabbing a handful, Aria pinched one piece between her chubby thumb and pointer finger, then placed it in her mouth. She nodded her head as she chewed, grunting at its goodness.

Arlo, a.k.a. Arson, and Cora had already bought a bunch of presents for the kids. Rayna and Asher added a few of their own but didn't go overboard. They were piled under the tree, waiting for River to wake up and see what Santa brought. Asher was waiting upstairs for the boy as was his habit. He didn't want River to be alone when he first woke. He also made sure River hadn't wet the bed. If he had, he would get him cleaned and changed before they came downstairs.

It was a learning curve for everyone involved, but Rayna wouldn't change anything about it other than wishing she could take away River's confusion and sadness. All she and Ash could do was love the kids and give them the tools necessary to move forward without their biological parents. After the adoption, they sat with River and Aria, playing on the floor, and explained how they were now the kids' parents. That they were a family. It was a lot for the little boy to take in, but he asked Asher, "Do I call you Papa and Momma now?"

"If you want to." That's what he had called Arlo and Cora. "Or you can call us Dad and Mom, or anything else you pick. Just know we love you very much, so it doesn't matter what you choose."

As of that moment, River hadn't called them anything, so when he ran down the stairs ahead of Asher, he rushed into the family room where the tree was and yelled, "Momma Ray, look! Santa comed!"

Rayna's eyes filled with tears, but she wiped them before meeting her son in front of the tree where his presents were on one side with Aria's on the other.

"I see that." Rayna felt Asher behind her before he wrapped his arms around her.

River grabbed one of the miniature cars and pushed it along the track. "Daddy, will you play with me?"

"I sure will, Buddy." Asher kissed Rayna's temple before dropping to the floor beside their son.

From the kitchen, Aria banged on her tray, yelling, "Mama!"

"I think you're being summoned." Asher smiled, his eyes glassy.

Rayna went to the kitchen and lifted Aria from her highchair, then took her to the family room and placed her on the floor next to her toys. Gran followed with her phone so she could take pictures and video. Aria toddled into the middle of her things, plopped down, and chose a stuffed rabbit. "Bun?"

"Yes, that's your bunny." Rayna sat next to her daughter. Aria passed the bunny over, then grabbed another present. This one was a hardcover book featuring animals. Aria climbed into Rayna's lap and patted the book. Rayna opened the cover, and as she pointed out each baby animal, Aria did her best to mimic the names and the sounds they made after Rayna made the noises. The kids played with their new toys for an hour before Gran announced breakfast was ready.

"Pancakes?" River asked.

"With smiley faces," Gran assured him. River loved bananas on his, so Gran added them in fun ways. Rayna had always been grateful for her grandmother, but having Fern help her and Asher with their new family gave Rayna insight into how Fern had dealt with Rayna as a small child. She was loving and patient. She wore a perpetual smile and gave the best hugs. Even Asher got in on Fern's embraces.

A few hours later, they were getting ready to go see Glory, Ripley, and his parents, when Gran's phone rang. Rayna figured it was Regina, but after a few minutes, Fern's raised voice carried from downstairs.

"Why would I tell you I moved, Colette? You haven't been a part of my life in years."

Rayna wondered why her mother was calling now. She hadn't spoken to the female in... Damn, she couldn't remember how long it had been. Five, six years?

"Rayna's fine. Actually, she's better than fine. She has a wonderful mate and two beautiful children."

Rayna hadn't bothered letting Colette know about her new status of being unemployed, married, moved to a new town, anything. She didn't feel her mother had a right to know. She also hadn't informed her of her new phone number, so Colette couldn't contact her if she wanted to.

"Why would she tell you? You abandoned her a long time ago." After a beat of silence, Fern huffed, "No, I'm not telling you where she is. If Ray wanted you in her life, she would have called you herself. I have somewhere to— Don't you threaten me. You have no idea the family Ray and I have now. Stay the hell away from us, or I promise things won't go your way. Ray is my daughter, not yours. You gave up the right to make demands when you left her with me to traipse around the world seeking fame. So go back to your friends, if you have any, and leave us the hell alone."

Asher and River met Rayna in Aria's room where she was getting the girl's coat on. "You okay?"

"I'm better than okay. I have the best mate in the world, two beautiful children, and the fiercest Gran in existence. What more could a girl ask for?"

EPILOGUE

Ace

10 Years Later

ASHTON GIGGLED WHILE blowing on Ace's fingernails. His six-year-old daughter thought it was hilarious to paint her papa's nails. "You're next, Uncle Rip."

Ripley wiggled his hand. "Gracie got there first," he said, showing off his own daughter's artwork. Where Rip's were navy, Ashton had chosen forest green for Ace. Just like the two males, their youngest were thick as thieves, having been born two months apart.

Gracie ran up to Rip, dropping a small snake onto his lap. "Isn't it cute?"

Rip rolled his eyes and picked the reptile up, jabbing toward his daughter's face. "You're cute." Gracie laughed, grabbed the snake in one hand and Ashton's hand in the other.

"Blow on 'em, Papa," Ashton demanded, then took off with her bestie. Ace did as his girl commanded, even when Rip smirked at him.

"What? I don't want bugs messing up my girl's hard work."

Rayna sauntered over to the picnic table with a beer. She twisted off the cap and set the bottle down. With a wink, she returned to where she, Glory, and Charlotte were sitting with Rhi and her three-month-old son, Rowan. Ace admired his mate's tanned legs topped by the usual cutoff shorts she preferred. In a couple of months, she would need something less constricting since she was pregnant again. Ten years had passed, and he was still as enthralled by the female as he'd been since that day at Haven when he saw her the first time.

When Ace and Rayna had went to dinner at Spyder's, his mate and Charlotte had become fast friends, both loving plants. Glory had recorded another album, only this time, she convinced Rhi and Rayna to sing with her. The three females harmonized beautifully. When the record was finished, Aria insisted on listening to it every night when she went to sleep.

Adopting River and Aria had been a blessing. After getting River the help he needed dealing with his parents' deaths, the boy flourished, becoming an amazing big brother and a loving son. There were photos of Arlo and Cora around the house so the kids never forgot their biological parents. Fern stayed with them for the first six months, but then she went back to Ace's old house, saying they needed privacy. Ace and Rayna became experts at making love quietly.

The campground was filled with Hounds, mates, and kids during their annual camping trip. Instead of visiting the campground close to Haven, they'd found a new one with more acreage and a creek where they could play in the water. The Lazlo brothers, along with several Hounds, had pooled their money and bought the place. It had cabins as well as tent and RV sites. There was a covered picnic area they had upgraded that now had several grills as well as a pizza oven. A kitchen had been built on where they could store the food and drinks they brought.

The MC rode together often, and the rest of the Hounds rode when they could. There were now more bikes with sidecars than without, and Hayden designed them all according to the child or children riding along. Ace currently had two. One for River, which was decorated with his favorite superhero, and one for the girls, which had books on one side for Aria and bugs, plants, and reptiles on the other side for Ashton. His baby loved digging in the dirt.

Having so many kids of different ages made it difficult to synchronize their schedules, but their August gathering was one event they all made time for.

River, Mateo, and the twins – Major and Marshall, because there were now three sets of twins – were tossing a football. Nadya and Nahla, Mav's second set, were trying to get the football from their brothers as Natalia and Kerrigan sat talking not far away. Surprisingly, Mav's own twin only had a son, Wyatt, who was chasing after Ashton and Gracie with a frog.

The other twins, Theo and Ollie, were home with Sultan and Tegan since Tegan had given birth a few days ago to their new daughter, Rosalee. Ace loved his kids, but he wasn't sure he could handle having two newborns at one time. Ashton had been a handful all on her own, and Rayna's last checkup proved there was only one baby in her tummy, thank Zeus.

Aria and Patrick were stretched out on a blanket under a tall tree, reading. His oldest girl was his quietest child. She'd found a kindred spirit in Tank's son who also preferred to read instead of running amok. Aria and River had welcomed Ashton, but it was River who wanted to hold his baby sister and feed her. Aria read books to Ashton and was the first to run to her if she was crying. They hadn't told the kids they were going to have another sibling yet, but Ace knew they would all be excited. When Ashton met Rowan the first time, she looked at Rayna and said, "I want one."

Daisy, who had taken after Rhi with her affinity for living things, was with Hallie, Hayden and Sadie's daughter, and it appeared they were listening to the trees. Both girls were touching the bark with their eyes closed. It wouldn't surprise Ace if they were, since Daisy often foretold of things yet to come after playing in the woods. She also alerted her older sister, McKenzie, that the baby in her tummy wasn't happy. It turned out the umbilical cord had been wrapped around Everett's neck, and they did an emergency C-section to save the boy. Ace might not understand the gifts bestowed upon Rhi and her daughter, but neither did he question them.

Ryker and Rhiannon were careful about who knew of Daisy's abilities. Once David Spencer moved overseas, they still didn't let down their guard. Abraham, when voiced, said he hadn't told anyone about what Rhi could do, but that didn't mean his wife hadn't let it slip.

The serum Lucy and Jonas developed had been offered to any of the human mates who wanted to take it. When those humans stopped aging, it appeared to be successful. Ace was thankful Rayna was a shifter and didn't have to worry about her lifespan. When she laughed at something Glory said, Ace glanced at her. As usual, she felt his eyes on her, and she turned his way. Love shown on her beautiful face as she blew him a kiss. Ace caught it and placed it over his heart.

After making sure his polish was no longer gummy, he turned to his best friend. "My nails are dry. Want to go hit the creek?"

"Yes, you diva." Rip punched his shoulder. They strolled over to their mates, kissed them, and told them where they would be, grabbing towels from the stack piled on one of the tables, then made their way along the dirt path through the woods. Ace heard laughter before the water came into view. Rip's son, Anders, was splashing in the water with Kayden, Kyllian's son. Kyllian and War were kicked back in lounge chairs, watching while drinking beer.

"Hey, Pop! You coming in?" Anders called out.

"Yep." Rip dropped his towel on the ground beside War and waded into the knee-deep water. Ace was right behind him. He plopped down, letting the cool water refresh his heated skin. It wasn't long before Kayden was sending small waves of water Ace's way. Out of all the kids, he was the most mischievous, giving Major a run for his money. He rarely smiled, but when he did, there was this look behind it that let the recipient know the kid was up to something. Ace loved the boy, but he was thankful River was less angsty.

"Where's Havyck?" Ace asked Kyllian.

"He and Sadie ran to town for stuff to make smores. They brought a big-ass birthday cake, but when Hallie was at Lucy's for Harlow's birthday party, Harlow had smores, so now Hallie thinks she should have them too."

"Smores are dumb," Kayden muttered.

"Yeah? Then that means there'll be more for me," Kyllian said, pointing his bottle at his son. Looking at War, he asked, "Was I that much of a punk when I was eight?"

"You were worse. At least that's what Pop told me when I called to wish you a happy birthday. He was ready to ship you off to Siberia until you were twenty."

"Huh. Then I guess I'm paying for my raising, as the saying goes." Kyllian drained his beer and snagged another from the cooler at his side.

"He's not that bad," War chided just as a low growl sounded behind them.

Kyllian looked over his shoulder at the large wolf stalking toward him, its teeth bared. "Now, now, Pretty Lady. I was only joking."

Another wolf, only slightly smaller than the first, bounded through the woods, past her parents, and jumped in the water, landing next to her brother. Kayden threw his body at Nikita, attempting to tackle his sister. When that didn't work, he climbed on her back. Nikita gave a yip, which must have been Kayden's cue to hang on because he wrapped his arms around her neck. When he was secure, she jumped out of the creek and took off running through the woods. Nikita had grown from an awesome teen to a brilliant young woman, and she doted on all the kids whenever she joined them for family outings.

Quinn shifted to her skin, fully clothed. Ace still thought it was unfair that dire wolves didn't have to strip when shifting. She sat on Kyllian's lap, taking the beer from him, and downing it in one go. "Don't call my son a punk."

Anders climbed on Ripley's lap, placing his hands on his pop's shoulders. "I want to play." Ripley grabbed his son around the waist and stood from the creek. He climbed out, set his son on his feet, and stripped out of his clothes after telling Quinn to close her eyes. Rip shifted to his Lion, and Anders climbed on. Rip shook his mane, which Anders grabbed hold of, then the father and son took off in the same direction as Nikita.

"How long?" Kyllian asked.

"I'd give it about thirty seconds." Ace stood and stepped onto the bank. He walked behind Quinn and removed his clothes, shifting so he was ready when his son emerged from the woods. Being a teen, River climbed on easily, throwing his leg over his dad's back. This was another reason they had bought the campground. It gave them privacy to shift without worrying someone would see them. Bishop somehow made it so that no drones could fly over the area. Ace wasn't sure how he did it, but

Ace was glad for it.

The next couple of hours were spent with the adults running in their animals with the kids on their backs. It was one of Ace's favorite things to do with his children. After everyone had a turn or five, everyone shifted back and dressed. By that time, Rory, Sutton, Regina, Conrad, Fern, and her new boyfriend, a Gryphon named Hank, had arrived. When Rayna asked Fern how it was possible to date someone after having a mate, Fern explained she would always love Rayna's grandfather, but after being alone for over fifty years, there was no reason not to date a male as handsome and sweet as Hank Ferber. Rayna hugged her gran and said she was happy for her. Ace was too. Hank was one of the best males he knew.

Dinner was organized chaos as always with a group their size. They enjoyed grilled steaks and burgers with all the sides you could imagine. When it was time for dessert, Hayden brought out the cake, and they all sang Happy Birthday to Hallie. Even Kayden joined in in celebrating his cousin. After cake was devoured, the kids helped clean up while the Lazlo brothers got the firepit ready. And by firepit, Ace meant the eight-foot-wide space surrounded by a stack of pavers. The wood had been gathered earlier, so once cleanup was finished and the ingredients for smores was lined up on a table close by, Ryker did the honors of lighting the kindling.

Rayna sat on Ace's lap and held out the chocolate treat. He took a bite, then Rayna did the same. There was plenty to go around, but his mate liked sharing with him. Once the treat was gone, Ace lifted Rayna's hand and licked the chocolate from her fingertips.

"Get a room," Hayden crowed from across the pit.

"That's a wonderful idea." He stood, cradling Rayna to his chest. Looking over at Fern, he asked, "You got the kids?"

She arched a brow. "What if *I* want to get a room?"

The adults howled with laughter, Hank blushed, and Rayna shook her head. "So sassy."

Fern waved them off. Ace didn't have to tell their kids to behave, so he stalked toward the cabin he and Rayna were using for the weekend. When they were locked inside, he took his mate to the bathroom where they showered together before round one of lovemaking. For so long, Ace thought he was broken. He never imagined getting to be with a mate the way he was with Rayna. Now, his libido was as insatiable as anyone else's, and he couldn't remember being any other way. In the early morning hours, after round three, he kissed Rayna's belly, telling their little one how much he loved them, then he kissed his mate.

Life was good. Their families were growing. The kids were happy and healthy, and Ace couldn't wait to see what the next ten years brought.

THE END

A Note from the Author

Thank you for your patience while I dealt with life trying to get Ace's story out. Things are still uncertain in my world, dealing with a parent with dementia as well as some other personal things. It took much longer than planned to finish Ace and Rayna's story, but I didn't want to rush it and give you something less than. As I said in the foreword, this concludes the current arc with The Ministry. The four horsemen from Sultan's books may get their own books, or they might get one together. They aren't talking, so I'm putting them on the back burner while I focus on the kids' books in The Rebel Moon Shifters series.

ACKNOWLEDGEMENTS

It's been a rough few months, but my core group of friends, Candy, Katie, Kerstin, and Nikki, have kept me going. Without their support, this book would have taken even longer to get out into the world, and I may have put Luna the writing partner in my car and driven far away to hide out in the woods. Just kidding. Kind of. They all listen when I need an ear, make sure my words make sense, talk me off the ledge, and basically keep me going on a daily basis. I love you all.

As always, I have to give credit where it's due with the cover. Golden's photo of Alex has been waiting forever to grace one of the Hounds' covers, and he was my perfect Ace. Jay did another fabulous job putting it all together.

To my reader group, Faith's Furies, thank you for following me on this journey. I appreciate you all. To my ARC readers, your feedback is not only appreciated but necessary. Thank you for reading the early copies and helping make the finished product even better.

And to the man... We've still got this. I love you.

ABOUT THE AUTHOR

Multi-genre author Faith Gibson began writing in high school, and through the years, penned many stories and poems. Since she was a child, her dreams (and sometimes nightmares) were vivid constructs, making her shake her head and ask, "where the hell did that come from?" Many of these nighttime escapades have led to a line, a chapter, or even a complete story.

"Love is love, and there's not enough love in the world." This belief she holds strongly, and it's the prevailing theme in her works, all of which come with a happy ending.

Faith believes her purpose in life is to entertain the masses, even if it's one person at a time. Aspirations of becoming a rock 'n' roll drummer didn't come to fruition, but she's fulfilling a different dream, and that's bringing stories to life one book at a time.

Faith lives just outside of Nashville, Tennessee, with the love of her life and her American Staffordshire pup, Luna, the writing partner. When she's not hard at work writing her next adventure, Faith can often be found reading, cooking up something in the kitchen, listening to live music, or off on an adventure of her own.